Best wus

Ja Winterford

Fall from Grace

JA Winterford

ISBN: 978-1-914933-27-1

Copyright 2022

All rights reserved. No part of this publication may be reproduced, stored in a retrieval system or transmitted in any form or by any means, electronic, mechanical, photocopy, recording or otherwise, without prior written consent of the copyright owner. Nor can it be circulated in any form of binding or cover other than that in which it is published and without similar condition including this condition being imposed on a subsequent purchaser.

The right of JA Winterford to be identified as the author of this work has been asserted in accordance with the Copyright Designs and Patents Act 1988.

A copy of this book is deposited with the British Library.

Published By: -

i2i

PUBLISHING

i2i Publishing. Manchester.
www.i2ipublishing.co.uk

Dedication

Fall from Grace

For Neil, my one true love and my rock. Also, for Joanna, David, Matthew, Harry, Jessica, Ava and Bruce.

Prologue
Derbyshire 1970

Jennifer walked tentatively into the classroom. Her mum had ushered her in gently through the main doors on her first day at the new school. She looked around the room at children hanging up their coats and hats, chattering and laughing. The atmosphere was just like her old school in Derby, which made her smile momentarily, but the obvious difference was that she couldn't see anyone with brown skin.

The class teacher, Miss Hawkins, approached her and showed her to the coat peg that already had her name written on a piece of card above it. She then led Jennifer to the front of the class and shouted for the attention of the children.

"Can everybody please settle down now? Please sit at your tables, arms folded!" Jennifer became very self-conscious as thirty pairs of eyes were now looking at her.

"Children, this is Jennifer Williams, it's her first day at Greenway Primary and I want you ALL to make sure you look after her, be polite and helpful while Jennifer settles in."

Jen wanted to die at that moment. She tugged at the grey pinafore that her mum had made and looked at the floor. The pupils at her last school were from more diverse backgrounds; like her, some were born into families from the Windrush Generation, some were children of first generation Indian and Pakistani immigrants, still a minority in an inner-city classroom, but they were there.

Miss Hawkins then looked around the room for a gap to slot her new pupil into. She spotted an empty chair next to Grace Farley. "Perfect," she thought to herself. Grace was a quiet and gentle girl who applied herself to class work and seemed to have good relationships with the other children.

As Jennifer sat down alongside Grace for the first time, Grace couldn't help studying her new classmate. Jennifer Williams was tall, slim and elegant. Her hair was short, and she had tiny plaits in lines all over her head. She noticed how white her nails looked compared to her dark skin and the fullness of her mouth. Her eyes were chocolate brown and almond-shaped and when she smiled at Grace for the first time, she could have lit up the room. Brilliant white teeth, high cheek bones and a knock-out smile. If the term 'supermodel' had been around in 1970, Jennifer Williams would certainly been considered as having the potential to become one.

Their friendship blossomed over the next few months as the girls got to know each other. Their backgrounds couldn't have been any more different. Jennifer's parents were born in Jamaica and her grandparents still lived there. Her father worked at Rolls Royce as an engineer and her mother was a talented seamstress. They had started out in high-rise flats in Derby and now they lived in picturesque Chinley following years of saving for a deposit on a house.

Grace looked up to her friend, (not just physically, as Jen was taller by a few inches) she was very bright, she drew figures and clothes during boring lessons, and she knew how to use a sewing machine. They had the same taste in music. The Motown tsunami from across the Atlantic dominated the charts and they spent many evenings dancing around in Grace's bedroom to vinyl records, the sounds struggling through the speaker of Grace's monogram record player. Diana Ross and the Supremes, Stevie Wonder, The Temptations, Marvyn Gaye, all played to death and cherished, as together, the girls danced their way from childhood to early puberty.

When they both passed their eleven-plus exam, they were lucky enough to be placed in the same form at the Grammar School in Chapel-en-le-Frith. Grace was definitely more academic than her friend, and as she swotted away for exams, Jen was making clothes and excelling at sport. Jen seemed to know where she was destined to be in the fashion world while Grace resigned herself to her future being nothing more exciting than a bank clerk or a secretary. Grace fell hopelessly in love with John, a beautiful boy from school when she was fourteen, while Jen stayed aloof and uninterested in male attention. Her parents were very strict about dating, so while Grace was crying in the school toilets because her boyfriend had just ignored her on the corridor, Jen was perfecting her clothing design and seamstress skills. It wasn't that she didn't like male attention, which seemed to increase year-on-year, she knew that dating wasn't an option, not till she was out of sight at university, then there would be no stopping her.

Their paths parted temporarily when Grace left school at sixteen and started an Office Junior position at the Midland Bank. Just as Jen had predicted years previously, Grace was suffering the drudgery of being a bank clerk and hated every minute of her time there. Jen was studying for a diploma in fashion and design at the local college and went on to Newcastle Polytechnic to graduate with a BA honours degree in fashion.

They stayed in touch throughout Jen's amazing years at the polytechnic, where she was truly out of sight from her strict Christian parents and didn't waste any time when it came to socialising and dating. When she could, Grace loved getting on the train to Newcastle to spend time with her friend, who would commiserate with her about the fact that she should never have taken up her boring and uninspiring job with the Midland Bank. The student life was fast-paced, mayhem, booze-fuelled and fun, and Jen was fully immersed.

After three years at the bank and as many failed relationships, Grace started to think about getting another job. Her parents were quite old, and she desperately wanted to leave home. Unfortunately, on her salary she couldn't afford the smallest of basic bed-sit accommodation. Life was becoming greyer until one day she looked up from her till and saw Mr D. Hearn of Hearn Logistics leaning on the counter, writing out a cheque. It was quite a new account and she had heard from some of the other cashiers that Mr D. Hearn was quite a looker. They weren't kidding. He was tall and broad shouldered, he had thick, dark wavy (borderline curly) hair and his eyes were menacingly beautiful. He wasn't wearing a wedding ring and the smell of expensive aftershave was wafting over the till. He smiled at her and pushed the cheque over the counter. To her complete horror, Grace immediately blushed. It was a sure sign that she found him attractive, so she bowed her head as she reached into her till for the £50 cash he was withdrawing.

"Thank God I washed my hair this morning!" was all she could think as she fumbled about with the notes.

After that first meeting, she noticed that he came in on the same day and time every week, which was great as she could get herself ready for him. Her hair had more highlights, she wore a touch more make-up, but not overdone, she engaged him in small talk while she counted money and stamped things. He had a lovely smile, and he seemed a little shy, so, after four or five weeks of blushing and small talk she wondered if anything was going to happen. Eventually, he very awkwardly asked her out for a drink sometime, if she wasn't too busy.

Grace didn't hesitate to accept, even though dating customers was a complete no-no. If he became her boyfriend, then she would be transferred to another branch, but that was fine. Mr D. Hearn was not getting away.

Chapter 1
New Year's Eve 2010

The car was moving slowly in the bottleneck that had formed on the dual carriageway. It had become a tedious crawl towards the single lane of the bridge. The wipers were dancing vigorously to the tune of the driving rain that was pouring down the windscreen, barely achieving a clear view of the car in front. All he could see was the distorted blur of two red rear lights. He had passed the sign warning that high-sided vehicles should take an alternative route. He turned up the music to drown out the screaming in his head and gripped the steering wheel so tightly he could feel his arms shaking.

The ferocity of the music forced the lyrics from his mouth, and he slammed the steering wheel as he sang:

Push my senses to the limit
While you hide just who you are
And sing to me your phoney lyrics
To paper over ugly scars
Done with all your bullshit now
And the wreck you really are

The full effects of the ecstasy pill he'd taken a few hours earlier were kicking in. His heart was racing, he was feeling invincible. From a pathetic, injured puppy to not giving a fuck about anything or anyone. He'd left the campus at Aberystwyth to drive somewhere, anywhere. He had decided to drive to Manchester to visit some friends he'd made at uni, the sort of students who went home for the holidays. The family party at his parents' was a consideration, he hadn't seen his brother for months and he missed him a lot, but he didn't want them to see him in this state. Not tonight anyway.

Earlier that day he had stopped at Chester services to buy bottled water. He looked around at the few people sitting at the various food outlets and sighed as the thought flit through his mind, "What kind of a sad fuck is hanging around this place on New Year's Eve?" And almost instantly agreeing with himself that he *was* that sad fuck. He wasn't just sad, he was trying to process the events of the previous evening that had launched him from a place that was safe and warm and (for what seemed like the first time in his life) acceptance, to a sink-hole of despair. His mobile rang and he tried to ignore it. How could he sound normal right now? The caller persisted, so he answered.

"Hi it's me,"

"Hello."

"Just checking, are you planning on coming tonight?"

"Er, I wasn't going to."

"Are you OK, you sound a bit weird?"

"I'm, I'm OK."

"We've missed you, your brother's missed you, please think about it."

"OK, I suppose yeah, I'll see you in a few hours."

"A few hours? Where are you?"

"Please, don't worry, like I said, I'm on my way."

"On your way how? Are you on a train?"

"Why so many questions? I wasn't going to but now I am."

He went and sat back in the car. It was too quiet, so he started up the playlist from his phone. Maybe running away wasn't the solution, maybe a party would facilitate getting monumentally pissed with his brother who he'd missed so much, despite the changes in his life. He decided to drive to Anglesey as quickly as he had decided to run away. There was no lateral thought process, just chaos and pain in waves and waves, each one bigger than the last.

The queue for Britannia Bridge had ground to a halt. He wound down the window to try to see what the delay was. The rain soon pelted him, chased by a formidable wind that was raging through the Menai Strait. The dangerous currents roared as the fiercely paced tides rushed in from opposite directions. He could just about make out a blue flashing light in the distance after the first tower of the bridge.

He quickly wound the window back up. He could feel the car shake as the storm pushed against it.

"Shit shit shit!" he said aloud as he assaulted the steering wheel. A lorry driver had decided to ignore the warnings and had been stopped by the police. He was starting to feel the panic of being trapped. No way forward, no way back and high as fuck. He noticed his phone screen light up on the passenger seat. It was a notification that somebody had posted on Instagram. He lit a cigarette and slowly drew on the first lungful. Maybe it would calm him down as he sat captive in the car?

He picked up his phone and tapped on the notification. It was his brother's post depicting a video of a struggling marquee tent being battered by wind and rain. Fairy lights swinging, mud on the floor, rain leaking in. Then the camera panned round to hay bales. He could hear his brother's voice, but he wasn't aware of what he was saying exactly, just something about a surprise. Then he saw a figure in the shot. He played it back several times to make sure he knew who he was looking at. There was no doubt in his mind who the person was.

The mounting pressure in his head was reaching an unbearable level. He pulled up his hood, sprang out of the car with his phone in his hand and started to run towards the bridge. He couldn't feel the cold or the driving rain, he didn't see the police officer who had started to give chase, abandoning the lorry driver he'd stopped. He had never in his life experienced how focused he was right now. He clambered up onto the left-hand side of the bridge, stood upright in the gale force winds with arms outstretched and let the force of the gale push him unmercifully over the side and into the inky swirling void below.

Chapter 2
New Year's Eve 2010

Grace stood at the window looking out to the Irish Sea in the distance. After a fairly promising start to the day with broken cloud and the intermittent twinkle of sunlight on the brooding winter sea, the weather had started to turn. Dan's insistence that the New Year's Eve party was happening and his 'sod the weather' attitude had worn her out to the point of abandoning her opposition. All hope of the micro-climate of Anglesey Island taking the gathering dark grey clouds and catapulting them over to the mountain tops of the Snowdonia National Park were pretty much gone.

The sides of the outside marquee were starting to flap with increasing speed and tiny spots of rain were beginning to splatter the canvas. She could see Dan walking in and out of the marquee carrying boxes and boxes of wine and beer for the long list of invited guests. It was doubtful now if everybody would show up, so they'd just have to make the most of it. According to Dan it was one of those occasions where, "We can't have a New Year's Eve party on any other bloody date can we Grace?"

Dan could be forceful sometimes, especially when organising their social lives. Grace was not the sort of person to throw herself into a gathering to soak up the experience. She had been an only child to older parents who would stay up till midnight *only* on 31st December. Dad would have a couple of whiskys, open the door at midnight to let the new year in, then everyone would go to bed.

Dan loved a party. He loved the planning as much as he loved the gatherings and he looked after his guests very well. In the six months they had lived on Anglesey in what was supposed to be 'semi-retirement' for him and Grace, he had been very busy. He sought out the local village pubs and restaurants and he made sure he frequented them, with Grace by his side more often than not. She was understated and shy, but even she knew that she needed to create new friendships having moved a couple of hundred miles away from their former home and social circles.

As she continued to watch Dan in his element she couldn't help thinking, "Oh well what Dan wants, Dan gets..." Anyone who knew him knew that much. Despite knowing this fact, she couldn't think of anyone that didn't like him. He was adored by his friends and family, especially their twin sons Gabriel and Michael. He was the sort of father that she could have only fantasised about when she was growing up in Derbyshire. He was smart, funny, strong, attentive and loving. His less endearing qualities were a streak of impatience and a tendency to interfere in situations where he wasn't always wanted. Without Dan's drive and impatience, Grace would not now be the lady of a seven-bedroomed Georgian farmhouse set in 22 acres of grounds with sea and mountain views. They lived on the outskirts of Beaumaris, the prettiest town on Anglesey, brimming with restaurants, bistros, cafes, art galleries, boutique shops and having a Royal Yacht Club and a medieval castle. It was a place she had visited with her parents every year, sometimes two or three times a year from being two years old till her teenage embarrassment factor put a stop to the traditional family holiday.

Dan approached Grace from behind and put his arms around her waist. His bronzed forearms could more than accommodate her slight frame. He was still in great shape for his 57 years.

"Stop worrying," he whispered, "if people can't make it there's more booze for us!"

"I'm not worried about people Dan; I'm worried about the boys. They're both travelling a long way for your, er, our party. The weather's absolutely crap and it's going to get worse."

Dan turned her around and cupped her face with his huge hands.

"Please try and enjoy whatever today brings. Michael sent me a text about an hour ago, he's about two hours away."

"And Gabriel?"

Dan hesitated and sighed. "Gabriel is being Gabriel. Not answering texts and not picking up. You know how he can be, Grace?"

Grace knew absolutely how Gabriel could be. He could be amazingly interesting company at times, not the life and soul, nor the party animal in the family. Identical in looks and build to his brother Michael, but an entirely different creature. The only way she could tell them apart when they were young was that Gabriel had a small strawberry mark on the side of his face, level with his right ear. Both boys had blonde corkscrew curls and chocolate-brown eyes. The only real resemblance to Dan was the give-away Hearn nose. Quite large with a slight hook, but not unattractive.

Grace only had Dan's word for it that the boys had the 'family nose'. His family were a mystery and family photos were non-existent. His parents had both died before she met him. He had a brother that he was estranged from, and Grace had never pushed it. There were obviously deeply buried issues and problems that he didn't want to talk about.

Before Dan returned to organising the struggling marquee, he said to Grace, "The boys will be here, Jen will be here and you're going to have an amazing night. Trust me, maybe even be a surprise…"

When Dan said surprise, he meant surprise. He could keep a secret and loved to ambush her with the unexpected. It started with their wedding in Scotland, everything including the dress was organised without Grace having a clue. She'd had cars, jewellery, holidays, pets… all manner of loveliness thrust on her when she was least expecting it.

Her best friend Jen had said over and over, "It's guilt or control or both, Grace." Jen was the only person close enough to give that level of honesty, without Grace thinking she was just jealous. Not Jen, she was possibly the most perceptive person Grace knew.

Whether it was guilt or control or a mixture of both, Grace trusted him. They had been together for twenty-five years, not all of them great but they had worked together to build a successful haulage business that Dan had built up from being fifteen years old. It wasn't a romantic 'rags to riches' story, as the first ten years proved, however, the eventual sale of Hearn Logistics had provided them with more than enough money, a stunning coastal farmhouse and a lifestyle that was still in its infancy, while growing in quality as every day passed.

Grace's underlying anxiety around guests and both their sons arriving safely was temporarily suspended as she relaxed under Dan's gentle grip. She moved his arms away to turn and face him. Before she could say anything, they heard the jangle of the front-door bells, that were actual bells that chimed in the hallway.

"Please let this be at least *one* of the boys."

"Probably not Grace, why would they ring the bell? This is their home."

Grace hurried into the hallway to greet the first arrivals. Before she got to the door, she could hear the familiar voice of her closest friend.

"Gee! Tell your butler to get a wriggle on, it's pissing down out here!"

Grace opened the door while Dan looked on to see who had arrived. There was Jen, tall and slim in a bright orange faux fur coat, sunglasses (despite the lack of sun) and killer-heeled patent black boots. Dan forced a welcoming smile while Grace hugged her friend. He could feel the resentment rising up from his stomach like a snake, writhing and turning as it ascended. Jen had been living in New York for the last three years, but she was back in the UK and she looked as formidable as ever. Three years of distance and space had been enough for Dan to put their last conversation behind him and just seeing her face over Grace's shoulder made him feel like it was yesterday when he ended their affair.

"What a fucking cliché," he thought to himself as Jen approached him with arms outstretched, "your wife's best friend, you fucking moron."

"God, Dan do you ever look anything other than gorgeous?"

Grace didn't flinch as Jen paid Dan the usual compliment. She was flirty, that was Jen, but Grace always believed that Dan was secretly terrified of her. He wasn't comfortable around strong, confident women.

Chapter 3
New Year's Eve 2010

Grace hadn't seen Jen for three years. She had moved to New York to continue an already successful career, writing fashion columns for a major newspaper. They called each other from time to time to catch up, and Grace more often than not let Jen do most of the talking. The world of haulage lacked the glamour and sparkle that the fashion world held in spades and Grace was always ready to hear the latest events in Jen's life and work. Jen's social media presence was pretty full-on, and she never missed an opportunity to promote herself. In that respect it was fairly easy for Grace to be a voyeur on the sidelines as Jen's life played out on Instagram and Twitter.

Dan took Jen's coat and the two women linked arms as they walked off down the hallway that led to the huge farmhouse kitchen. He had known for at least a month that she was back, and he had struggled with his strategy. Grace knew nothing about their brief affair, nothing at all. His strategy was *not* to avoid Jen, so not inviting her to the party wasn't an option. There was a remote hope that she would be too busy in London, especially on New Year's Eve. Jen must have had plenty of invites to a higher stratum of social events than this? He tried not to get angry. He could hear the girls chattering and laughing in the kitchen, the chink of wine glasses, and he could feel the resentment still rising. What kind of a bitch screws her best friend's husband behind her back? What kind of low-life scum screws his wife's best friend? He had never felt this guilty and conflicted before. Grace had already forgiven him for a drunken 'mistake' with one of the office girls several years ago and a very difficult few years in their marriage had ensued. That hadn't stopped him from scratching a very old itch just a couple of years later. Jen had been recently separated from the musician she'd married, and she had worn her fake devastation in the guise of a vulnerable kitten in need of rescue. He had slept with her four or five times during their six-month affair. It had been too easy for him to slip away for a few hours without Grace questioning anything. A meeting here, a conference there. Jen knew that his and Grace's sex life was nowhere near back on track after his 'mistake', of course she did, because Grace told her everything. She was smart and manipulative and she had led Dan into her bed by his stupid male ego.

He decided to keep his distance as far as he could and concentrate on looking after the other (so far absent) guests. Yes, she still looked amazing, but he was done with the risk-taking of complicating his life. If Jen was back for an encore, she wasn't going to get one. He loved his wife and their two boys, and he was lucky that Grace was still by his side, twenty-five years after they married.

As Dan walked through the kitchen to access the outside marquee he tried not to glance sideways at Jen. She was sitting with Grace at the huge rustic dining table, large glass of red in hand, filling Grace in on her new home and job in London. It was three o'clock in the afternoon and Jen was downing the first of what may well lead to many large Merlots. Dan tried to escape the room without being noticed, damn it, why didn't he just walk out the front door and walk around the house?

"Hey Dan, Grace was just telling me the boys are coming home."

"Er, yes, both boys here for the first time since we moved in." Dan carried on walking towards the door that led to the marquee area.

"I'm really looking forward to hearing about their uni exploits! I'd know more if they'd accept my friend requests."

"I'm not sure if they know you're here actually, we haven't exactly published the guest list."

Jen took another swig from her rapidly emptying glass. She was nervous so this cheeky Merlot was calming self-medication. This was a party after all.

"Then again who wants their ancient godmother prying around social media?"

"Jen you're 47, that's not ancient." Grace knew when Jen was fishing for compliments. "If you're ancient then I am too, but I'm not," she said, defiantly shaking her long blonde waves away from her shoulders.

With Dan out of the way, Jen leaned towards Grace whispering,

"Is Gabriel still gay?"

"What do you mean still gay, and why are you whispering?"

"Because the last time we talked about Gabriel you said Dan didn't know. I just didn't want to blurt anything out. You know me Grace, I'm forever putting my big feet in it."

"Dan does know yes. I'm not saying he's happy about it, but he knows."

"How long has he known?"

"Not as long as I have Jen. I think I've always known really." Grace poured the remainder of the Merlot into the two glasses.

"Come on Gee, it really shouldn't be a thing. Gayness isn't illegal anymore. Hasn't been for a long, long time!"

"It's not the legal thing really, it's well, it's Dan's thing."

"What's Dan's thing for God's sake?"

"It's just the way he was brought up, you know, a cultural thing?" Jen shook her head.

"Nope, don't understand the 'cultural' thing."

Grace was struggling to find the right words. Dan was a great father and loved his sons in equal measure. Literally his two angels, Michael and Gabriel were his life and joy. His miracle babies were born prematurely following years of trying and hoping, and expensive IVF treatment.

Their 'monozygotic twins' were a rare occurrence. The last embryo was implanted, and their last hope of a single child became two. They were told by the consultant that although it seemed like a miracle, there was a higher risk of complications and poor outcomes. Despite all the worry the twins arrived at 30 weeks, both weighing a little over three pounds but otherwise both healthy.

Grace shuddered as the trauma of their delivery, just over nineteen years ago, flit through her mind.

She was woken from her thoughts by Jen.

"Come on Gee, what cultural thing?"

With a sigh, Grace replied. "It's a cultural Romani thing." Jen's eyes widened in disbelief.

"You're telling me Dan's a Romani?"

"I'm telling you that Dan's family, the family that I've never met, are Romani Gypsies. Dan doesn't acknowledge them or talk about them. His parents died before I met him, and he refuses to talk about his background. It's like he's ashamed or something. I didn't know anything till our wedding day. I thought I was marrying *Daniel* Hearn. Turned out he's Danior Hearn."

Jen was shaking her head. "So, you've known about his background all this time and never said a word to me about it?"

"He just doesn't want anyone to know, not even his sons. It's never made sense to me but please Jen, not a word."

Jen shook her head. "Not a word."

"Thanks, you're one of the few people I can trust."

"I'm a bit shocked Gee, to be honest, Dan is from Gypsy stock?" Jen was waving her empty wine glass at Grace. Jen said what Grace had expected her to say, well who wouldn't be shocked? She thought about the intimate tattoo at the top of Dan's right thigh, that he'd declined to explain to her during their affair. She had looked it up and it was definitely a Romani symbol. She started to say something as her mouth, mixed with two large glasses of Merlot, raced ahead of her mind. She stopped herself referring to the tattoo just in time. Then she remembered something.

"God, Gee you've certainly got an unconscious type."

"What on earth Jen? Unconscious type?"

"Remember John? That boy you fell for at school?"

"What about him?"

"I'm sure he was from a travelling background."

Grace did remember John. He was so beautiful but so aloof. She had followed him around, hoping he would take notice of her, which he eventually did. He was friendly enough, but he could blow hot and cold without a moment's notice. He was dark haired, almost black, with brown twinkly eyes, he could have been a young version of Dan, only Dan wasn't a bastard.

Both women were then distracted by a blue canvas holdall that flew across the tiled floor towards them from the direction of the hallway. It had been hurled like a bowling ball and it stopped abruptly at Grace's feet.

"Michael, you made it!" Grace was ecstatic to see one half of the sainted duo walking towards her.

Chapter 4
Nevi Wesh

Two-year-old Danior was sitting outside with his mother, Annie Hearn. Between them was a basket full of holly. He didn't know at the time what the green prickly leaves were, but he knew not to touch them as they would bite. His mother worked with moss and holly, fashioning wreaths that she would be taking to market the next day. His hands were cold and he could see his breath in the chilly November air.

The caravan was parked in a lay-by a few yards away and the door was open. He craved the warm sanctuary of his home and the thick wool blankets within. As he pushed himself up from the floor his mother spoke softly.

"No Danior, I'm nearly finished here. A few minutes that's all."

He looked up and smiled at her suntanned face, lined with years of working outside and her long black plaits that were looped and fastened behind her ears.

Annie Hearn was around twenty-eight years old. She didn't know her exact date of birth, only her place of birth, the Nevi Wesh, the New Forest. She was born in a place that for centuries had drawn Romani and Irish travellers to its green spaces, abundant wildlife and freshwater springs. The camp at Shave Green was her home till she married her first cousin Patrin on her sixteenth birthday. She was a 'black blood', considered the purest of the Romani gene pool. She had grown up alongside Patrin who was two years older, the son of her mother's brother.

She had never doubted that Patrin would be her husband, she adored him without really knowing or understanding the emotional connection she had with the boy that she played in the forest with, gathering firewood, picking blackberries, and hunting rabbits.

The first time she kissed Patrin was on her wedding night. A Romani union could only be consummated after marriage and the bride had to be pure and untouched by any other man. An unmarried Romani girl who was not a virgin was considered unclean and would struggle to attract a husband that wasn't a Gadjo, a non-Romani.

Patrin was not a virgin, which was an acceptable status for unmarried men. He met girls from the outlying villages at horse fairs and markets. With his dark skin, almost black curly hair and twinkling brown eyes there was practically no effort required when it came to attracting a farmer's daughter. They were far more accessible than even his own kind and seemed less inhibited than the Romani girls of the camp who were strictly controlled, wearing long skirts so as not to expose their legs to the gaze of the young Romani males.

Annie smiled at Danior as he obediently sat down on the ground when asked. At two years old Danior, her only child, was gentle, inquisitive and intelligent. He looked a lot like Patrin, especially round the eyes, his untamed curls already brushing his tiny shoulders. Annie's two younger sisters had already produced six children between them, four of them boys, all of them boisterous and feral. Danior continued to lay twigs on the ground, counting them up to fifteen, gently laying his finger on each one as he counted. The stark contrast between him and his male cousins was a concern to Annie and a major worry to Patrin. His boy followed mummy around, seemingly not very interested in the outdoor life.

His boy was articulate and smart for his age. His boy didn't like getting his hands dirty or helping with the animals. His boy cried when he took him out foraging.

"You need to put the boy down Annie," was a regular demand.

Annie was subservient to her husband in many ways, but Patrin's demands for her to be more distant and less attentive towards Danior were not fulfilled. Patrin was an impatient man. At eighteen he'd expected Annie to fall pregnant on their wedding night. Fertility had never been a problem in his family, who often produced more children than they could reasonably feed. Two years after their wedding, Annie's womb had remained fruitless and Patrin's drinking had increased with his despair.

The strong desire to produce a son, to carry on the Hearn name and traditions that could be traced back for centuries, was all-consuming. Fertility was essential to the survival of their race, many of whom had been corralled by the Forestry Commission into compounds similar to Shave Green. Pushed by the arrival of the motor car and the appeal of the New Forest to wealthy London dwellers, travellers were no longer permitted to move around the hundreds of square miles of broadleaved woodland, heathland and grassland. No permanent structures were allowed to be built and many multi-generational families were living in tarpaulin-covered wooden frames with no water, no sanitation, and in winter, an abundance of mud.

Annie had started to feel increasingly lonely as Patrin spent longer and longer hours away from their home. At best he was hard-working and determined, mainly in agricultural work, doing whatever the season demanded on the outlying farms, and at worst he was self-pitying and woeful that he and Annie remained childless. If he didn't arrive home by twilight, he often didn't come home to their van at all. She tried not to think about where he might be or who he might be with, and she certainly didn't dare to ask him directly.

One evening in May 1953, as she watched the orange embers of their campfire slowly fade to ash, Annie made a decision. She would ride one of the horses a couple of miles into the fading light, made darker by the forest canopy and seek out Lizzy Cooper. Lizzy lived alone in defiance of the rules and would not be moved from her dwelling. She had been born in the Nevi Wesh and in her advanced years the authorities decided to leave her alone as it was only a matter of time before she died, and they could reclaim the area that Lizzy considered was her right to occupy. The more superstitious people in authority were quite happy to leave Lizzy well alone.

One thing was certain – Patrin could never know about her visit to the 'Coxani'. Like the majority of travelling families, the Hearns had adopted the faith of the host country and were Catholic at heart. Some families mixed Catholicism with ancient beliefs in Gypsy magic, using either to suit their needs, however, Patrin was suspicious and uneasy around witchcraft which is why he drew a firm line in the sand when it came to occult practices. As desperate as he was to produce a child, he would never expose his vulnerability to a practising witch.

Annie knew approximately where to find Lizzy Cooper, who lived a solitary life and was well known for her dislike of children which is why, as she was growing up, Annie and her siblings took great care not to wander into Lizzy's part of the forest. They took heed at their mother's warning, "She'll catch you and skin you, then she'll put you into a stew."

She took a battery torch, one of the very few modern implements they owned and shone it over the horse's head, following the twisting paths deeper into the forest. The evening chorus had started, song-thrushes, blackbirds, the occasional shriek of a tawny owl, all welcoming the dusk and the night ahead. After an hour she came to a clearing and saw a campfire whose flames were caressing a cooking pot that was hung over it. Beyond that was a bender tent, a simple dwelling made of flexible branches, bent and woven together and covered in tarpaulin. She stopped the horse and waited. She could make out the shape of the bender tent but that was all. She turned off the torch and watched. Before she could dismount, she saw Lizzy Cooper emerging from the tent. She was very small, no taller than five feet, probably due to the curve of her spine. She moved slowly towards the fire and sat on a wooden box, she then reached into a pocket in her long skirt and pulled out a tin of tobacco. As she started to roll a cigarette she called out into the dark.

"What brings you to *me*?"

Annie froze as Lizzy lit her cigarette on the fire. She stepped into the clearing. Before she could say anything,

"Nothing other than trouble is what it is."

Lizzy motioned her to sit beside the fire. Annie could see by the firelight that Lizzy was wizened with age, her bent arthritic fingers looked like they had set solid and as the fire reflected in her eyes, they illuminated an inner light blue ring in contrast to the deep outer brown of her iris.

"What are you seeking?"

"A child."

"You have a husband?"

"Yes."

"But no child. Why?"

"He doesn't always come home from the farms. They pick crops and sometimes they drink into the night. He's a troubled soul."

"As are you, as are you." Lizzy nodded to herself as she puffed on her rapidly shrinking cigarette. Then she let out a loud laugh which made Annie flinch. "You wouldn't ride here without trouble following you!" She rocked backwards and forwards, her feet barely touching the ground.

She then took Annie's wrist and locked her gauntlet-like hand around it. "Do you want a boy or a girl?" But before Annie could answer, Lizzy threw her head back, her eyes rolling upwards, the flames grasping at the dark as if an accelerant had been poured over them. If Annie had any doubts about this woman's status, they were gone.

"You'll have a child by the harvest, a boy."

Annie shook her head as Lizzy turned to face her, still holding her wrist tightly.

"A child in three months? It's not possible I'm not with child."

Lizzy tightened her grip and Annie could feel her long, thick fingernails digging into her arm. If it got any tighter, she would draw blood.

"Please, please, I... I can't have a child in three months, please let go!"

Annie lessened her grip and the flames lowered. As she started to let go Lizzy repeated what she'd said.

"You'll have a child by the harvest. A boy."

As soon as Annie could wriggle free from the immensely strong grip of this tiny, seemingly frail woman, she ran across the clearing and grabbed the reins of her horse, mounted and turned him into the dark. A baby boy before the harvest? There's one every year. Maybe she meant next year's harvest?

Whatever had just happened it was not part of the physical realm. She looked over her shoulder to make sure Lizzy or any of her potential minions were not chasing her. All she saw in the clearing was a much younger, naked woman with very long black hair, dancing around the fire with a dark, formless shape and no sign of Lizzy.

Three months later, Annie woke at dawn in the green bow-shaped van. She was alone again as the first light had started to creep through the wooden shutters. Patrin had not returned from the harvest last night. She sighed and decided to hold back the sorrowful tears that were welling. The noises from the waking forest were multi-layered but they were all noises she was used to. Then something stood out among the birdsong, insects and rustling trees. It sounded like a small, wounded animal. Had a fox attacked the poultry again? She heard somebody coming up the wooden steps to the van. As the door opened, she saw Patrin, weeping and pale, holding out a bundle of grey rags. Wrapped in the rags was a new-born baby.

"It's a child Annie, he's ours."

She sat upright and gently took the bundle.

"It can't be ours Patrin! Where did you get this child?"

"It's my child," Patrin confessed as the tears rolled down his face. "Please help me Annie, he needs a mother."

The baby flinched and threw his arms out as Annie demanded loudly, "And which Gadji whore had your child?"

"It doesn't matter Annie," he said, shaking his head, "she's dead."

Annie's mind went back to her encounter with Lizzy Cooper. She felt a tingle in her breasts as she watched the baby trying to suckle his own fist. Without hesitation she lifted her night shirt and put the tiny mouth to her nipple.

The baby latched on with determination and she felt pains in her lower abdomen as if she had given birth and her womb was contracting down as the baby took what he desperately needed. Her body was giving up milk that she didn't have ten minutes before Patrin put the baby in her arms. She knew it was the result of a spell cast by Lizzy three months earlier.

"See, it's a miracle Annie, I've prayed for a miracle over and over and he's here."

"And what do we tell the family Patrin? They know I've not been pregnant. They'll think we stole a baby."

"That's why we've got to leave, Annie – today."

Chapter 5
New Year's Eve 2010

Grace looked up to her son, towering above her. His already untamed hair was wet and pushed back over his head. His smile as dazzling as ever, he hugged Grace tightly.

"Jeez Mum, I thought I'd never make it!"

"Well, you were two hours away at least three hours ago."

"The traffic is mental out there, honestly. Everybody's trying to get somewhere."

"Oh well, your father's obsessing over his bar," Grace motioned to the back door. "He probably hasn't read your message."

"The pace this storm's going he'll be lucky to have a marquee in a few hours, it will be on its way to Dublin. Is Gabe here yet?"

"No, but I spoke to him earlier and he's on his way."

Michael went to hug Jen. "Hi Jen, you pissed already?" Jen held up her wine glass.

"Not by a long way darling, but I'm working on it."

Michael was looking forward to spending a few days with his brother. They were as close as twins could be, so following their separation in September when Michael started his law degree at York and Gabriel started his fine art degree at Aberystwyth, he had missed having his brother by his side. They had taken their gap year together, travelling through Australia and New Zealand, pursuing their joint passion for surfing. Not being physically close to Gabe since September had been strange. It had been an inevitability that they would pursue different career paths. Michael was outgoing, competitive and down to earth, with a realistic approach to life whereas his brother was the quieter of the two boys, happy to lurk in his brother's shadow and 'under the radar' of society in general.

Michael made his way outside and darted through the entrance to the marquee to avoid becoming re-drenched. There he saw his dad, arranging bottles of wine, beer, spirits and mixers on a makeshift bar that was basically a trestle table. The marquee was strewn with fairy lights and the makeshift seating consisted of several bales of straw. Music was (for now) playing quietly through the several speakers that lined the inside of the venue. They greeted each other with a strong hug.

"Jesus Dad, why didn't you and Mum just have a house party, I mean it's big enough?"

Dan held his hands up in defence. "Because you can't do *this* inside a house!"

"Looks like we're in for a hose-down not a hoe-down."

"Thanks, and I've missed you too son, and now you're here you could give me a hand setting up."

Michael shook his head. "Nah, looks like you're bossing it without me, anyway I need a shower and a drink."

"Have you spoken to Gabe today? Your mother's starting to worry, he was supposed to be here yesterday, but he didn't show."

"Did he say why?"

"No just a lazy text message, something about a change of plan."

Michael shrugged his shoulders. "You know Gabe, likes to keep us all guessing. I reckon he's seeing someone. He thinks I can't sense it, but I've got a feeling he's up to something. It's weird he hasn't even told *me*."

Dan tried not to let his face give away his internal response. Accepting his son was gay had been a difficult process, unlike Grace who typically embraced Gabriel for his courage in 'coming out' to his alpha-male father. Acceptance was one thing, what else could he do really other than reject his son? Cheerleading Gabriel's lifestyle choice was something he wasn't going to do. Love him, yes, be there for him, absolutely, but not encouraging. He just wasn't ready.

Michael could see the tell-tale signs of strain on Dan's face.

"Look Dad, I don't think Gabe's going to spring a secret boyfriend on you tonight. He's a flake, he knows how you feel, and he's, well, he's sensitive to your..."

"My what Mike?" Dan interrupted impatiently.

"He's not going to fuck your night up with the Anglesey glitterati. Sounds like some of them have braved it. Catch you later."

Michael made a run for the kitchen. Dan smiled to himself knowing that if he had said 'fuck' to his father, he would have had his teeth knocked down his throat, nineteen or not. Part of accepting Gabriel's homosexuality was imagining how Patrin would have reacted if Gabriel was *his* son. If Dan had been attracted to males, would he ever have been able to tell Patrin? His honest answer to himself was no. And Annie? Well, she wasn't allowed an opinion about anything. The travelling community, plagued with rejection, targeted by hatred and discrimination from non-travellers had its own internal prejudices that were positively flammable.

Dan could hear chatter from the kitchen getting louder. At least some of the guests had arrived, hopefully enough to fill the marquee. He and Grace had been careful to invite an eclectic mix of guests from the area, not just as his son had put it, the 'Anglesey glitterati'. From local people who they liked to spend an hour or three with in the Admiralty

Arms or the Black Sheep to Royal Anglesey Yacht Club members, shop owners, rib-ride skippers, fishermen and women. People who wouldn't normally be at the same parties despite their shared love for this beautiful place.

He put the last champagne bottle in the huge tub of ice and decided it was time for him to greet their guests. The exit to the marquee was blocked by Jen.

"How's the Marquis of Anglesey getting on?"

Dan was immediately irritated. His plans to avoid spending any time alone with Jen had already gone south.

"Very funny Jen, now I need to help Grace, so if you'll excuse me."

Jen didn't move. She took a breath as if she were going to make a speech.

"There's somebody else arriving tonight. Totally uninvited I know, but the thing is, he's my husband."

Dan didn't flinch. "You got married again. Great, Jen, that's really, really great, now can you let me past please?" Dan was relieved to hear the news. A single Jen in his home, drinking with his wife was a potentially unhealthy cocktail. On the other hand, a married Jen waiting for her new husband to arrive, albeit uninvited, was a much better scenario. He could relax and enjoy the party he'd spent so long planning.

"So, you got married without anyone knowing? How?"

"Thing is Danior, my new husband is my old husband."

Dan didn't even register that she'd called him by his real name. Her old husband meant Nick Foster. Song writer, musician, ageing rock star and premier league wanker. He could only say one word.

"Why?"

"That business with the inquiry was an utter farce Dan, and we all know it. He was completely vindicated. It should never have happened - it almost ruined his life."

"So what changed?"

"We met up by chance in New York a few months ago and we tied the knot in Vegas two weeks ago. We've realised we're soulmates, always have been."

Dan couldn't quite process what he was hearing. "OK Jen, do me a favour, when he gets here just make sure he's wearing a muzzle for all our sakes."

"Don't worry Dan, he's two years clean now, well, when I say clean, he's drug-free at least. He's a changed man."

"You'd better go and put the kettle on then. Distract him from the free booze."

Before Jen could leave the marquee, Dan heard the echo of her words from seconds ago.

"How do you know my real name?"

"Well, Grace is already a little tipsy, and I know about your little problem with Gabe."

Dan felt the already simmering disdain for Jen's very presence in his home start to bubble.

"And do you know Dan, it's obvious to me now why you lost it with Nick that time, you know when you floored him? Remember?"

Dan remembered all too well the evening several years ago when Jen and Nick hosted a pre-tour party at their Grade 1 listed Elizabethan Gothic pile in Surrey. Nick's band were still touring, refusing to grow old gracefully and strangely still in demand. Their catalogue of hits was modest, born from the Punk era of the mid to late seventies and their appeal was to old and young alike. They were one of several support acts for a major rock band on their world tour and the party's guest list read like an excerpt from

Who's Who. Lords and ladies, models, actors, actresses, TV show hosts and Dan and Grace Hearn, Managing Director and Operations Director of Hearn Logistics, Chapel-en-le-Frith, Derbyshire. Completely out of their comfort zone. While the host and hostess mingled, Dan and Grace had stuck together in a corner of the room watching a parade of vacuous, attention-seeking luvvies, just Nick's sort of people.

When Dan had eventually got talking to an ordinary-looking man who described himself as a 'life coach', Nick appeared with a bottle of champagne in his hand. He interrupted the conversation without blinking.

"Hey, Dan my man!" All Dan could think was, "God, I can't stand him."

"We're doing Glasto next year. Just to round off the tour. Do you and Gracie-face fancy VIP tickets?"

Who the hell was 'Gracie-face'? Why does everything have to fucking rhyme? God what a moron.

Grace had suddenly become animated. "We'd love to Nick, thank you."

"OK, yes, thanks Nick, that will be very, er, nice. We could hire one of those massive campervans, you know, do the glamping thing?"

Nick had shaken his head, laughing. "Dan, my man, don't be such a fucking pikey! You'll be in the hotel with us."

It had been a long time since Dan had been called a 'fucking pikey'. Not since he was a child in Hayfield. He hated the label then and he hated it as an adult. Without hesitating, he had grabbed Nick by his shirt and thrown him to the floor. He was considerably taller and stronger, so the altercation had been over very quickly.

Without any explanation or apology, Dan had left the celebrity-strewn mansion alone, leaving Grace in shock and in tears. She couldn't understand why he had lashed out so suddenly with no warning. Yes, Nick was annoying, mouthy, loud – a prize prick really – but in Grace's eyes he didn't deserve to be laid out in front of his guests. Nick had got to his feet very quickly and turned to walk back into the crowded room, arrogantly brushing off his embarrassment.

"Touched a nerve there," was all he said.

Dan had been in a mini trance recalling that evening. He was snapped out of it by Grace walking into the marquee, followed by about twenty assorted guests. It was only half the number of people invited but it was a start. The winter storm was cranking up outside, and as he greeted his guests he couldn't help wondering where Gabriel was. As he had that thought, Grace approached him, smiling and obviously a bit tipsy. He reached out to hug her with his strong reassuring arms.

"Let's have a lovely night," he whispered to her. "Despite our uninvited guest."

Grace gave him the all-knowing look. "No fireworks please, just actual real ones, you know, at midnight?" Dan nodded obediently, just as Nick Foster made his entrance, linked by his blushing bride.

Chapter 6
Hayfield 1964

Annie was collecting eggs from the chicken coop when she felt her waters break. Not what she had expected at all. No great gush of amniotic fluid, more a warm, small, steady but uncontrollable trickle that lasted a few seconds. The baby wasn't due till mid-September, and it was only mid-August. The sun was losing its intensity as it gradually hung lower in the sky and the sweet scent of autumn was in the air.

After hastily leaving the New Forest in 1953, they had travelled day and night in their horse-drawn van to put as much distance between themselves and the Nevi Wesh community as they could. Within a few months, they had arrived in Derbyshire, both weary and worn-down. Their aim to settle in northeast England was starting to fade as they struggled to rest in any one place, constantly being moved on by the local police. Their van was very distinctive and invited a lot of attention. It was old fashioned even for Traveller standards and with Danior growing by the day, Patrin decided to trade in their family home and their horse for a modern caravan and a car to tow it. That had been relatively easy as the transaction was agreed with a dealer from a travelling background. He planned to put the van in his back garden and live in it while his wife stayed in the house. That seemed like a perfect plan to him.

Annie had never asked where Patrin got his money from. There was very little farm work going into the winter, so all their usual sources of income had started to diminish. Nevertheless, they now had a car (even though Patrin had not got a driving licence, he had driven all manner of farm vehicles so that was enough for him) and the caravan had lighting, heating and cooking facilities all powered by bottled gas. It felt like a palace to Annie and accommodated the three of them comfortably. What Annie didn't know wasn't something she worried about. She made sure the caravan was clean, she looked after Danior, and Patrin supplied the money. He was a gambler and a drinker which was something that had always blighted their marriage, but he always provided for his family.

Patrin and Dan had set off early that morning for the livestock market in Bakewell, hoping to buy a tup for their smallholding. Their ramshackle farmhouse was surrounded by four acres of land and sat just above the village of Hayfield in Derbyshire. There was no modern plumbing in the property, their water came from a spring nearby and there was no bathroom. Just an outside toilet in a separate brick-built construction that had a cut-off wooden door. Not a modern WC, however, it offered the user a panoramic view of the village below with the backdrop of Kinder Scout, the highest point in the Peak District.

Annie knew that once the protective waters had left her body, she would be giving birth probably within the next twenty-four hours. She didn't have any way of contacting Patrin unless she was prepared to walk into the village to use the public phone box. Even then, she would have to hope that the operator could put her through to the market manager at Bakewell. As she stood up, she felt a deep ache in her lower back as her abdomen started to tighten up. She made her way slowly to the house and lowered herself onto the threadbare couch. Within a few minutes, the same ache started but this time it increased in intensity and her swollen abdomen tightened harder. Annie knew this wasn't a rehearsal as the contractions continued. She took deep breaths and silently prayed that her child would be born alive. Her first child, her miracle child, conceived after twenty-one years of marriage to Patrin. She was around thirty-seven years old, her hair was greying and her face was lined due to years of working outside. The chances of giving birth to a healthy child were slim given her age and the fact that, unlike in the Nevi Wesh community, there was a lack of knowledgeable midwives in Hayfield. There was one doctor in the village who spent most of his spare time in the Ploughboy public house. She had a deep mistrust of medical doctors and had only visited him once for him to confirm the pregnancy.

After twenty minutes, Annie felt she couldn't stand the pain any longer. She managed to remove her underwear as she felt the urge to push. She stood upright and put her hand between her legs. She could feel the top of her baby's head. As she lay down again, she couldn't stop herself from bearing down. First came the head that made her shriek in pain. Then the shoulders that felt like someone had taken a sharp knife and cut her lower half in two from front to back. As she watched her abdomen lower, she knew that her baby had arrived. He had announced his arrival with a loud shrill cry. He was perfect. Smaller than expected, but after all he was a month early. His head was covered in thick black hair, and she instantly recognised the strong resemblance to Patrin. Nature's way of reassuring a father that the child was from his seed.

By the time Patrin and Dan had returned, Annie had cut the cord and clamped it with a wooden peg. She had cleaned and dressed the baby in a tiny white gown and wrapped him in a shawl. He had taken to her breast as well as she could have expected and as the colostrum flowed into the mouth of her child, she felt a tsunami of love wash over her and baby Jack, the name they had chosen for a boy. This was a love she had never experienced before. She recalled when

Patrin had held out his child to her she didn't feel *this* feeling. She cared for Danior and had grown to love him without knowing what a birth-mother's love felt like from the inside.

When Patrin walked back into the house he saw his wife sitting in front of the open fire, swaying gently backwards and forwards with a bundle in her arms. He rushed to see their first child together that had arrived into the world two hours before he and Dan had set off back to their home. His eyes were awash with tears as he took the child gently in his arms.

"Our miracle Jack, that's what you are," he whispered gently as the tiny baby slept contentedly. "I knew our miracle would happen one day."

Hadn't Danior been their miracle several years ago? Annie didn't try to contradict him at this moment. She didn't want to remind him that Danior was handed to him on the day he was born by an angry farmer whose fifteen-year-old daughter had given birth to him in a barn. A farmer who didn't want anything to do with the child of a Gypsy. Danior was half Romani, half gorger and not what Lizzy Cooper had foretold. Jack was a black blood through and through, born before the harvest.

Chapter 7
Hayfield

Dan welcomed his baby brother. His eleven years of life so far had proved to be lonely. He had been an only child for what seemed a long, long time and he didn't make friends easily. Even the local primary school he'd attended hadn't offered up a group of friends or even one true friend he could trust. There was no shortage of kids from poor backgrounds in his school but even he felt that they were a different kind of poor compared to the Hearns. At least most of them lived in houses with electricity and bathrooms. Dan was very aware that he was different, not just because of his traveller heritage, it was more than that. Deep inside for as long as he could remember, he had a feeling that he didn't belong in the family he was born into. He had vague memories of living in a caravan and moving around from place to place, just as the travelling community did, not being tied to or identifying with any one place on earth. The feelings that he was an imposter were compounded by an intense fear of disappointing his father, that somehow if he didn't behave in a certain way he would be 'found out' and rejected by Patrin. He loved his father and respected his skills and knowledge around farming and trading, his love of horses, his love for Annie and his determination to provide a better life for his family than he himself had experienced as a child in the New Forest. Dan loved listening to his parents talk about their young lives at Shave Green and how they left to pursue a better life for themselves and their baby.

Dan believed that he had been born in a green, wooden, bow-shaped van that was heated by a wood-burning stove and pulled by a horse. He understood his parents' journey from the traditional Romani home in the New Forest to a smallholding in Hayfield had been difficult. Nobody wanted gypsies in their villages, towns, fields, lay-bys, car parks or wastelands. They were not trusted and quite often feared by the local people. They were labelled 'Gypos', 'Pikeys', 'Tinkers', 'Diddycoy' and 'Nacker'. Making a living in the traditional Romani ways started to get harder and harder for Patrin and Annie as they were increasingly shunned by 'civilised' communities, safe in their centrally heated homes with their television sets and record players.

Dan was aware that his father was a gambler and a drinker. Not a violent drunk, not that he had witnessed, more a jolly, mischievous drunk who liked to mark any occasion with an abundance of alcohol. Of course, celebrating anything was the excuse to drink to excess. Patrin was a religious man and firmly believed that part of the human condition was an inherent desire to celebrate. It was a gift from God that he embraced as often as he could.

One night when Dan was about three years old, Patrin arrived back at their caravan in a drunk and joyous state, waving a piece of paper at him and Annie. It wasn't unusual for Patrin to fall through the door and pass out on the bench seating after a particularly heavy night on real ale and whisky chasers, so seeing him so animated meant he was probably celebrating something.

His garbled tale was that he had joined a game of poker at the Ploughboy Inn, a place he preferred to frequent when they were on the outskirts of Hayfield. He knew a few of the regulars which included a couple of farm labourers, the village doctor, a local JP and a member of the Derbyshire Constabulary. Their shared habits unified them in their pursuit of the thrill of gambling, accompanied by the love of their chosen libation. Social status outside the pub didn't count while a game was underway, as it was played on a level field, both socially and morally.

Patrin had had a very good night. Frank Shaw, a local drunk, had joined the game, a man with money from an inheritance who didn't have to work for a living. Patrin had played well and taken every hand until there was just him and Frank left. There was twenty pounds on the table and Frank had run out of cash. In an attempt to win back his money, Frank, witnessed by the local JP, wrote a pledge stating he would stake an empty farm building with land that he owned to play another hand. The result was he lost the hand to Patrin and the written contract was now in force. Frank was a drunk, but he was a gentleman who kept his word. Patrin was now the owner of a run-down farmhouse with four acres of land. Frank would eventually go on to lose everything he owned.

Annie was thrilled to hear about the acquisition. The caravan was starting to leak and Danior was growing by the day. She didn't care if the farmhouse didn't have electricity or a bathroom, it had land that they now owned, and that land would be the key to their future. The twenty pounds would be enough to buy basic second-hand beds and furniture as long as Patrin didn't decide to carry on his celebrations in the Ploughboy Inn.

Chapter 8
Danior and Jack

Danior adored Jack. They resembled each other physically, both with dark curly hair and dark eyes like their father, however, Jack seemed to have a spirit that was in complete opposition to Dan's. As the baby started to move around independently, Dan became Annie's second pair of eyes, constantly watching his brother who could rapidly move from one room to another, sometimes vanishing in seconds. His determination to leave the confines of the farmhouse was on a grand scale, but Jack seemed void of fear. The outdoors seemed to call him from sitting on the rag rug, playing with wooden clothes pegs, to crawling around outside in mud and chicken droppings. He could climb before he could walk, which was particularly terrifying for Annie. Patrin had started to service and repair farm machinery. Beyond the aged and fallen dry stone wall that surrounded the farmhouse, there could be tractors, harvesting machinery, hay balers, all with their own dangerous parts, whether stationary or not.

When Jack was two and a half, he let himself out of the house while Annie was cooking and Dan was trying to do his homework. He was studying for upcoming gruelling exams that were a regular occurrence at grammar school. He had sat his eleven plus exam a few years earlier, without any encouragement or interest from his parents, and when he passed there were no celebrations. Just shrugs of indifference. He had been desperate to leave behind his tormentors from primary school, hoping life as a grammar school pupil would be different. But it wasn't.

Annie raised the alarm when she walked into the sitting room and Jack was nowhere in sight.

"Jesus Dan, where's your brother?"

He looked up from his open book. The side door to the house was swinging open. Annie was first out of the house, swiftly followed by Dan. There was no immediate evidence as to where Jack had got to. There was a yellow plastic brick on the path that led to the garden gate, but beyond that he was nowhere in sight. Annie was panicking in a way Dan had never witnessed before. He was calling out to Jack, but his mother was screaming hysterically above the noise of the wind and rain. Jack wasn't around any of the farm machinery, which he would usually head for. He wasn't in the field where the few sheep and horses were still gorging away on the land, oblivious to the weather.

Dan started to race towards the far fencing that was just about adequate to keep the animals from entering the stream that eventually flowed into the river Kinder. The relentless rain would have turned the gently tuneful, meandering water into a fast-flowing torrent of white noise. Not a threat to an adult, but certainly enough to take the body of a two-year-old child. When he reached the fence, he could see a scrap of material caught in the lower strand of the barbed wire. It was Jack's 'comfort rag'; a muslin square that he carried around by day, chewed on, and slept peacefully with at night.

"Oh God! Oh God! Please not Jack, please don't take him, not our baby please!" Dan shouted out loud.

Then he spotted the frame of his little brother. He was standing on the bank of the stream, very still and trance-like. He seemed fixated on the torrent that had transformed since the last time Dan had taken him there to paddle in the relatively safe water, looking for sticklebacks and minnows.

Dan approached Jack slowly so as not to startle him. When he'd got within a few feet, Jack seemed to wake up out of his trance and threw up his arms in delight at seeing Dan, motioning Dan to pick him up. That was when he started to slide towards the stream. He was on a bend where the water had cut deep, and the drop was a few feet high. Dan launched himself at Jack and they both tumbled into the cascade. It wasn't too deep for Dan as he clung onto his brother and swept him up in his arms. As he stood up, he could see his mother clambering through the barbed-wire fencing, and he could hear her screams above the rumble of the fast-flowing water.

"Give him to me now!" She was gasping for her own breath after running the half-mile from the house to the outer fence.

Dan was spluttering from the water he'd inadvertently ingested as he had entered the stream. He passed the child up to his mother. She took off her long wool cardigan and wrapped it around Jack who was by now crying from the shock of suddenly being very cold and very wet. Without another word she turned to carry Jack back to the house, leaving Dan standing up to his thighs in cold running water. There were no comforting words from his mother, no warm garments offered to stop his body shaking and his teeth from chattering. He had been left to pull himself out of the stream and make his way back to the house.

Annie didn't look back to check on Dan. With Jack in her arms, she made her way to the caravan that was parked up behind the house. It had seen better days; the axle was rotting and there were a few holes appearing in the floor. Despite the decline in its condition, Annie took comfort in her 'safe place'. She had spent many nights alone in the caravan since they acquired the house from Frank Shaw. Patrin's habits hadn't changed much since he was a farm labourer around Hampshire. Some nights he stayed out very late, some nights he didn't come home at all. She found the farmhouse cold, draughty and soulless. In contrast, the caravan, despite its age-related imperfections, was comforting and familiar. Now she was calm and rocking her black-blood child to sleep after his ordeal.

When Dan appeared at the caravan door sometime later, he could hear his mother gently singing a familiar song to Jack:

> *'Last night I lay in a well-made bed,*
> *With silken hangings round me,*
> *But now I lie in a farmer's barn,*
> *With the gypsies all around me.'*

She looked up and motioned Dan to stay outside. His tear-stained face didn't move her at all. She knew in her heart that there was no contest between her feelings for the two boys. Dan was the son of a Gadji whore and never more than right now did she want him to know it. As angry as she was, she wouldn't betray Patrin's secret, not unless she had to.

Dan thought his mother may be grateful that he had plucked his baby brother out of the stream, but he was wrong. All she whispered aggressively was, "Why did you try and kill your brother?"

More tears started to flow from his already pink eyes. From that moment he didn't just wonder if he was different and misplaced by the universe, he could actually feel it in his very essence.

Chapter 9
New Year's Eve 2010

Grace looked around the temporary room that seemed to be holding out quite well against the storm. Most of their invited guests had arrived, which was a relief, and they all seemed to be having a good time. The straw bales were adorned with the backsides of local characters and the dance floor was taken up with a few guests who had already passed their tipping point with alcohol, two of them being the newly-weds. She couldn't believe that Jen had not just taken Nick back, she had married him for a second time. She watched as they danced around each other, drinks in hand, laughing and pawing at each other. It was starting to make Grace feel very uneasy. The fact that Jen who couldn't keep a secret if her life depended on it, had not mentioned in the run-up to the party that she had re-married Nick? Some of the guests had already recognised the 'Shit Joe Strummer' (as Dan called him, but not to his face) and asked for selfies. Nick wasn't happy to oblige, which seemed odd. In Anglesey he was a celebrity for the evening, in London circles he was a has-been, practically nobody and probably skint, unlike Jen.

Dan tapped Grace on the shoulder and motioned towards the embarrassing duo on the dance floor.

"It's only nine o'clock for fuck's sake."

Grace had to raise her voice to be heard above the music.

"Exactly. Where are the boys? Michael went upstairs to change, and he hasn't come down. Gabe said he was on his way hours ago!"

"Stop worrying please Grace. They're both students now, probably nocturnal, you know?"

Grace nodded while Dan continued to try to reassure her.

"You see, we old farts like to be tucked away before midnight. *They* probably won't appear till then. It's what students do, we've just forgotten..."

"OK, do me a favour then. Just go upstairs and see if you can get Michael to get his arse down here and socialise. Oh and ask him to find out where his brother is. They're still as thick as thieves."

Dan left the marquee and dashed towards the kitchen door. The wind was still fierce but at least it had stopped raining. There were a few people sitting around the huge table, mostly older people enjoying the relative calm of the kitchen. Marquees and straw bales weren't for everybody.

He called up the stairs to Michael. No answer. The boys' bedrooms were on the second floor, two flights up. He shouted again, this time louder. No answer. He cursed as he ran up the stairs and stood outside Michael's room. Should he knock? As far as he knew, Michael had arrived on his own, so it wasn't very likely he had company. Dan reasoned with himself out loud. The wine was taking effect.

"Fuck it, it's my house, I don't need to knock!"

He opened the door to see Michael asleep on his bed, wrapped in a fluffy white bathrobe. He groaned as he opened his eyes.

"Sorry Dad, I had a shower and got on the bed, I, I'm knackered."

"OK, at least you're here, knackered or otherwise. Your mum's worried Mike, where's Gabe got to?"

Michael sat himself up and reached to his bedside table for a pack of cigarettes. Dan held up his hand.

"No smoking in here, that's the rules."

Michael wasn't about to challenge his dad. He knew how much it upset his dad that he and Gabe were both smokers.

"I spoke to Gabe around lunch time. He seemed a bit down, a bit non-committal. Like he's looking for a better offer?"

"We thought he was making his way from Aberystwyth yesterday. What do you know?"

Michael sighed again.

"Dad I honestly don't know."

Dan shook his head. "Look son, you know Gabriel better than me and your mum. We think he may be trying to hide something. We've hardly heard from him since September."

"He's not hiding anything Dad, I'm sure. You know Gabe. He's, well, he's..."

"Homosexual and vulnerable?" Even Dan couldn't believe he just said that out loud.

"He's found some freedom at uni and he's enjoying it, you know, without me for a change. We've been co-dependant for too long Dad. It's weird not having him around but it's OK. He has to find out who he is. Don't you think that's important?"

Dan knew exactly how important it was to know who you were. He instantly had a flashback to the day he pulled his brother Jack out of a flooded stream, his mother's anger that day and seemingly every day after. At eleven years old he was crying himself to sleep, if he slept at all, for weeks after the potentially tragic event. He had never forgotten the fight his parents had when Patrin returned from the pub that night. They thought Dan was asleep, but he had left his bed and was listening at the top of the stairs. As far as he could tell his father was trying to calm Annie down while she continued with her accusation that Dan had deliberately pushed his brother into the water. Patrin was drunk but coherent.

"He's not jealous of our son Annie, he cares for him, can't you see that?"

"He could never love Jack like we do. He's a curse Patrin! A curse that I invited so *you* could have a son."

"He's no more a curse than the air we breathe Annie." Patrin had shouted angrily. "Now you've got your own child you're forgetting how much you wanted...." Annie cut in, "A child yes Patrin, not your child, *our* child. A black blood, not half gadjo! He needs to know who his real mother is and stop telling me she's dead!"

Dan's memory had started to produce a knot in his stomach. He needed another drink.

"I know Gabe has struggled, God knows I haven't helped him much, but I get it Mike."

Their unusually intimate conversation was interrupted as the bedroom door slowly opened. There stood Nick Foster, swaying in his black jacket, black t-shirt, black drain-pipe jeans and sharp pointed black shoes, his very outdated signature look.

"Oh, sorry guys I'm a bit lost. This gaff is ma-hoosive! Where's the toilet?"

"Down one flight, second left."

Nick gave the thumbs-up. "Cheers, Dan, I badly need a piss, see."

"More like – where can I go to do a line?" whispered Michael.

Dan followed Nick down the stairs and watched him walk into the bathroom. God, he despised that man. That man who was pissed already, with the potential to be coked-up to the eyeballs (despite Jens's claims that he was now drug-free) right here in the house, completely uninvited. What did he know about Dan and Jen's affair if anything?

He waited outside the bathroom, subjected to the sound of the heavy flow of urine, clearly audible from the landing. Then a fart. He heard Nick chuckle to himself.

"Whoops, steady Nick. Not in this gaff."

He came out of the bathroom still zipping up his flies. He hadn't washed his hands. Dan waved him passed but Nick stood for a moment. He tapped the side of his nose and whispered, "You always had great taste Danny boy, especially the women." Then he sauntered off down the landing. As cocky and arrogant as ever.

Was that a threat? Dan now had a reason to suspect that Jen had told Nick about their affair, and Nick wasn't the kind to bury that calibre of information.

Chapter 10
New Year's Eve 2010

PC Ian Roberts was approaching fifty years old and was a few months away from retirement. He didn't like working New Year's Eve as a rule, but as a team his shift tried to let the younger police officers have the time off over Christmas and New Year. Family time was precious when working a gruelling shift pattern and in the past he had had the benefit of spending time with his wife and young children over the festive period. In three months' time he would be free to put his plans to sail around Britain into practice. He and his wife could take their time and enjoy their lovely boat together and their joint passion for sailing.

The storm was as awful as any he could remember. The wind and rain coming in from the west was potentially hazardous to the high-sided lorries that usually flowed in their hundreds every day across the Britannia Bridge, heading for Ireland via Holyhead. The signs on the A55 warned the HGV drivers that the bridge was closed to high-sided vehicles, and it seemed to be working. There was no way they could make their deliveries on time if they couldn't cross the bridge so many of them had started to pull up in lay-bys praying for the wind to drop so they could carry on their journeys.

Of course, there were always chancers who ignored the signs and PC Roberts was not enjoying the soaking he was experiencing as he tried to reason with a lorry driver who spoke very little English. He knew he would have to let the lorry pass as any hold up on the bridge could cause massive queues, so he was going to be quick. The lorry was left-hand drive and had already made its way onto the single file road.

The driver opened his door and gestured with his shoulders and up-turned hands. More or less, "What is your problem?"

"No ferries from Holyhead tonight," Ian shouted. "All the signs say don't go to Britannia Bridge!"

The lorry driver looked bewildered. Then he pointed and shouted at PC Roberts, who was at this moment wishing his retirement date was January the first. What the lorry driver saw was a male in jeans and a pulled-up hoodie running past.

"Look sir, look!"

Ian turned and saw the man running. He immediately gave chase. There were very few reasons for any member of the public to be running across the bridge here in the midst of a forceful winter storm. Whoever this guy was, he didn't look like a typical local who liked running to keep fit, whatever the weather. His years of giving chase to younger, fitter people were pretty much behind him, but when he saw the guy stop and throw something very phone-shaped over the side of the bridge he tried to run faster. Like a bad dream, his legs didn't seem to respond to his thoughts. When he saw the young man step up onto the side of the bridge, he felt a surge of panic. In his career with the North Wales Police, mostly based in Llangefni, Anglesey, he had witnessed many situations on both the Menai and Britannia bridges when highly distressed people were looking for a way out. Thankfully, due to extremely well-trained negotiators they had all been talked down. Right now, there was no time for any sort of negotiating. He got within a couple of yards of the young man, now standing swaying up on the side of the bridge, arms outstretched and shouting into the gale force wind. He didn't make any attempt to jump, he didn't have to. One huge gust took him over the edge and out of sight within seconds.

PC Roberts was in shock and out of breath as he held on tightly to the side of the bridge. He slid to the floor and reached for his radio. Not surprisingly, the lorry had gone on its way and some cars were passing by slowly, but he was oblivious. He reported the incident as calmly as he could although his voice was shaky and tears were trickling down his face. He hadn't seen enough detail to properly describe the male that had just been pushed to his certain death by the gale. At a guess he was quite young.

A man appeared shouting and pointing at an abandoned car that was now holding up the queue.

"You need to get this shifted mate." The man was clearly angry. He had no idea what had just happened on the bridge.

PC Roberts got to his feet and shouted back.

"Get back in your car now and stay there! DO NOT go near the abandoned car."

"I don't think you understand officer, I have to get across this bridge, I'm due at a function."

It wasn't often Ian Roberts lost it with members of the public.

"You do as I say right now, OK? Or you *will* be attending a function mate, in a wooden box!"

"You can't talk to me like that! What's your collar number?"

PC Roberts ripped an epaulette from the left shoulder of his police issue waterproof jacket and threw it at the whining shit standing in front of him, dressed in a (now drenched) dinner suit.

"Whoever owns that car just went over the side of the bridge. Now get back to your car and stay there till we can get this cleared."

Obediently the man turned to go back to his car. He dropped the epaulette in shameful defeat.

The sound of approaching sirens was getting louder. Ambulance, Coast Guard, more police cars, but he knew that it was impossible for the young man to have any sort of positive outcome.

At least they had the car. The driver door was open wide, the wipers were still trying to clear the windscreen in vain, and a cigarette was still burning in the ashtray of the 1990 VW Golf. PC Roberts had requested a PNC check on the abandoned car. He listened intently as the radio operator at the control centre in St Asaph returned a result in minutes. The car was registered to a Mr Jamie Fellowes, 520 Caernarfon Road, Bangor, Gwynedd. Not currently taxed.

Chapter 11
New Year's Day 2011

Grace woke to the sound of Dan snoring rhythmically. Not loudly, just annoyingly regularly like a half-muffled pile-driver. Sun was seeping through the tilted blinds and the breeze outside was audible but gentle. It took her a few seconds to establish her bearings as the bedroom door seemed to be in the wrong place. When she looked up and saw the light fitting, she realised they were in the holiday lodge that was in the grounds of their coastal farmhouse. It wasn't the first time they'd woken up in this very modern, beautifully furnished, glorified caravan, that the previous owners had let out, making a small fortune in the process.

She reached over for her phone but unusually it wasn't there. All that stood on the bedside table was an empty bottle of red, an empty wine glass and her reading glasses. She lifted her head to see if Dan's side of the bed was giving up any evidence of the previous night. She could see his phone and an empty whisky tumbler.

She spent the next few minutes lying still, trying to recollect how she and Dan had started the night in their house and were now in the lodge. The patchy recollections started to appear like flashing images in her mind. Just snapshots of people, mostly drunk people dancing and generally enjoying the setting of the marquee. Jen and Nick's embarrassing antics on the dance floor, the Commodore of the yacht club and his wife letting their hair down, their guests generally enjoying the hospitality laid on by their hosts.

Grace momentarily smiled to herself but then in an instant her lovely fuzzy recollections of the night were annihilated completely. Gabriel hadn't arrived at the party.

She sat up quickly, waking Dan as she moved. He rolled over and groaned.

"Happy New Year..."

"Is it Dan? Did you see Gabriel last night?"

Dan was also beginning to recollect the events that led them to retreat to the lodge. He just hoped that Grace couldn't.

"I don't think he did love."

"We should call the police Dan."

"We discussed this last night Grace, don't you remember? After the fireworks? Me, you, Michael and that friend of Gabe's that turned up?"

A young man had turned up just as Michael had decided to join the party. Nobody knew who let him in. He had stood shuffling around awkwardly in the marquee until Dan approached him.

"And you are?"

"Oh, hi, I'm Jamie." He had offered his hand politely.

"Are you from the rib ride crew?"

"Er no, sorry, I'm a friend of Gabe's. He's not expecting me. I thought I'd surprise him."

"A friend of Gabe's from?" Dan had never seen him before.

"Oh sorry, from uni, I'm an art student. Aberystwyth."

"That's a long way to surprise somebody."

"Er yes, no, sorry, my mum's in Bangor so not far really."

Dan hadn't been too impressed by the gate crasher. Was he Gabe's secret love-interest? Hopefully not. He could just about recall Michael appearing in jogging bottoms and a hoodie. No effort made whatsoever. When Jamie saw him, he froze as Michael walked right past him to grab a drink from the bar. Dan had motioned to Michael.

"Do me a favour Mike? Could you ask our uninvited guest a bit more than he's willing to tell me? He said he's a friend of Gabe's but he's not giving much away. He could be anybody! We need to put your mother's mind at rest."

He couldn't hear what was said but he watched Jamie's face turn from bewilderment to smiling and then very nervous-looking but laughing. He was shaking Michael's hand and nodding. Then they left the marquee together, drinks in hand. As Michael passed Dan, he had made a strange remark.

"Honestly Dad, you couldn't make this up. He thought I was Gabe! He didn't even know Gabe had a brother, never mind a twin."

Grace was still struggling despite the prompt from Dan. Now both sitting up in bed, Dan decided to give her a version of the truth that was plausible.

"The fireworks were a disaster remember? Hardly anyone wanted to venture out to see them. There was me, you, Michael, Gabe's friend Jamie, Jen, Dick... I mean Nick, and a few other people. The umbrellas weren't holding out, the grass was turning into a bog. It was game over before it started really. We all went back to the kitchen to warm up. Does anything ring a bell?"

Grace recalled sitting at the kitchen table flanked by Nick and Jen. She was checking her phone to see if Gabriel had made contact. She was upset to see nothing incoming, just unanswered calls and texts from her phone to his. She remembered fighting back the tears as she announced she was calling the police. There was some resistance from Dan who tried to reason with her even though he was beginning to feel uneasy. Gabe was probably unconscious at another party, he may have mislaid his phone, he didn't know his friend was planning on showing up otherwise he'd be here, surely? The police wouldn't even start looking for a student, probably drunk or high at a so far unidentified party on New Year's Eve?

"Did we have a row in the kitchen?"

"Sort of yes. Jen was trying to comfort you, but you were insistent. Drunk and insistent that we report him as missing. You were starting to get so wound-up that you had a go at Jen. Remember?"

Grace closed her eyes and nodded. She recalled snapping at her friend which was very uncharacteristic.

"How would Jen know what it's like to feel the pain of not knowing where your child is?"

"That's pretty much what you said to her, Grace. Only not that calmly."

"So how did we end up here?"

"Well, I could see where things may have been heading. We were all pissed and well, you know, I didn't want Nick to join in the conversation. He's usually ready to crank things up, pissed or not. I just thought if we broke away…"

"There'd be less chance of you attacking him again?"

"Yes. I told Michael to get rid of all the guests, at least those that lived locally, and I persuaded you to walk over to the lodge so we could talk privately, in peace."

What Dan left out was Nick Foster had started to follow them from the house. He had been unsteady on his feet and his speech was slightly slurred when he called to them from the front door.

"Not very sociable leaving your own party. You need to put more lemonade with it Grace! Anyway, where the fuck are you going?"

Dan had asked Grace to carry on towards the lodge. At least it had stopped raining and the path was lit with solar powered lights. She had tottered on robotically.

He turned back towards Nick Foster.

"I'm taking Grace to the holiday lodge Nick; she's upset and she's drunk. Just get back to your wife for fuck's sake. We'll see you in the morning."

"A holiday lodge Dan? Prefer your temporary accommodation then? That figures."

Dan remembered wanting to knock him clean out. What a circus that could have turned into. Nick was baiting him, and he knew it. He couldn't afford an assault charge against him, and he couldn't afford his affair with Jen getting out via Nick Foster's stupid, uncaring, moronic mouth.

Sitting in bed in the holiday lodge he now picked up his phone and called Michael. It took a while, but he answered, hardly awake.

"Mike, it's Dad."

"Er yes, I know it says 'dad' on my screen."

"This isn't the time for sarcasm Mike. Did Gabriel show up?"

"Nope."

"Are you sure he's not somewhere in the house?"

"Dad it's 10 am and I've been in bed for two hours. Gabe isn't here."

"OK, me and Mum will be over soon. We spent the night in the holiday lodge."

Dan's heart was sinking as he called 999.

"Yes, police please, I want to report my son missing."

Chapter 12
New Year's Day 2011

PC Roberts sat in the refs-room at Llangefni Police Station. He had two hours left on the shift from hell, that had started with a tragedy he couldn't prevent, and had continued through the night. Domestic violence, pub fights, drunk and disorderly. The cells were full. In his nearly thirty years policing he had never adapted to the usually tranquil semi-rural patch in North Wales shapeshifting into a raging beast. The storm hadn't made much of a difference to the obvious excesses of alcohol and drugs being ingested by its citizens 'celebrating'. Christmas had been tough too for the on-duty officers. Having two historic feats of engineering connecting Anglesey to the mainland brought in flocks of tourists for sure, but they were probably unaware of the extent the bridges played in facilitating desperate people to end their lives. Nobody ever survived a jump from either bridge into the beautifully deceiving Menai Straights. Within a few hours of the incident he had witnessed, his colleagues were called to the Britannia Bridge again to speak to a man reported using the Samaritans phone at the Bangor end of the bridge then smashing the handset against the wall. He had been persuaded to get into the police van, he was lucky that somebody had the compassion to care about his state of mind enough to alert the police. He would see the new year.

The VW Golf had been taken to the police vehicle compound for examination. It probably wasn't a crime scene, but it would be held for forensic confirmation of who may have abandoned it on the bridge. Despite being extremely tired and hungry, he was going to drive to the address at Caernarfon Road, Bangor, before his shift ended, to enquire about Mr Jamie Fellowes. If the car wasn't taxed, then there was more of a chance it was stolen? Even though it hadn't been reported as such. Not a great start to the new year for this family - whoever they were.

It was 6.00am when he knocked on the door of number 520. It was a traditional, small, terraced house with pebble-dashed walls and a Welsh slate roof. It was a nice front door, a new trendy grey colour. There was a lot of student accommodation on this road, but it looked too nice and orderly to be that. He was accompanied by his younger, fitter, more awake colleague PC Andy Davies. A slight middle-aged woman in an over-large fleecy bath robe answered. She took a breath when she saw the two officers.

"If you're looking for Owen, he left six months ago."

PC Roberts shook his head. "Sorry love no, we're not here about Owen." Andy Davies cringed. Calling women 'love' was not part of modern Police training. The lady didn't flinch, she breathed a sigh of relief.

"Could we possibly come in Mrs...?"

"Fellowes, Angela Fellowes, yes of course, but I can't think why you're here. Sorry about the mess."

The room was clean and tidy with an empty wine bottle on the coffee table and one empty glass.

PC Roberts cleared his throat; this was never easy no matter how many times you sat with relatives that may have lost a loved one.

"Erm, Mrs. Fellowes, do you know a Jamie Fellowes?"

He expected her to look worried, but she just nodded and said, "He's not in trouble, is he? Only he's not like his father, useless scumbag."

"Er, so he's your son?"

"Yes." She still wasn't flinching. Usually at this stage the tears are welling up in anticipation. Two police officers sitting in your lounge at 6.00 am on New Year's Day was never a good thing.

"Does he own a car?"

"Yes, a white Golf? Is it? I'm no good with cars, I don't drive myself."

"When was the last time you saw your son?"

"That would be, er, September-ish when he left for uni. He drove himself there. I wasn't happy really, the car's a bit crappy but I couldn't be bothered arguing with him. He's a bit headstrong see. Why? Has he been in an accident?"

She still didn't seem particularly worried about the questions. PC Roberts felt a slight twinge in his guts. He took a breath.

"Mrs. Fellowes, the car that Jamie's the registered keeper of was abandoned on Britannia Bridge last night."

"So?"

The driver that abandoned the car jumped off the bridge." He braced himself waiting for the response.

"Like a suicide or something?"

"Well, I can't really say that it was anything else. I witnessed it myself Mrs Fellowes."

"When you say last night, what time was it?"

"It was 19.45, er quarter to eight in the evening."

Angela Fellowes smiled as she was shaking her head.

"Not my Jamie, he wouldn't do that. He's happy at uni, Aberystwyth. He's a fine art student. We speak every few days. Real mummy's boy, only don't tell him I said that..."

"So can you remember when you last spoke to your son?"

She got up and excused herself from the room. She went upstairs and returned with her mobile.

Within seconds she was replaying a voicemail message, timed at 1.30 am 1/1/11. There was music and loud voices in the background, but it was a male voice clearly speaking up above the din.

"Hi mam it's me. Sorry I didn't ring earlier, I'm at a party. Real posh place. Hope you're OK. I'll be over tomorrow sometime. I'm at Gabe's. Bit of a last-minute thing. Happy New Year! See you soon. Love you!"

"That's my Jamie at half-past one this morning. He's not your jumper. That's definitely his voice."

PCs Roberts and Davies were both extremely relieved to hear the voicemail, although it left a lot of unfinished business.

"Do you think he drove up from Aberystwyth yesterday?"

"Not a chance, he's a good boy, that car's not taxed or insured now so he wouldn't drive it anywhere I'm sure of it."

"OK, we're not accusing him of breaking the law Mrs Fellowes, we just need to establish who was driving his car yesterday."

PC Davies cut in, "Do you know who Gabe is?"

"He's a friend from uni. An art student, like Jamie. He's mentioned him a few times. His parents live near Beaumaris, well-off from what I can tell."

"Do you have a second name for Gabe?"

"Sorry, I can't remember. Tell you what, I'll ring Jamie now if you like."

Angela rang her son and put the phone call on speaker. It rang out and rang out till, "Hi it's Jamie here. Please leave a message and I'll get back to you."

"He's probably asleep Mrs Fellowes. If we could have his number, we can call him again later. Is that OK?"

"Absolutely fine. Please let me know if you find anything out. I know my son and he wouldn't harm anyone. Do you think his car was stolen?"

PC Roberts gave the standard answer, "At this stage we're still trying to establish the facts, but thank you for your time and your co-operation Mrs. Fellowes."

"No problem at all. What about the person that jumped? My God, they must have a family, how terrible."

"Like I said, we're trying to establish a few facts and hopefully your son can help us."

Chapter 13
New Year's Day 2011

Grace looked around the kitchen trying to remember where she had left her phone. The place didn't look as bad as she'd anticipated. The floor was a bit muddy. Bits of straw here and there but at least somebody had attempted to throw some empties into bin liners. The house was very quiet except for the low hum of the central heating boiler. She wasn't entirely sure who had stayed the night apart from Michael. She was hoping that Jen and Nick had vacated early, still under the influence or not. It wasn't out of the question as they both had form for drink driving, they just hadn't been caught yet.

Dan had already called her phone, but it was going straight to voicemail. He had gone upstairs to change but Grace had no inclination to do anything till the police called back. She wanted to know exactly what they were going to do and when they were going to do it. Dan had left his phone with her while he showered and changed. She carried on looking for her phone in desperation. It may have something on it that would give a clue as to Gabe's whereabouts. The time he rang her yesterday, text messages over the last few weeks. The police could tell a lot from mobile phone activity, even pinpointing where the phone had been at certain times. A very small glimmer of hope started to unfold in her mind when she heard the muffled sound of a phone ringing in another room. It was a familiar ringtone but not hers. She followed the sound to the sitting room and saw a figure flat-out on the couch, covered by a quilt.

"Gabriel, oh Gabe we've been so worried!" Grace was filled with relief. Michael hadn't checked the sitting room. Gabe had got here and crashed out.

The figure turned and a head peered out from underneath the quilt. The phone was still ringing out.

The instant relief was fast-tracked from her toes and out through the top of head when she realised that it wasn't Gabriel. She could see a dark topknot and a short, dark beard.

The young man was trying to locate his phone whilst half asleep. He looked up and saw Grace staring at him.

"Jamie?"

"Er yes, sorry I shouldn't be on your couch, so sorry, I'll be leaving soon." His phone had stopped ringing. He threw back the quilt and tried to put his jeans on without falling over. Grace watched the young man as he grabbed his clothes, hopping around in his boxers in a rush to get dressed. He was stunning, like her boys but in a totally different way. The hairstyle, the beard and the tattoos gave the appearance of somebody not to be messed with, while his face exuded a form of male beauty that she had never seen before. Thick dark but shapely brows laid over deep-set dark eyes and a full exquisite mouth. She was transfixed for a moment as she caught a glimpse of his perfect, lightly tanned torso. He looked older than Gabriel, by a few years, but was that just the beard? He started to apologise again.

"I'm sorry Mrs Hearn, I thought Gabe would be here, I'll be gone in five..."

Grace shook her head. "No, please stay Jamie. We need to find Gabriel. Please, I'll get you a coffee."

She motioned him to follow her into the kitchen. She hadn't even registered the night before just how utterly beautiful Jamie was. It was darker in the marquee which was the only time she'd glanced at him. He seemed to disappear with Michael after that brief sighting. If he was Gabriel's lover she understood why.

"When did you last see him?"

Jamie was about to answer when his phone rang again. He didn't recognise the number, so he ignored it.

"Why don't you answer it Jamie, it might be Gabriel?"

"I don't recognise the number. Thing is I don't answer if I don't recognise the number."

Then his phone notified that he had voicemail.

"Sounds like *somebody* wants to talk to you."

The same caller had left a voicemail message. He reluctantly decided to listen to it.

"Hello this is PC Joanna Draper from North Wales Police. I'm trying to contact Mr. Jamie Fellowes. Please could you call this number back as a matter of urgency. Thank you."

Grace watched Jamie's face as he listened to the voicemail message. She looked for a sign that the caller had good news, Gabriel-related information, anything that might put her in contact with her son. Jamie just looked puzzled. Grace couldn't wait for him to volunteer the information on who was trying to contact him.

"Well?"

"Ehm, I have to make a call Mrs Hearn, I'll just go out the back if that's all right?" He was already thinking, "What the fuck did North Wales Police want?"

"Yes of course, the marquee is still standing, miraculously. You could make your call in there if you like."

Jamie sat down on one of the few straw bales that had stayed intact. Was it his mam? Had his waste of space dad Owen done something terrible? He pressed call. It was answered very quickly.

"North Wales Police, PC Draper speaking."

"Er hi, it's Jamie Fellowes, you rang me?"

"Oh, hi Jamie, can I ask where you are at the moment?"

"I'm in Beaumaris."

"Exactly where?"

"Llanddona. Cae Mawr Road I think. I'm at a friend's house."

"OK, your friend is?"

"Gabriel, Gabriel Hearn. I came over to a party at his parents' place. Why do you want to know?"

"Right, do you own a VW Golf, registration H703 LCC?"

"Yes."

"Jamie could you please stay put for the next hour or so? I'd like to come and talk to you."

"About my car?"

"Yes mostly. It was found abandoned yesterday. I'll tell you more when I see you."

"I haven't driven it for months, honestly."

"I understand what you're saying Jamie, but we have to try to establish who was driving your car yesterday. Please just stay put and I'll head over now."

"Fine."

When Jamie walked back into the kitchen Dan had re-emerged from upstairs. He was holding Grace and stroking her tangled unkempt hair.

"That was the police. They found my car abandoned yesterday. They want to come here and talk to me, is that OK?"

"Abandoned where?" asked Dan.

"She didn't say, she's on her way though."

Grace and Dan looked at each other. Jamie had arrived at their party and Gabriel hadn't. Jamie's car has been found abandoned. Simultaneously they had the same thoughts, hoping desperately that the two things were not connected.

Then Dan had to inform Jamie, "The thing is Jamie, we've reported Gabriel as missing a few hours ago. The sooner the police get here the better."

Jamie sank onto a kitchen chair and put his head in his hands. Now he would have to tell the police everything he knew.

Chapter 14
New Year's Eve, Aberystwyth, 2010

Jamie had woken up on New Year's Eve with a jolt. He was in a single bed, alone, in the basic but functional student accommodation block. It was very quiet, due to most of the students going home for the holidays, with just a handful deciding that Christmas and New Year in Wetherspoon's was preferable to going home to their families.

It was already 10.00 a.m. and he started to wonder where Gabriel was. He could have gone to the shared bathroom along the landing for a shower, but he couldn't hear any running water. The clothes Gabriel had been wearing the night before were in a pile on the floor, alongside his.

He rolled over and sighed, re-running the conversation they had in the pub, reliving the painful emotions they both endured and feeling the effects of a heavy dose of regret.

Gabriel had come into his life just three months earlier. Jamie knew a lot of Fine Art students, most of them passionate and expressive, talented and special people who made sense of their surroundings in such a beautiful human way. He had always been attracted to art and it was the world he was happiest in.

When he saw Gabriel walk into the room for the life drawing class in September, he was instantly attracted. For the first time in his life, he experienced a ridiculous rush of adrenaline and joy, happiness and sadness, all in a few seconds. Like he'd loved him and lost him already.

Gabriel was tall and lean; his skin was perfect and sandy coloured from a part-faded tan. His blonde hair was shoulder length and twisted tightly into corkscrew curls that swayed seductively as he walked. His shoulders were slightly stooped which didn't give Jamie the impression that he was an over-confident person. He didn't smile at anyone, and he didn't talk to anyone. He sat at his easel, which was nearest to Jamie and listened intently to the lecturer. Jamie had tried to make eye-contact without success as Gabriel concentrated on his life drawing. He could see that Gabriel had large brown eyes, like pools of melted chocolate. He didn't know the boy's name or his sexual orientation but as far as Jamie was concerned, an *actual* angel had just walked into the life-drawing class.

Within a few days Jamie had decided to act on his experience rather than let it float off into the soulless realm of 'what might have been'. These feelings were strong, so surely it meant something. He waited after the next class and followed Gabriel, who headed towards the refectory alone. All he had to do was accidentally cross his path, and maybe share a table?

He bought a coffee and looked around the room. Gabriel was sitting alone, reading a book while he was eating pasta with a fork. Jamie was determined he was going to have a conversation with the shy, mysterious blonde and cringed inside at himself as he approached, struggling for an introduction that didn't appear corny and contrived.

"Hi," was all that came out. "Do you mind if I join you?"

Gabriel looked up and smiled a completely knock-out smile that transformed his already beautiful face into a joyous masterpiece. His teeth were white and perfect, he had dimples in both cheeks and his brown pools of chocolate twinkled with complete menace.

Jamie tried to play it cool as he offered his hand.

"I'm Jamie, from the life drawing class?"

"Oh, hi I'm Gabriel, Gabe. I prefer Gabe, it's less angelic. Yes of course I remember you."

An hour had passed very quickly that afternoon. The conversation was mostly about the course and the book Gabriel was reading, *The Art Spirit* by Robert Henri. From what Jamie could deduct, Gabe was probably gay but lacking any confidence in himself. Pretty much how Jamie had been several years earlier. There were few personal details exchanged during their conversation. Gabe was from Derbyshire originally and his parents lived in North Wales. Jamie lived in Aberystwyth so having the university on the doorstep was more than handy, given his love for all things art.

The conversation had ended with a loose agreement that they should meet up so Jamie could show Gabe the 'bright lights' of Aberystwyth. Jamie could tell that Gabe was lonely and at the same time, trying to cover it up. He had seen the young women in the class orbiting the shining star that was Gabriel Hearn and he knew that they were all going to be disappointed, one by one.

What followed in the next few weeks was a fast-paced, mutual, crazy and intense experience. Gabe wasn't ready to be openly gay, and Jamie had a flat, a girlfriend and a baby. He was living the lie that his father was happy with and the life that he was increasingly *unhappy* with. Gabe couldn't know about Ceris and their baby daughter who was not even a year old.

They met in bars that were miles away from campus, they booked hotels for the afternoon, Gabriel even sneaked him into his cramped student accommodation so they could hold each other in the confines of the barely adequate single bed. Jamie had never felt love like this for anyone in his life, his angel was loving and kind, gentle and intelligent, shy and unassuming with a phenomenal artistic talent. Jamie had had short-lived affairs with other men whilst living with Ceris but he couldn't compare his feelings now to those gay hook-ups, which were satisfying part of who he was but falling so short from the completion he needed as a living, breathing human being.

The nagging doubts that sat in the back of Jamie's mind were that he had a huge responsibility as Gabriel's first love. He was five years older, he wasn't being honest about his situation and his excuses for not taking Gabe back to his flat were already wearing thin. The months were passing by with no let-up on the intensity of their relationship. Gabe was already talking about staying in Aberystwyth for Christmas and New Year as he couldn't bear the thought of leaving Jamie for three weeks. He could feel the pressure mounting and like all pressurised situations something, sometime or other, would have to give. He couldn't facilitate the lie over the holidays, he had to tell Gabe the truth, he had to tell Ceris the truth and he had to make sure that him and his angel survived and continued their lives together whether either family approved or not.

Lying in a student bed, on the morning of New Year's Eve he recalled the look on Gabriel's face when he confessed about Ceris and the baby. Gabriel had closed his beautiful eyes and slowly shook his head. Tears had started to slide down his face as he sat down on the bed in the Premier Inn they had booked. He recalled the conversation clearly.

"Gabe, please, I'm going to tell her about you I promise. You're everything to me, please believe me."

"So, the flat that's damp and embarrassing is just a cover-story? The flat you share with your girlfriend? You have a child? Jamie you're just a fucking liar!"

"No, no Gabriel please, my life is a lie, a huge pathetic lie, to keep other people happy. This, this is real, it's who I am and I'm going to put it right I promise."

"No Jamie, you just want me to fuck off to North Wales while you play Santa to your child."

"Gabe listen to me. I'm going to go home tonight and I'm going to tell her about you, us, everything! I'll be back in the morning and we can do anything you want."

"You'll be fucking homeless Jamie."

"We could go up north together, you know, I'll take you to meet my mam, she's in Bangor. She knows about me, she knows what I've done to keep dad happy, but he's gone now, they split."

"No Jamie. If you love me, you go and tell her right now."

Gabriel had snatched up his holdall and left the hotel.

In the early hours that followed, Jamie had let himself into the student accommodation block and made his way to Gabriel's room. He had found him practically unconscious with an empty vodka bottle on the bedside drawers. He undressed and gently climbed into the bed, taking Gabriel in his arms and stroking his hair. He had whispered gently.

"Don't worry angel, it's going to be fine."

Gabriel opened his eyes, trying to focus. He smiled a drunken smile and put his arms around Jamie.

"You told her?"

Jamie didn't reply.

"No more lies Jamie please. You told her?"

"Shhhh."

"You didn't tell her."

"Tomorrow Gabe, I'll do it tomorrow, I promise."

Gabriel removed his arms from Jamie and rolled over into a foetal position.

"Just fuck off Jamie…"

Chapter 15
New Year's Day 2011

PC Joanna Draper pulled up outside the impressive farmhouse. She couldn't help feeling a slight twinge of resentment towards wealthy people from the mainland, sweeping in with their money, buying up the beautiful coastal properties, while genuine islanders struggled to get on the housing ladder. The feeling came and went in a second as she composed herself professionally and pulled on the handle of the iron doorbell. The briefing from her Sergeant had left her feeling that this enquiry had a strange vibe to it. A car had been stolen then abandoned by someone who went on to jump from the Britannia Bridge. The registered owner of the vehicle was apparently at the house of the parents who had just that morning reported their son missing. There had to be a connection, so her job was to be extremely careful, especially when talking to the anxious parents. Right at this moment the only potential crime was a stolen vehicle. She would have to talk to Jamie Fellowes first, in private. Dan answered the door. He had 'that look' Joanna had seen so many times. Tired, pale and low on hope.

"Hi, I'm PC Draper, I've come to speak to Jamie Fellowes."

Dan ushered her into the sitting room where Jamie was sitting with Michael. Joanna thanked him and asked respectfully if she could talk to Jamie in private. Michael stood up and followed his dad down the hallway. Even he was starting to feel very uneasy about Gabriel's whereabouts. He had spent most of the party in the games room with Jamie playing pool and talking. He had found Jamie really great company. He would only admit to being a friend of Gabriel's, a fellow art student at a loose end on New Year's Eve. Michael hadn't pushed him for anything more even though he knew inside that Jamie was definitely Gabriel's ridiculously handsome partner. He had wondered where his brother had got to but dismissed anything sinister because it was too unthinkable. He was happy for Gabe.

Joanna sat down opposite Jamie. She had some preliminary enquiry information and hoped that Jamie would co-operate. She noticed he was pushing back his hair a lot and stroking his beard. He was anxious and she would have to tread very carefully. She cleared her throat nervously.

"OK Jamie, I'm here to ask you a few things. You know your vehicle was recovered yesterday?"

"Yes." He nodded affirmatively.

"It's in the police compound at the moment but you will get it back eventually."

"I don't want it back to be honest, I can't afford to run it. That's why it's been sat on a car park for ages."

"Which car park was that?"

"The student parking at Aberystwyth Uni. I haven't driven it for months. Has it been used in a robbery or something?"

"No Jamie, and this isn't easy to say but whoever took your car left it on the Britannia Bridge, it was heading this way for sure."

"I'm sorry but I don't know how I can help you."

"We believe that the person who took your car jumped off the bridge yesterday evening during the storm."

"You believe? What do you mean you believe?"

"Jamie we have a witness, a fellow police officer who gave chase and tried to stop this person from, well from taking his own life."

Jamie closed his eyes and fought back the tears. He had woken up alone on New Year's Eve, just a few hours after arriving at Gabriel's student room. Gabriel had left a note that just said "Going home, can't deal with this. Enjoy the break with your family. Gabe."

Joanna interrupted his thoughts.

"Thing is Jamie we also have a missing person enquiry that we think may be connected to the theft of your car." She held out her hand to Jamie who was clearly starting to tremble. He didn't want to make that connection, but it was already there.

"Before you say anything can you confirm your home address please?"

"Flat 2, Bridge Street, Aberystwyth."

"OK that's not the address your car is registered to?"

"No, it's registered to my mam's address in Bangor."

"OK Jamie, when did you last see your car?"

"Before the end of the term, about mid-December."

"Jamie how do you know Gabriel Hearn?"

"He's in my cohort at uni, we met in September and we became friends."

"OK so he's a fellow art student?"

"Yes."

"But you're not an art student are you, Jamie? I've made some initial enquiries with Aberystwyth. You're on the payroll, not the student list."

Jamie looked up quickly, his body language was obvious, he wasn't expecting that.

He took a deep breath and wiped the tears from his face on the sleeve of his sweatshirt.

"No, I'm a part-time life model…"

"So why would you want to give the impression you're a student?"

"My mam thinks I'm studying for a Fine Art degree but I'm not. I moved down there a couple of years ago to get away from my dad, Owen Fellowes, you've probably heard of him... he's a proper arsehole."

"So how did you meet Gabriel?"

"He walked into the life drawing class three months ago and I was lying on a couch naked."

"Please be honest Jamie, are you and Gabriel a couple?"

Jamie couldn't hold back the torrent of tears any longer. He started to feel breathless and panicky.

"We fell in love, honestly he's the best thing that ever walked into my life."

Joanna started to fight back her own tears; this conversation was becoming harrowing.

"So, when did you last see him?"

"At his student flat on the campus early hours of yesterday. We have an issue to get through see and he got drunk on vodka. When I woke up, he was gone."

"Would you mind telling me what the issue is?"

"Thing is I had to tell Gabe about Ceris and the baby..."

"Ceris is?"

"A girl I met not long after I moved down there. We have a baby daughter together, but I was going to tell her about me and Gabe. Thing is she's gone to her parents for New Year, she went the day before yesterday, a bit last minute but she thought I'd be following her..."

"So you didn't get a chance to speak to her?"

"No, I mean this is major, isn't it? I've been living a lie for a long time, I wasn't going to dump her by text, *I'm* not an arsehole."

"Do you think it's possible that Gabriel took your car yesterday?"

Jamie nodded.

"Did he have the keys?"

"Nope, the car was unlocked and the keys were in the door trim. It was a bit of a joke really, I wanted someone to take the fucking thing. It was no use to me, not even roadworthy."

"OK Jamie, here's what I'd like you to do. Please try to stay positive. We don't know for certain who jumped off the bridge yesterday, we're going to look at the CCTV later but as far as we know the man had pulled up his hood. Not even the police officer who witnessed it could describe the person. It was dark and it happened really quickly. Gabriel is still a missing person until we know otherwise, and that's what I'm going to say to his parents."

"Will you tell them about me and Gabe?"

"No need to unless you're all right with it. Your business is your business. You're a friend, that's not a lie, is it?"

Jamie shrugged his shoulders. "A friend who spent his last fifty quid on train tickets to Bangor because I was so desperate to see him?"

"Like I said Jamie, how you describe your relationship with Gabriel to his family is up to you. Now please dry your eyes and I'll take you home to your mam's when I've spoken to Mr and Mrs Hearn. Is that OK?"

Jamie nodded just as his phone rang. It was Ceris. He had ignored all her calls and texts for the last twenty-four hours. If he didn't answer now, she would probably report him as missing too. He answered tentatively.

"Hello,"

"Jamie, where the fuck are you? We've been worried sick!"

"I'm in Anglesey?"

"What? Why? What's going on Jamie?" It was now or never so he took another deep breath.

"I'm so sorry Ceris, there's someone else, I, I didn't want it to come out like this…"

She hung up immediately.

That was *one* confession. Sometime soon he would have to tell his mother about the granddaughter she didn't know she had. All the lies and cover-ups were crumbling around him as he wrapped his arms around himself for some kind of comfort.

Chapter 16
New Year's Day 2011

Dan found Grace sitting on the corner of the huge bed in their recently refurbished master bedroom. She looked so small and frail compared to the day before. She had tied her hair back and had no make-up on, looking every bit her age. He sat next to her and sighed.

"The police officer's here, she's talking to Jamie about his car. Then she wants to talk to us."

Grace shook her head.

"So a bloody car is more important than our missing son?"

Dan had to agree but he didn't say it out loud. He had to stay strong and supportive because if this was a nightmare it was only the start of it.

"Who is Jamie anyway? I mean Gabe hasn't mentioned him at all, then he just turns up to our party uninvited?"

"Gabe has hardly spoken to either of us since September Grace. He's always been the secretive one. He's not the open book that Michael is unfortunately."

"Where is Michael anyway? He spent most of the night playing pool with our surprise guest. Didn't Michael ask him any questions?"

"Like what Grace?"

"Like where's my brother. What have you done to him?"

"That's a bit harsh, Grace, we don't know enough to make that judgement."

Grace's nerves had been literally tingling since she woke up in the holiday lodge and she couldn't hold back.

"For God's sake Dan, what is *wrong* with people? Gabriel tells us nothing about his life, you tell me nothing about your past life, my best friend marries her *awful* ex without telling me. What is it about me Dan? Why is Grace not allowed to know things?"

Dan couldn't answer for his son or Jen, but he tried.

"Jen knew you, we, would try to talk her out of it, that's why she didn't tell us about marrying Nick again. Gabe has been secretive all his life Grace, he's probably still trying to establish who he is..."

"I don't care who he is, I care *where* he is Dan!"

"He's probably crashed out somewhere. Hopefully we'll know more when we talk to the police."

Dan left Grace sitting on the bed, blowing her nose that had started to drip along with the tears. He headed up the second flight of stairs to Michael's room. Surely Jamie had given something up to him during the previous evening? He walked in to see Michael standing at the open Velux window, head peering out, with a cigarette in hand that was quickly discarded when his dad walked in.

"Dad can't you at least knock?" Dan shook his head. He couldn't be bothered reprimanding his adult son this time.

"There's a police officer downstairs talking to Jamie."

Michael looked puzzled. Then he yawned.

"Talking to Jamie about what?"

Dan felt irritated about his son's apparent lack of concern.

"Something about his car being found abandoned."

"Abandoned where?"

"We don't know yet."

"He told me he came up on the train yesterday."

"What else did he say Mike, you spent long enough with him?"

"Why Dad? Why all the questions? He said he wanted to surprise Gabe so he came up. What's the big deal?"

Now Dan was shouting. "The big deal Mike is that your brother is missing, his mystery 'friend' turns up instead, your mother is in bits and you are yawning and scratching your arse like nothing's happening."

Mike's expression changed instantly. He now had a rare, serious look on his unshaven face. He wished that he was psychologically in tune with his twin, but he wasn't. Yes, they looked identical, but he didn't feel his brother's pain like some twins. They weren't telepathic, that was entertainment for documentaries, but right now he wished they were. He'd always known that he was the stronger twin, protecting Gabriel for as far back as he could remember, taking the lead, talking for him, allowing him to stay in his shadow. Not knowing his brother's approximate location was something he wasn't used to.

"I think Jamie came up to see Gabe because they're together Dad. He didn't announce it last night, but he didn't have to."

"But didn't you say last night he didn't know about you being Gabe's twin? Don't you think that's really odd?"

"Yes, I think it's very fucking odd Dad. I know when he looked at me, he thought I was Gabe. I've never had anyone look at me like that before apart from, well..." He stopped himself from saying who. "God he nearly died of embarrassment."

"So why would Gabriel not tell his, his, (he could hardly get the word out) partner, about his family set-up? We know he can be secretive but Jesus, Mike, this is off the scale. And how did he know our address?"

"Maybe Gabe just wasn't ready to spill his guts? Maybe he didn't want to introduce his partner to his identical, smarter, funnier twin?

"But he shared our home address? This isn't the time to joke Mike. Seriously I'm not happy about our friend Jamie. He's hiding something."

Mike, for all his apparent lack of empathy, commented with an unusual gem of wisdom.

"He's hiding something, Gabe is hiding something, everybody is hiding *something* Dad. I mean what chance do we have if everybody knows everything there is to know about us?"

Dan reeled inside at his son's statement. Of course, he was right, everybody, no matter how close they are to somebody, has something to hide. Sometimes on a small scale and sometimes on a colossal scale. His life hadn't been a complete lie but the need to distance himself from his past seemed to own him like a relentless curse. He could hear Annie's voice in his head echoing, "Tell him who his real mother is!" Dan had never met the woman who gave birth to him but right now he wished he had. Maybe his real mother, given a chance would have loved him. Unlike Annie.

Chapter 17
Hayfield 1968

Annie's mental health was declining quickly. Since she had given birth to Jack, Dan had noticed changes in her. They were subtle at first, not obvious to anyone that didn't know her. Patrin noticed too but to Dan, his father clearly had his head in the sand. He was busier year on year as his business grew and when he wasn't working he was in the Ploughboy Inn with his 'acquaintances' from the village. It was firmly his second home. If Annie wanted Patrin's time and attention she would send Dan running down to the pub with all sorts of tales and emergencies.

Sometimes Patrin would drop everything and run home, depending on how convincing the story was and sometimes he would shoo Dan away, too engrossed in his card game. It started with baby Jack's health, he had a fever, he was sick, he had fallen off the couch, he wouldn't wake up. All manner of false situations which in time, Dan was reluctant to convey and Patrin just stopped believing altogether. After Jack had fallen in the stream when he was two years old Annie's behaviour towards Dan changed. It felt to him like the event had triggered feelings of resentment in Annie that she couldn't or wouldn't hold back. Her focus became almost exclusively on Jack to the point that Dan had to look after himself. He had to feed himself, wash his own clothes, take himself to bed, wake himself up for school. Dan had acquired second-hand school uniform from the local JP whose son was a few years older and also attended the grammar school. Most days he didn't have the bus fare, so he walked the three miles there and back, whatever the weather. His determination to be educated was in him despite the lack of encouragement from his parents. He now knew Annie wasn't his birth mother which explained her apathy towards him. Not that Patrin and her had ever sat him down and talked him through his beginnings. No explanation came following Annie's outburst about his 'real mother'. Patrin wouldn't talk about her whenever Dan asked him the question. He always seemed irritated and snappy with his answers. The cruellest notion was that his mother wasn't dead. Patrin never admitted that Danior's birth mother had died in childbirth, like Annie had been led to believe.

Not long after his fifteenth birthday, Dan arrived home from school to see a fairly new caravan in place of the old one that had sat behind the house. It didn't hold much interest for him. Annie had been spending more and more time with Jack, eating and sleeping in the old caravan. She had been in and out of hospital for the last few years with a diagnosis of manic depression and it had become exhausting for him and his dad. There were periods when she didn't sleep for weeks, chattering at speed, sometimes incomprehensible. The periods of mania could be very unpredictable when the usually quietly-spoken Annie would become animated and sometimes violent. Jack's attendance at nursery school lasted all of three days, as Annie would wait outside for hours, refusing to go home till Jack's nursery class had ended. Sometimes, she took him on long walks, further than his young legs could cope with and would be brought back by the police.

She talked about Lizzy Cooper during her manic episodes. Dan presumed she was a traveller from the New Forest, somebody deep in Annie's past. He got the feeling that Lizzy Cooper was a real person that Annie could actually see when she was hallucinating and calling out to the woman to leave her alone.

That day, he changed out of his uniform, unknowingly to him for the last time. He found his dad loading up bags of clothes into his faithful Land Rover along with Annie and Jack's personal belongings, and some of his own.

"Dad what's happening?" was the obvious question.

"Look son, I've got to take your mum home. She's not well and she's going home."

"Home where?"

"Back to Hampshire, her sisters are still there. She can't stay here Dan, they'll come for Jack, the social services, they know she can't cope."

Dan was immediately fired up. He loved Jack and couldn't understand in the moment what his dad actually meant.

"I can take care of Jack, we can cope though..."

Patrin was shaking his head.

"I'm taking them back to the New Forest Dan, her sisters will look after them, make her well again. She never really took to this life. I'll be back in a few months trust me."

"A few months? What about the business? What about school?"

"You just did your last day at school son. Sorry. I've taught you everything I know so you can do the repairs till I come back. You haven't had a mother for years, you'll do just fine."

"No dad, I can't do it on my own. There's the animals as well. I don't want to leave school..."

His dad had fronted him that day as if Dan was already a grown man. Patrin had bought the caravan for Annie and Jack to live in. He was towing it down to Hampshire and re-uniting Annie with her family. There was no question of Dan going with them, the rest of the family didn't know he existed. Patrin promised he would be back in three months' time to 'sort out' the business, whatever that meant.

When Annie got into the Land Rover with Jack, she didn't even glance at Dan standing by with tears in his eyes. In just one day he had been forced to end his education at the same time as being saddled with the full responsibility of a smallholding and a mechanical repair business. His beautiful brother Jack was being taken from him and his (so-called) mother was leaving for good. As they drove away, Patrin wound down the window and beckoned Dan.

"Don't worry son, I've got you some help till I can get back. He'll be here soon, he knows the situation. He needs a place to stay see, his girlfriend's kicked him out. He can pay you a bit of board, but you make him do some work for his keep. He's a good man."

Before Patrin could pull away from the farm, a familiar figure came walking in full tilt down the muddy driveway. It was Frank Shaw. Dan had sighed in disbelief. How was he going to coerce Frank Shaw into doing anything? He stopped in front of Dan, swaying gently. He started singing:

"Oh Danny boy, the pipes the pipes are calling, from glen to glen and down the mountainside."

Dan led Frank into the house and watched him fall onto the couch. His trousers were pee-soaked.

He didn't know it at the time, but he would never see Patrin and Annie again.

Chapter 18
The Frank Shaw years

Dan despaired the first night his 'babysitter' had taken temporary residence. He left Frank snoring on the couch and took himself to bed. The next day wasn't a school day so he thought he would get up a little later, hoping Frank Shaw would not be where he had left him the night before. His bedroom was cold, and he had already decided that he would move into the larger bedroom with a larger bed that his parents had abandoned, along with him. He would take advantage of having a fireplace with a real fire and Frank Shaw would have to use the smaller, draughtier, damp single room.

As he lay in bed, he tried to make sense of what had happened the day before. He thought about Annie's illness and the strain it had put on them all, apart from when she was in hospital – then things were far less stressful. He had looked after Jack while his dad carried on the machinery repairs, missing school to the point where letters were arriving, querying his frequent absences and threatening expulsion. Well, none of that mattered now, he had officially left school and there was nothing he or the authorities could do about it, he was fifteen, he didn't have to go to school. He had probably been set to pass all his O levels, with a particular love for science, but that had been snatched away from him along with his brother. As Annie's love for him had waned, he knew he wasn't going to miss her too much. The tenderness he'd received from her was a very distant memory now, almost erased from his life-story. The ironic fact that he had been taken (or handed over) from his birthmother, then abandoned by his fake mother left an indescribable pain. He had to put all his trust in Patrin who, to this point, had never let him down in any sizeable way. He would step up and keep the place going till his dad returned from Hampshire.

An unusual but pleasant smell had started to rise up the stairs, accompanied by a faint crackle. Dan grabbed his trousers from the floor and ran downstairs to investigate. The couch was unoccupied and to his utter amazement there at the cooker stood Frank Shaw, frying eggs and bacon in a battered old frying pan. He was dressed in clean clothes, shaved, hair washed and sober. Dan had never encountered Frank sober before; it was completely unknown territory, so he stopped abruptly at the kitchen door. Frank motioned to the kitchen table that was set with cutlery and condiments.

"Please take a seat, your breakfast will be ready soon lad. Can't expect you to work on an empty stomach."

Dan wondered where Frank had acquired the clean clothes then noticed that the jeans and sweater were definitely part of Patrin's limited wardrobe. He really didn't know what he expected of Frank, but it definitely wasn't 'house trained'.

"Er, I just have porridge in a morning but thanks." He sat down as directed and started to feel extremely confused. To any person in the village, Frank was a waster, a drunk, a man from a privileged background, a man who was given everything on a plate, who pissed it all up the wall. That wasn't what Dan was witnessing this morning. As Frank set down two plates of cooked breakfast and took his own seat, Dan could smell last night's consumption on his breath. Frank cleared his throat then made his announcement."

"Danior, er Dan, do you prefer Dan?"

"Yes."

"All right Dan, here's what's happening. Your father has asked me to look after you while he's away. I urgently needed a place to stay so it was win-win. I know what you're thinking, Frank Shaw is a drunk and a gambler, how can he look after me?" Dan couldn't disagree. "Surely things will be the other way around? Dan will have to look after Frank?" Dan still couldn't disagree. "Well today, by the grace of God and your father's good heart, I Frank Shaw, have been given another chance. Now, I'm not going to give any assurances that I'll be sober. That would be foolish, I'm an alcoholic, but young man, what I can promise you is I will cook because I like cooking, I will help with the animals because I like animals and I will make every effort to be sober during daylight hours because I like you. I have a dwindling amount of money in the bank due to my philandering habits, but I will pay you seven shillings a week for my board and lodgings. Do we have a deal?" Frank held out his right hand.

Dan was taken aback at how articulate the sober Frank Shaw was. He knew that Frank had been very well educated at a private school and there were glimpses of who he actually was, minus the alcohol. He accepted Frank's hand and felt grateful that he hadn't simply claimed back his property and moved in uninvited. He felt he should mention it.

"Don't you sort of own the farm anyway?" Frank gasped and immediately replied.

"I may be a piss artist lad, but I'm a man of my word. When I put up this place as a stake it's because I was prepared to lose it. And lose it I did. Fairly and squarely to a fine upstanding man, your father. He has the deeds and I have no legal claim whatsoever."

That was reassuring for Dan to hear.

"I'm nearly sixty-eight years old, lad, and I could do with slowing down a bit. So, starting today I will not be visiting the off-licence for my usual bottle. I'll be visiting the off-licence for a half-bottle instead. I will make a meal that will be on this table for 6.00 p.m. and at 6.30 p.m. I will be taking a stroll to the Ploughboy Inn. I can't guarantee what time I'll return. Do we still have a deal?"

Dan nodded. Having Frank for company was better than no company. He cooked a great breakfast and if his pledge to reduce his alcohol intake actually happened, they could make a decent team.

"What about your clothes? Those are my dad's."

"Ah yes, sorry I don't have a lot of clothes but what I do have will probably be in the front garden of my last address. I'll collect them today and take them to the launderette, in fact if you want any of your clothes washing, I'll take them too."

Dan was trying to get his head around the difference in this man without a drink inside him. He *was* completely house trained after all, but would all that change in the evenings? He claimed to be nearly sixty-eight, but he looked twenty years older. That was probably his lifestyle, which hopefully was about to change for the better.

Chapter 19
The Frank Shaw years, continued

Patrin didn't return after three months as he had promised. Dan had waited at the village phone box every Friday at 6.00 p.m. for his father's call. He would update Dan on his mother's recovery, the aunties, uncles and cousins that didn't even know he existed and sometimes he would hear Jack in the background shouting to him. Hearing Jack's voice was the one thing that really hurt. He didn't miss Annie or Patrin, he was hurting from being abandoned, and the provision of the village drunk as his babysitter. The calls lasted no more than five or six weeks into the new arrangements. One Friday evening early in October, Dan waited for an hour at the red phone box on Market Street. Most of the villagers knew not to use this phone on a Friday at 6.00 p.m. On that occasion, Patrin didn't call, and on the next occasion Patrin didn't call. When it happened for a third time in as many weeks, Dan decided he wouldn't go to the phone box again.

Frank tried to stick to his pledge. Their lives became quite routine, starting with a cooked breakfast every morning, a sandwich for lunch and a hearty evening meal. As promised at 6.30 p.m., Frank would don a clean shirt and trousers and head over to the Ploughboy Inn, his half-bottle of brandy having been consumed during the day. Sometime between 11.00 p.m. and midnight, Frank would stagger through the back door and head for the couch, and occasionally he would make it to bed.

Dan could see himself filling out, now that his meals were regular and of a better quality than Annie could have provided. Working on the farm machinery and other agricultural vehicles was physically very demanding and he was starting to become toned. He liked the fact that it made him look older. The regular customers trusted him to carry out repairs properly, as Patrin's protege, however, new custom was starting to become a problem. In an effort to tackle the issue of potential new customers seeing not much more than a child running the business, Dan asked Frank if he could be the 'front of house'.

As long as he was sober enough, he could be the adult face of the outfit, while Dan stayed firmly in the background carrying out the repairs and services.

Frank had responded cautiously at first. He instinctively shied away from responsibility, his confidence in himself had eroded with every sip but he was willing to try. The half-bottle of brandy was still purchased daily and the 6.30 prompt stroll to the Ploughboy Inn continued. The minor miracle that started to emerge was that Frank's brandy bottles were not completely drained every day. He liked talking to the customers, mostly farmers and farm labourers, and not having alcohol on his breath started to become a little more important to him. Very slowly, Frank was losing his bloodshot eyes and sallow skin tone. Some nights he would return to the farm before 11.00 p.m. and if Dan was still up, he would sit and recount tales from his life story for as long as Dan could stay awake.

Frank had been the only child of wealthy farmers. His parents sent him to boarding school at the age of eight and he hated it. He wasn't really interested in farming despite having to help out during the holidays. When he left school his parents sent him to Sandhurst Royal Military Academy. They knew he wasn't going to take over the farm so they pinned their hopes on Frank becoming an army officer, something they could be proud of and justification for his expensive education. It was nearing the end of the Great

War and recruitment was still a high priority given the huge numbers of officer casualties from 1914-1916, and the potential to lose more was a reality.

Frank didn't complete his basic training. He was bullied and ridiculed by his peers who were mostly from aristocratic families. To them he was just a skinny farmer's boy with no breeding and a strange Midlands accent. After six weeks he left Sandhurst without permission. His distraught parents couldn't bear the thought of a dishonourable discharge and the gossip it would generate, so they had paid his way out of officer training, excusing him to their friends and family as having a 'weak chest'. He spent the next two years at his parents' farm, playing at estate management and developing a passion for cooking. In a last attempt at launching their only child into a career worth noting, Mr and Mrs Shaw sent Frank to Paris to Le Cordon Bleu culinary school. Once again, he was bullied and ridiculed by his peers and mentors, the difference being that this time he was determined to succeed. After graduation, he started as a commis chef at London's Savoy Hotel and rose in rank to sous chef in just two years. Mr and Mrs Shaw were happy to be able to tell their friends about their son, travelling to London occasionally to dine at the Savoy and marvel at the food he created. What they didn't know was the job demanded long working hours, relentless pressure and very little time off. Frank was spending his 'down-time' relaxing with his favourite friends Johnnie Walker and Jim Beam.

Tragedy struck in 1935 when Mr Shaw was killed in a farming accident, which left him impaled on a pitchfork. Mrs Shaw spent the next two years drinking while the business fell apart around her. By the time she died there was no business, just a large valuable farmhouse, a hundred acres of land and several outbuildings. As sole heir, Frank inherited everything and sold everything. He bought a modest house in Hayfield, with ten thousand pounds in the bank and never worked again.

Dan became very fond of Frank and enjoyed listening to the stories about his colourful life. He was an acquired taste for most people, but Dan learned that he was at heart a kind and sensitive human being. He was probably only half the man he could have been due to his alcohol intake, and he had trust issues due to people taking liberties with his money, borrowing but not repaying, and accepting his wild generosity in the pub. As the months passed by into winter, then spring, and with no word from Patrin, Dan accepted that his life was in his own hands now and the emotional wounds he sustained from being abandoned would heal in time. He was going to build up the business with or without Patrin and, when he was ready, he would find his real mother.

Chapter 20
New Year's Day 2011

PC Joanna Draper made some notes in her pocketbook before escorting Jamie from the farmhouse to the police car. She knew from her conversation with him that there was every possibility Gabriel had been in distress the previous day. What she didn't want was his anxious parents asking Jamie too many questions and making a tense situation worse. She asked him to stay in the car till she had spoken to Dan and Grace. She asked him to check his phone while he was waiting and make a note of any significant communication between him and Gabriel over the last twenty-four hours. That was easy for Jamie. He had made twenty or thirty calls, sent countless text messages and they were all unanswered.

She returned to the house just as two of the overnight party guests were leaving. A very striking woman in a bright orange faux fur coat, tall and slim with a look of Naomi Campbell, followed by a man dressed all in black, carrying two overnight bags and looking very much the worse for wear. He looked strangely familiar, but she couldn't think why.

Dan and Grace were waiting in the kitchen with Michael. Joanna could see that Grace had been crying but she was making the effort to compose herself, while nervously turning the rings on her left hand. A missing person case was nothing new, especially given the proximity to Bangor University. Students going AWOL after nights out, students just not going home in the holidays. Ninety-nine times out of a hundred they were found safe and well, but Joanna had a strong feeling that Gabriel Hearn was the male that abandoned the car then surrendered his soul to the Menai Strait. This was going to be difficult.

Grace spoke first, her eyes glistening with tears.

"Do you know anything? Has Jamie told you anything useful?" Joanna took a seat at the kitchen table.

"Mr and Mrs Hearn..."

"Please just Dan and Grace, we don't want formality..." Dan interrupted.

"Fine, Dan and Grace, I've asked Jamie quite a few questions and I'm satisfied that he answered most of them honestly."

Grace looked puzzled. "Most of them?"

"Yes, we had a bit of a shaky start, but I'm satisfied that what he told me about the last twenty-four hours or so can all be verified. This is still a missing person enquiry and the only possible crime that connects to the situation is Jamie's vehicle being taken from the student car park at Aberystwyth University in the early hours of yesterday and being driven untaxed and uninsured up to Anglesey."

Michael was quick to interject. "Where was it abandoned?"

Now Joanna's heart was starting to race a little.

"It was abandoned on Britannia Bridge, inbound at around 19.45 yesterday evening."

Michael interrupted again, desperately wanting to defend his brother. "So what? Gabe doesn't have a driving licence, he wouldn't steal a car, he just wouldn't."

Joanna turned to face Dan and Grace who were holding hands at the table. They had both closed their eyes.

"Whoever took Jamie's car and abandoned it, and I'm pretty sure at the moment that's one and the same person, er, he stepped up onto the side of the bridge and was well, literally blown over..."

Michael could see the terror on his parents' faces. He stood up quickly and thumped his hand down hard on the table.

"Gabe doesn't drive, so please what are you trying to say? That he's committed suicide?"

Joanna's training around delivering bad news seemed to be failing her.

"I'm so sorry but at the moment, we can't rule out Gabriel as being that driver. I'm going to see the CCTV footage this afternoon. It may or may not help us. The weather was bad and sometimes in those sorts of conditions it's hard to make out individuals."

Michael was becoming more and more agitated while his parents sat still, trying to digest what this police officer was trying to say.

"Like I said, my brother doesn't drive. You should be out there looking for him, in fact we should be looking for him, Mum, Dad..." Then he broke down in tears.

Grace tried to comfort her distraught son.

"We don't know anything yet Mike, but please let's face some facts. Gabe never took a driving test but he's had lessons in the past..."

Dan could feel his anger rising as he witnessed his wife trying to reason with his son. He had to ask the question.

"So where's Jamie and what does he know?"

Joanna switched her tone back to formal. "Mr Hearn, I've asked Jamie to wait in the car then I'm taking him to his mother's address."

"So, this Jamie character turns up uninvited to our home, sleeps on our couch, tells us nothing about his 'friendship' with our son and now you're his fucking chauffeur?"

"Please Mr Hearn, you'll get your chance to speak to Jamie, but in the meantime I'm asking you to sit tight till we find out more facts about the driver of the car. This isn't a criminal investigation."

"Well, I'll speak to him right now because I want some answers now!"

Dan left the kitchen at speed, swiftly followed by Joanna Draper.

"Mr. Hearn, please! This isn't going to help!"

Dan was pulling on the handle of the rear passenger door and banging on the window. Jamie stared straight ahead.

"What have you done to my son?"

"Mr Hearn! If you don't stop, I'll have to arrest you. Please go back into the house and as soon as I have any more information I'll get straight back to you."

Dan turned abruptly and returned to the house. He didn't want a criminal record.

As Joanna Draper drove along the B5109 towards Pentraeth, she tried to make small talk with Jamie.

"Were you at the party all night?"

"Yes."

"It's just that I saw two of the guests leaving earlier and I thought I recognised one of them."

"Nick Foster."

"The musician?"

"Yes."

"I thought he looked familiar."

"He's godfather to Gabe and Mike. His wife's their godmother, didn't you recognise her?"

"Sort of, looked exactly like his ex-wife to be honest."

"She's not his ex-wife. They just got married."

"Did you talk to him at all?"

"Yes, he's a total wanker."

The radio sounded, calling her collar number. Jamie had never sat in a police car, so he didn't pay any attention to the communication officer's message.

"Can you make your way to Llangefni station please.

Midday briefing regarding possible 10-56 at Ynys Llanddwyn."

Chapter 21
New Year's Day 2011

The tide at Newborough Warren had ebbed away enough to expose the path to Llanddwyn Island. The storm that had thrown so much debris onto the beach had passed in the early hours and by 10.00 a.m. a smattering of local people were enjoying walking in the sunshine and the stunning views over to Caernarfon and the Llŷn Peninsula beyond.

Dewi had offered to walk the dog before he and his wife made the annual New Year's Day trip to her parents in Conwy. Damson, their excitable, water-loving springer spaniel, didn't travel well so taking her with them in the car wasn't an option. He couldn't help smiling as Damson ran freely in her 'happy place'. Dewi felt very blessed to have this beautiful beach right around the corner from their house in Newborough. He loved his walks with Damson, although some days it was very difficult to keep her on dry land.

He decided to go as far as Llanddwyn to make sure the dog was suitably tired for the rest of the day. There was something genuinely magical about the tidal island that was accessible on foot for just a couple of daylight hours. He would walk Damson to the Twr Mawr lighthouse at the far end of Llanddwyn, a point that marked the western approach to the Menai Strait.

He ignored the signs requesting the public to keep their dogs on leads when on the island. There wouldn't be any ground-nesting birds at this time of year, so everything was just fine. He tried to keep up with Damson, who was running away from the path, backwards and forwards, nose to the ground as always. She was a family pet but her natural instinct to find and retrieve anything she found interesting was at best amusing and at worst gruesome. Dead fish, dead sea birds, parts of animals that couldn't be identified because of decomposition. It could be a really smelly and unpleasant experience, but hopefully not today.

As Damson disappeared from view for the umpteenth time, Dewi felt a little irritated. He couldn't be late back, and he didn't want any doggy-drama to interrupt their plans. He still couldn't see her, but he could hear her distinctive bark. Loud and persistent, she had probably found a dead gull or maybe hopefully just a rubber ball, the reaction would be the same regardless.

He followed the familiar noise down towards the small beach that lay to the left of the lighthouse. He could see Damson in the distance. She wasn't moving around as she focused on what looked like a large piece of driftwood. Her barking was interspersed with a whine, and the odd growl. She was very excited, and he would have to get her back on the lead if he wanted to get back home on time.

As he approached the stationary object, he could see that it was definitely not driftwood. There, face down in the sand was a body. He didn't panic, he was a paramedic, so he knew that life for this person was extinct. Due to his profession, it wasn't the first time he'd witnessed a body washed up around Anglesey and it probably wouldn't be the last. He knelt down gently next to the partially-clothed corpse, who was naked from the waist down and shoeless. It was a male, probably in his early twenties, blonde hair peeking from the black hoodie and a small, red mark on the right side of his face, in line with his right ear.

Dewi had become a little hardened to death over the years due to the numbers of dead or dying people he came into contact with. One thing he never got used to was seeing the lifeless body of a child or young person. His eyes filled with tears as touched the side of the boy's face. This was a tragedy, either accidental or suicide, either way this boy's life was over, and a family somewhere would have to be informed. He sighed as he reached in his pocket for his phone. "Police please, I've found a body, Ynys Llanddwyn." As he finished the call, an uninvited raven landed on the beach and let out a loud almost mocking squawk, alerting other potential predators to the scene.

Chapter 22
New Year's Day 2011

Joanna Draper had dropped Jamie off at his mum's address and hastily made her way back to Llangefni. Everything in her experience as a police officer was telling her that the briefing was going to be sombre and stressful at the same time. Any suicide was extremely difficult to deal with, from seeing the body either at the scene or in a mortuary, to the immense responsibility of informing a family that their loved one has ended their own life.

Her Sergeant, Bryn Edwards, was waiting in one of the interview rooms. They were joined by one other male colleague who had been at the scene. She listened to Bryn as he described the events of that morning. A local off-duty paramedic had discovered the body of a young male on one of the small beaches at Ynys Llanddwyn. The coroner had attended the scene and was satisfied that there was no crime to investigate. The body had been transferred to the mortuary at Ysbyty Gwynedd awaiting a formal identification. Photos taken at the scene and the mortuary by the mortician were now on Bryn's laptop and he turned the screen around to show his colleagues.

Joanna knew instantly who it was. She had been in the company of his identical twin just hours earlier. There hadn't been anything on the body or around the scene that could identify the tragic soul, but she was certain.

"Jo, is this our misper?" asked Bryn Edwards.

"Definitely Sarge. It's uncanny how much he looks like his brother."

"Right, well, we'd better get over to his parents' place and give them a chance to formally identify."

Joanna felt very uneasy at the thought of returning to an already semi-grieving family, to deliver the sad news. Why was it always harder on a sunny day? This wealthy family with their huge property, sea and mountain views and showbiz friends were not exempt from tragedy. Mrs Hearn had looked very frail earlier so what would happen when her worst fears were confirmed? That prompted her memory of seeing Nick Foster and his wife leaving the house.

"I spotted a celebrity leaving the Hearn's house earlier."

"Oh really, like who?"

"Like Nick Foster, you know, the musician?" Bryn had to think about it.

"Erm, kind of rings a bell. Is he current?"

"Well yes and no really. His band still tour but they're all getting on a bit now. Remember Cult Rebellion? Quite big in the seventies apparently?"

"Ah, yes, if you can call him a musician. How come he gets invited to parties in Anglesey? Do his band do private functions?"

"Nope. Apparently, he and his wife are godparents to the twins. According to Jamie Fellowes."

Bryn's memory started to kick-in. "Wasn't he the one who had the messy divorce from that fashion designer, what's she called... er... Jennifer somebody or other?"

"Jennifer Williams."

"That's the one. She's well rid of him, he was punching."

"He was with her this morning."

"Are you sure it was her?"

"Absolutely, she's a good friend of Grace Hearn, why wouldn't she be there? And according to Jamie she's the current Mrs Foster, not the ex."

"Well, there's no accounting for taste that's for sure. Fancy marrying a creep like that twice?"

"A creep that was never charged with any crime Sarge." Bryn rolled his eyes. "Yeah but…" He didn't finish what he was about to say as they pulled up outside the Hearn's luxurious farmhouse.

A very dishevelled-looking Michael answered the door. His blonde curls looked lank and greasy and his face was pale. His clothes smelled of weed, a very familiar smell to the two police officers, but this wasn't the time to comment. He invited them into the sitting room and apologised that his parents had gone out for walk. Just to try to calm their nerves. Probably to Llanddona beach. He offered to make them a drink.

"Oh, no thank you," Joanna declined before her Sergeant could say anything. "Could you give one of them a ring please? Let them know we're here."

"Why are you here? Have you found anything else out?" Then Michael noticed the stripes on Bryn Edward's shoulders. Why send a Sergeant? He knew why.

"You've found Gabe?" This was the cue, but the timing wasn't great. Bryn cleared his throat nervously. This was never ever going to be an easy thing to say.

"Er, Michael, I can confirm that the body of a young man was discovered this morning at Ynys Llanddwyn. His description matches your brother, but we still don't know for a fact who it is."

Michael sank into an armchair and covered his face with his hands.

"We're so sorry to have to tell you Michael, but we need someone to formally identify him."

Michael was shaking as he pushed his hair back and exposed the tears rolling down his face.

"You don't understand, he's not just my brother, he's the other half of me. I, I can't just be me on my own, I can't."

It was obvious how hard this information had hit Michael, but they needed to inform the parents, and quickly. News travelled fast on this small island off northwest Wales, so they had to be located.

"Do you want me to call your dad?" Joanna offered.

Michael shook his head. "No, please just leave it with me."

He left the room very quickly and ran upstairs. Within a couple of minutes, he had re-emerged in a change of clothes.

"I know where they are, please don't call them." And with that he ran out of the house.

Michael ran the half-mile to the beach, twisting and winding down the steep narrow lane, along the flat beach-side road, past the cafe and the car park, then he turned right onto the sand dunes. He could see several couples dotted around, mostly with dogs. The beach stretched for three miles around Red Wharf Bay as far as Benllech, but he was doubtful they'd walked that far.

He took a left and carried on running. To an onlooker he was out for a New Year's Day jog, to blow away the excesses of the night before. After about half a mile he spotted them in the distance walking towards him. His dad was so much taller than his mum and he had his arm tightly around her. Michael started to wave his arms as he ran, now almost breathless, he couldn't say anything.

Grace spotted him first and smiled. It was him, he was alive and well and he'd come to find his parents. She broke free from Dan and started to run towards her son.

"Gabriel, oh Gabriel! Thank God you're OK..."

Dan carried on walking at the same pace. He could see Michael running towards them. He had a slightly different gait to Gabe and Dan recognised it immediately, unlike

Grace who was blind with hope. As she got within a metre of her son, she knew she'd made a mistake and her knees gave way beneath her.

Dan ran to help her as Michael crouched beside his mother, crying, not able to say a word, but he didn't have to. "They've found Gabe?" was all Dan could say. Michael nodded, still sobbing into his mother's hair.

When Grace looked up, she saw two uniformed police officers walking towards them and she let out a guttural, haunting groan.

Chapter 23
New Year's Day 2011 (evening)

Dan was sitting on the decking of the holiday lodge. He had lit a fire in the fire pit that was crackling and spitting, the flames grasping at the darkness. He had spent the last two hours lying with Grace on their bed, stroking her hair while she sobbed, waiting for the valium to kick in. It was fairly old medication that was kept in reserve, just in case it was needed. Eventually her breathing slowed to a more gentle intake, and he knew she was asleep. He had left her a note in case she woke up and wondered where he was.

That afternoon he had had the worst experience of his entire life. Accompanied by Michael he drove to Ysbyty Gwynedd to formally identify his son's body. Just his face, for a fraction of a second, through a viewing window had been enough. Michael asked if he could go into the room to get nearer to his brother. He was advised against it, but he insisted, and he had gone in alone. Dan had watched through the glass as Michael bent over his brother's body and put his head next to the still form. Gabriel hadn't been in the water for too long, so his body was intact. He looked as though he was asleep and would sit up any time soon when he heard Michael's voice.

As Dan sat wrapped in a quilt on a recliner, whisky in hand, he saw Michael coming up the wooden steps. He was carrying a bottle of Jack Daniels in one hand and a long, thick roll-up in the other. Dan didn't question the contents of the roll-up; he didn't care right now. The lack of light pollution in Anglesey facilitated the most beautiful, star-filled night skies, and this was one of them. Dan had spent the last ten minutes watching the breathtaking display of shooting stars, hurtling across the dome-like structure above. The Milky Way was clearly visible, and the warmth of the whisky was going some way to block his pain. Michael had entered the lodge and emerged with another quilt. He sat opposite Dan and said nothing for a few minutes. He didn't look up, he just stared into the fire. Then he asked Dan the biggest question of all.

"Where is he Dad? Where's Gabe gone to?"

Dan poured himself another glass.

"Honestly Mike, I don't know for sure."

Michael took a long drag on his spliff.

"Do you believe he's somewhere though, not like he was, but somewhere?"

"Yes, I think I do Mike. Otherwise, what would be the point in any of us?"

"I talked to him today Dad, but he wasn't there."

"What did you say?"

"I said, stop fucking about Gabe, this isn't funny anymore."

Dan's eyes glistened in the firelight. He knew how close the boys had been and just how difficult life was going to be for all of them, especially Michael. He and Gabriel had shared a bed till they were five years old and separating them had been difficult. Tears and tantrums, mostly from Gabe who refused to settle without his brother by his side. They had tried as parents to encourage different hobbies and activities as individuals, but it never seemed to work. Michael led the way and Gabriel followed, that was just the way it was. When they applied to different universities it had seemed like a big breakthrough to Dan and Grace. They were confident that Mike would crack on and embrace uni-life and new friends, and they were nervous about Gabriel's ability to survive emotionally without his brother. Just three months in and all their fears had been realised on an unbearable level.

Dan couldn't help thinking about Jack, his own brother. He was still alive, somewhere, but he wasn't missed. In the fog of whisky thoughts, he tried to gather some wisdom, something that could help his grieving son.

"You know Mike, I've got a brother somewhere, well a half-brother anyway."

"I know Dad, but that's all I know. Why don't you ever talk about him?"

"Because he's never been worth mentioning."

"Why is that Dad? You've still got a brother. What happened? What was so bad that you can't talk about him?"

"It depends what kind of brother you've got Mike. He was taken away from me when he was four years old. I was fifteen when my parents went back to Hampshire. Up to that point I loved him, I looked after him – a lot. I knew he wasn't my full brother, but it didn't seem to matter."

"Why did your parents go to Hampshire?"

"They were, we were travellers."

"From Hampshire?"

"From the New Forest. That's where I was born."

"Travellers? Why have you never told me? Are you embarrassed or something? Because you know Dad, you shouldn't be, really, that's not cool."

"I'm not embarrassed in any way believe me. I was left to more or less fend for myself at fifteen. You couldn't even tie your shoelaces at fifteen Mike! No, I'm proud of my heritage. Self-sufficiency and making money, that's been their legacy to me, and you can't say I didn't embrace it."

Mike was intrigued. His dad had never ever opened up about his early life before, so he listened intently to the alcohol talking.

"The next time I saw Jack was when he turned up at the haulage business, we were in Chapel by then. Right out of nowhere, without invitation or notice, he walked into my office and introduced himself. I was twenty-eight and running my own show, he was barely eighteen and destitute, or so he told me. Then he told me that our parents were both dead. Mum took her own life during a psychotic episode and Dad had drunk himself to death in his grief. None of that surprised me, but when you're abandoned at fifteen, believing that you've been the result of some kind of curse, it's easy not to care much."

"So, what happened next?"

"I found him a flat and gave him a job. I loved him and I wanted to look after him. I was so happy that my kid brother was back in my life. I put him through his HGV training with the understanding that he had to start at the bottom and learn the business. He seemed fine with it at first. Everything was going great. God, I even got a tattoo, a Romani symbol. It's never been on public display but it's there." He pointed to the top of his right thigh.

"Everything was going great till?"

"Till he stopped showing up for work. A few days at a time, then whole weeks. When I questioned him, he got angry, said I was playing God with his life and that he was entitled to have a share of the business that his father started. Of course, that was bullshit. The business that *I* started with money that was left to *me* (he raised his glass to the stars), Frank Shaw, what a man, I'll tell you more about him another time, anyway, he was wrong. He was greedy and lazy and entitled. He wanted everything on a plate, and I wasn't going to give it to him. I'd worked too hard for too long for somebody, even if he was my brother, to give away half of my business."

"Holy shit Dad, I never knew any of this."

"Well, after about six months of me telling him how it was, he decided he'd quit. He knew he didn't have any real claim, but he'd been more than willing to try. What a chancer. He started making noises about knowing who my birth mother was, you know like, fancy bargaining with that sort of information?"

"Bargaining?"

"Absolutely. He told me it was my dad's dying wish that I knew who my birth mother was. He said if I paid him five thousand pounds, he'd tell me her name and he'd be on his way. Out of my life. Of course, I didn't believe him, why should I?"

"So, what did you do?"

"I willingly gave him half the money and told him to piss off, basically. He wasn't blackmailing me. He could have said any woman's name, couldn't he? How would I have known if he was lying or not? Anyway, he left the flat and I haven't seen him since. I don't know where he went, or what he did next. A few weeks later there was a letter delivered to me at the office. It was post-marked Poole in Dorset. All that was in the envelope was a piece of paper. All that was written on it was a name – Marianne Fletcher, and a short note saying, "Thank you for the money Dan, if I can ever do you a favour let me know."

"Your real mum?"

"Yes, as it turned out. I didn't waste any time looking for her. She was born in 1938 on a farm in the New Forest. That meant she was fifteen when she gave birth to me. Fifteen? It made me feel sick. I hired a private detective to find her. It didn't take too long really. She was still living on the farm and running it with her husband. As far as I know she's still alive. Fletcher was her maiden name and she's called Hobson now."

"So, I have a grandmother?"

"Yes."

"So why have I never met her? Why Dad? Why all this pain and bullshit?"

"Because when the private detective approached her, she didn't want to know. He reported back that she didn't deny giving birth at fifteen, but her irate father had given the baby away within hours of it being born. A boy. The man she eventually married knew nothing about the baby and neither did her legitimate children. She wanted things to stay that way. She also confirmed that the baby had been handed over to its father – Patrin Hearn."

The fire was beginning to die down so Dan stood up, a little wobbly, and headed for the wood store. As he placed the logs in the fire pit, he tried to sum up what he was trying to convey to Michael.

"You see Mike, in your lifetime you've experienced what it's like to be truly loved by a mother and father and brother. Gabe too. Please just try to hold on to that fact and cherish it."

Michael had lit another spliff. Nothing his dad could say right now would make any difference, but he filed the words carefully in his memory.

"So, do you think you'll ever meet Marianne?"

"Probably, but not yet."

It was 11 p.m. when a few spots of rain started to fall on the decking. Without thinking, Dan walked back into the lodge, sought out the bed that was unmade from the night before and fell into it.

Chapter 24
January 2nd 2011

He was running through a field, feeling panicked and scared. He was looking for somebody, but he couldn't find them. He could hear the sound of the rush of running water and he followed it over a fence and along a riverbank. Then he saw who he was looking for, standing near the edge of the steep banking, staring. It was Gabriel but he was a toddler, chatting to himself and delighting at the sight of the flowing water. Dan was running but his legs were hardly moving. He had to get to his child quickly, but it was hopeless as his legs became heavier and heavier.

Then he saw a woman kneeling down next to Gabriel. She was old and crooked, and she was whispering to him. He was listening to her and nodding as if he understood what she was saying.

Dan stared in horror as the tiny woman took Gabe's hand and jumped into the torrent. He could hear the child voice of Gabriel, "Daddy, help! Daddy, help! I don't want to go!"

He was sitting up rigid in bed, he was sweating and his heart was racing. The clarity of the images in his nightmare had been in high definition. The loss of his son, mixed-up with the incident years ago when he had prevented Jack from meeting an almost certain death had Dan not got to him in time. He tried to recall the image of the old woman, but he didn't see her that clearly in his dream as he focused on Gabriel. He didn't know who she was, or the significance of her presence in his sub-conscious mind.

It was dark and the air was still, apart from the humming of the fridge. He looked at the bedside clock, it was 5.30 a.m. For the second time in as many days Dan had woken up in the lodge, this time without Grace. He cursed himself for getting drunk with Michael. Everything he had kept inside for so long had come pouring out as easy as the amber liquid had transferred from bottle to glass. He had never let his guard down before about his ethnicity. His boys had been privately educated and he had wanted them to never suffer the cruel abuse that he had tried to contend with during his school years. In Dan's mind the only way to guarantee a safe passage through their education was to hide behind a false narrative. The narrative being that their father was born in Hayfield and his parents died before the twins were born. He then inherited a haulage business from his father and had gone on to build it up to a very successful level. Now Michael would have more questions than Dan cared to answer, he might even be angry, in fact he didn't know where Michael was right at that moment. He had to get back to the house before Grace woke up and establish where his only remaining son was. He knew that he would have to summon up all his reserves of emotional strength to carry these two precious people through the next days, weeks, months, even years if that was what it was going to take. He would fall apart when his emotional reserves were depleted to zero.

When he got to the house, he checked Michael's bedroom first, but the bed was unoccupied. He tried the next bedroom, Gabriel's room. He could just see the outline of a body and the bed covers gently rising and falling. He felt a twinge of adrenaline as he gazed at the scene, it could have been Gabriel, but it wasn't. Michael had chosen to sleep in his brother's room and that was fine, however he was coping, it didn't matter. He smiled when he recalled the bizarre recurrence of Gabriel sleepwalking back to his brother's bed for years after they had separate bedrooms. Michael would often have to get out of his own bed and leave Gabriel sleeping. He would then make his way to Gabriel's empty bed and finish off his sleep there. Thankfully, it had stopped, eventually.

When he entered the master bedroom, Grace was just stirring so he undressed quickly and lay next to her. She woke up almost immediately.

"What time did you come to bed?"

Dan sighed, there was no point lying to her.

"Just now."

"I can smell the alcohol Dan. Why? Where did you sleep?"

"Me and Mike, well, we went to the lodge, we talked and well, I woke up there."

"And where's Mike now?"

"He's asleep upstairs, I just checked."

Grace sat up. She looked dark around her eyes and her eyelids were red and swollen.

"We need to speak to Jamie. He knows something that we don't, and we have to find out ourselves Dan. The police won't tell us anything. Not even his address."

He tried to calm Grace down. "Ok, we'll find Jamie somehow and we'll ask him ourselves."

"Do you think he knows what happened to Gabe?"

"Probably by now Grace, but please, let's take it easy today, try and stay calm if we can..."

"Stay calm?" Grace was raising her voice now. "Stay calm? Our son is lying in a mortuary and you want me to stay calm? He stole Jamie's car and he was driving here, to our party, and, and, before he got across the bridge, he decided that jumping off it and dying was a better option? Jesus, Dan how can you be so calm?"

"I'm not calm inside Grace. I'm trying to make sense of it all too. I think he was involved with Jamie and for some reason something went wrong. I'm sure Gabe didn't know that Jamie was at the party, bur how can we know what was said between them on the day? Gabriel's phone hasn't been recovered so..."

"So why hasn't anyone looked at Jamie's phone? He must have sent messages to Gabe."

"The police have probably looked at Jamie's phone. We don't know for sure, do we? There's been no crime committed, they're satisfied that Gabe intentionally took his own life."

"For what reason though Dan? It's not making sense at all. Please can we find Jamie, today, please?"

Dan was losing the battle to keep his wife calm.

"Fine Grace, I'm hoping Michael has his number, we'll see. Don't forget we'll probably get a visit from PC Draper today. She said she'd let us know about the toxicology report."

Grace shuddered at the thought of her beautiful boy being opened up then sewn back together. She ran to the en-suite to be sick as Dan stayed put and fought back his tears. There was so much to do, so many people to speak to, including Jen and Nick. They had left on New Year's Day just as PC Draper had arrived. They knew that Gabriel had been reported missing and they both expressed their concerns but as far as Dan knew they hadn't been in touch since. It seemed a bit strange that the godparents to his boys had left Anglesey for London two days ago and hadn't called for an update. This would be a huge shock for them, and despite Dan's feelings towards Nick 'the prick' Foster and Jen Williams – his biggest regret – he was dreading making that call. When emotions run high, pressure can blow the lid off a secret like an erupting Roman candle, enlightening everybody within striking distance. The further away Jen and her husband were from him and Grace

and the whole ridiculous nightmare, the better. Nick Foster
especially was not to be trusted.

Chapter 25
January 3rd 2011

The car pulled up on the opposite side of the road to Jamie's address. Most people were still on their Christmas break from work so the parking opportunities on Caernarfon Road, Bangor, were scarce. There was a car parked directly outside number 520, a black Suzuki Vitara. A middle-aged-looking man sat in the driver seat with a younger woman sitting beside him.

They knew Jamie was expecting them. Michael had his number and he had given it to Dan. Jamie hadn't hesitated when he agreed to meet Dan and Grace, as long as they could pick him up and they could talk privately. Jamie knew what time to expect them, so they didn't have to go to the door to knock.

Before Jamie emerged from the house, the young woman got out of the car and approached Jamie's house. She started to bang furiously on the front door, shouting his name, challenging him to answer.

Dan and Grace sat still and watched what was playing out in front of them. A pale-looking Jamie opened the door, he looked dishevelled and tired. The young woman continued to shout in Jamie's face, but he didn't seem to react. He was saying something, but they couldn't hear exactly what was being said. She was very angry and she slapped his face before returning to the Suzuki Vitara and slamming the door. The driver shook his head slowly as they drove away at speed. Jamie disappeared again, then re-emerged with a coat in his hand. He had seen the black Range Rover parked across the road and he was ready to talk to Gabriel's parents. He got into the car and sat behind Grace.

"Did you see that?"

"Yes Jamie, we did, unfortunately." Grace couldn't help feeling sadder than she had been ten minutes previously. Dan didn't want to talk in the car. He wanted to see Jamie's body language when he talked. He set out the plan.

"OK, thanks for agreeing to this Jamie. I don't want a conversation in the car, we need to sit down somewhere and talk things through together. Is that all right with you?"

"Er, yes, yes, of course, anything you want, I'm fine."

"Do you know the Ship Inn at Red Wharf Bay?"

"Yes, I think so. I had a friend who worked there years ago."

"OK, we'll head over there. It shouldn't be too busy, out of season and so on."

The journey was relatively silent. Dan had taken the Menai Bridge route to and from Bangor, purposely avoiding the Britannia Bridge. Grace hadn't glanced sideways whilst they drove over. The two bridges had clear sight of each other, and she couldn't bear to see the place where her son had ended his life.

They found a table in a corner of a back room at the Ship Inn. It was quiet, apart from Radio Four being played at a gentle level. Grace had visited this pub many times in her life, both on holiday with her parents, and with Dan. It had been the Quay Inn for years, from its origins in the eighteenth century to the early twentieth century, and was a real pull for locals and tourists alike. The familiar sight of the hanging pub sign, depicting a steam clipper in stormy seas, would normally invoke a feeling of contented familiarity. Not on this occasion. The ship depicted on the sign was destined to become a wreck, and Grace never thought she'd be sitting in this lovely place, feeling like a shipwreck herself, washed up and broken.

"So, Jamie, erm, who was that woman at your door? She seemed pretty angry with you?" Dan began the conversation.

Jamie sighed and closed his eyes. "That was Ceris, I used to live with her, till recently."

"How recently exactly?"

"Just a few days really."

Grace couldn't wait to cut to the chase.

"Jamie, who was Gabriel to you?" Jamie hung his head; the tears were already starting to fall.

"He was the love of my life Mrs Hearn. We met back in September when he walked into class. I was the life-model, see?"

"So where does Ceris come into this scenario?"

"Ceris was a mistake. I've tried to kid myself that I'm bi, but I'm not. I slept with her once and then she tells me she's pregnant a few months later. I tried to do the right thing, you know? I let her move into my flat, I felt obliged, see."

"So, you have a child?"

"Yes, Bronwen, she's six months old now."

"You see Jamie, we want to know why our son did what he did."

"So do I, honestly, it just doesn't make sense. Yes, he was upset when I told him about Ceris and the baby. He slipped away in the morning without me knowing, but I thought he was just angry, you know, off to clear his head. I promised him that I would tell Ceris the truth the night before, but she'd already gone to her parents. I wasn't about to let Ceris down via a mobile phone, I wanted to tell her to her face. I don't hate her, I didn't want to end things in a cowardly way, and I love Bronwen so much. See, if I wanted a future with Gabriel *and* keep contact with my daughter, with her mother's consent, I had to try to do it right."

Dan was listening and watching. Grace had gone to the ladies to get toilet tissue for Jamie as his nose was running as fast as his tears. There was nothing about Jamie's words or behaviour that made Dan think he was lying about anything. He was genuinely grieving and as a family they would have to try to help him too, he was as much a victim as anyone who loved Gabriel.

"Why did you come to Anglesey if you didn't know for sure that Gabe was here?" Grace didn't seem as sympathetic as her husband and her tone was slightly tinged with suspicion.

"Well actually, he did leave a note that he was going home, and he had mentioned a few weeks before that you were having a party. He said he was going to stay in Aberystwyth for the holidays anyway, to spend it with me. I couldn't do that, see? All I asked was a little more time, just a few days to sort my life out and then we could have faced the world together, no matter what. I just presumed he'd gone home, like his note said. I couldn't get hold of him on the phone, so I was desperate. I took a risk that he'd still be mad at me, but I thought it was a risk worth taking."

Grace was now convinced that Jamie's heart and intentions were in the right place. Either that or he was an Oscar nominee for best performance. Gabriel didn't know that Jamie was at the party, but he was making his way there anyway, so what happened on Britannia Bridge? There was something missing from the tragic tale, and without Gabriel's phone they would probably never know what it was.

Chapter 26
January 28th 2011

The function room at Chateau Tryfan was almost full to capacity. As requested by Gabriel's family, all the funeral guests were wearing white. Dan and Grace had to some extent taken a step back to let Michael, the person who knew Gabe better than anybody, organise the aesthetics. There was to be no black, no mournfulness, no weeping and wailing about a tragedy. This was to be a party, with a party-like atmosphere. Michael wanted everything Gabe had loved about life, to be known to his friends and family. He had set up a projector from his laptop that showed a new image every few seconds from Gabe as a baby, family holidays, school days, christenings, weddings, their gap year together, surfing, Gabe's amazing artwork – everything that brought joy to his brother.

As Grace sat at the bar, she looked around the room at Gabriel's student friends all chattering and laughing, bubbling with life, and she knew that she really couldn't take it. Mike had done his best to keep the sadness away and he had done such a fantastic job, but she wasn't feeling it. This was a 'no expense spared' occasion that Dan had insisted on. A five-star hotel on the Menai Strait with mountain views, a free bar and Michelin Star cuisine for their guests. Grace was dressed head to toe in Chanel – an outward sign of wealth that she wasn't comfortable with, and certainly not an outfit she'd ever wear again. The funeral was another example of Dan's typical, over-the-top hospitality that was ingrained in his being. Mostly modern music was playing, and the guests all seemed in good spirits, exactly as Michael had planned. She watched as he mingled, never without a drink in his hand and she thought an awful, irrational thought – what if Michael got so drunk that he died of alcohol poisoning? Or, what if he went outside and fell into the exact same body of water that had claimed his brother's life? Irrational as she knew it was, it gave her the fear. A fear that was no different to losing sight of your toddler in a supermarket or waiting for them to get in from meeting their teen friends. It was the type of fear that nobody except a mother could feel.

She turned herself away from the giant screen that was projecting images of Gabriel. All she had to do was get through the next few hours, then she would continue to mourn her son in her way, in her own time.

Jen approached and sat beside her at the bar. Whenever Grace felt that she'd made the effort with her choice of outfit, Jen would more often than not walk into the room and make her feel like a drudge. She only wore her own designs and she knew how to rock her own style, which was sort of Vivienne Westwood meets Jasper Conran – very classy, fitted and chic with additional edgy touches. Jen took Grace's hand.

"I'm so sorry Gee, Nick's had to go back to London, it's a contractual thing, you know how it is?"

"He was at the service though?"

"Yes, late, but he got there about five minutes in. He sat at the back."

"I don't remember seeing him."

"He slipped in and out pretty quickly, you know, there's a lot of students here, he probably wanted some anonymity, today isn't about him, is it?"

"So Nick left just in case somebody recognised him?"

"Oh, no, not exactly, he's recording this evening, he just can't wriggle out of it."

"Not even for his godson's funeral?"

"These contracts are pretty fierce Gee, honestly, you'd think Nick could get out of things easily but sometimes he just can't."

Grace sighed and rolled her eyes. She still couldn't understand why Jen had re-married him just three years after they divorced. She especially couldn't get her head around Jen wanting to be with a man like Nick. At best he was arrogant and outspoken and at worst a D-list has-been still trying to be relevant. It had been more than a surprise when he turned up to the party as Jen's new husband. How had they re-married without even the media finding out? It was one mystery after another. Grace had drunk the best part of a bottle of wine, and she could feel herself loosening up to some extent.

"I suppose things can't be easy for him since... you know... since..." She didn't have to say it.

"You're not kidding Gee. All that stress put a massive strain on our relationship. They even interviewed me! He was never charged with anything, but you wouldn't believe how quickly the work dried up for him. He was treated like a leper for years, like he's a genuine creep. It's bullshit. I know him better than anyone and he's a lot of things Gee, but he isn't like *that*."

Grace nodded, but she understood why somebody in Nick's position would be shunned and labelled, despite never being charged with any offences. The police had decided that his explanation of carrying out 'research' was plausible, and they let the matter go.

"Look Jen," said Grace. "And don't take this the wrong way, but even me and Dan had some nagging doubts and you couldn't blame us for that really. I mean, all the time the boys spent with you and Nick in the summer holidays while me and Dan had our 'parent breaks'."

Jen's face got serious at this point.

"What are you trying to say? You thought Nick may have harmed one of them?"

"No, no, God no Jen, honestly. Please. What I'm saying is when Nick was named as somebody the police wanted to interview, well, it crossed my mind. Of course it did."

"All what time anyway? It was the odd weekend here and there. Most of the time Nick wasn't home. What the fuck, Grace?"

She only called her Grace when she was rattled, and she said it loud enough for Dan to hear as he approached the bar. He knew that Jen was not to be messed with when she was upset so he tried to intercept whatever she was going to say next.

"Jen, er, where's Nick?"

He couldn't have pitched it any worse. She didn't answer.

"Can I get you ladies anything?"

She turned and faced Dan.

"Yes darling, you can get me a cab. I'm going to yours to pick up my car and I'm going home."

Dan was now terrified inside.

"Jen, please whatever it is, please. We're all tired and emotional. Please don't leave, not today."

"Sorry Dan, thing is, Nick has been nothing but a wonderful godfather to the boys and he's suffering too. There's not a chance he would ever have even thought about harming either of them!"

Dan immediately knew what she was referring to. The Met's Operation Starling had reared its ugly head. Today of all days, the day of Gabriel's funeral. The angel that had taken his own life en-route to their party. The toxicology report had confirmed that Gabriel had taken ecstasy on the day he died, but there were still a lot of unanswered questions. This just wasn't the time or the place to ask them. Grace tried again to apologise but Jen was already heading for the exit.

"Just let her go Dan, she's upset. You know me and Jen. We fight occasionally, then we're OK."

"But not today surely. Where the hell *is* Nick anyway? I haven't seen him. Was he at the service?"

"According to Jen he was there. He was late but he was there, sat at the back. I didn't see him. I don't think anyone did."

Dan was relieved that Jen had left the hotel. He was always on edge when she was around, and it made him feel vulnerable. What she knew, and could prove, would wipe out his marriage. He turned his back to the bar and watched the huge screen at the end of the room that was projecting the images from Michael's laptop. It was a hard watch, seeing the boys happy and full of life in almost every shot. Grace still had her back to the room, she couldn't bear to see any of it. Then he noticed an apparent glitch in the slide show. It wasn't a still photograph, it was a few seconds of a video. A little dark but he could make out Michael talking to what he presumed was his phone's camera. There were some fairy lights being blown by the wind and Dan realised the video was from the party. In just a few seconds the slide show moved on to still photos. Then he saw Michael making his way back to the younger people in the room. He'd probably been outside for a smoke.

He stopped Michael and put his arm around him.

"Don't worry about your mum. The slide show Mike, it's amazing, but you know it's so hard…"

"It's fine Dad, I'll turn it off soon. Jamie's here too and he's, well, he's a bit overwhelmed."

"Must have taken you ages to put together?"

"Yep, it did. I think I must have dozed off doing it, that video clip got on there by accident. I only noticed it today."

"The party one?"

"Yes, I posted it on Instagram, but it wasn't on long. I was asked to delete it a few minutes after."

"Why would anyone ask you to take it down, it's not offensive?"

"It was Nick. He insisted. Something about privacy. His social media's carefully managed so he didn't want any private stuff out there."

"Nope, still don't get what your social media has to do with his?"

"Well, he was in the shot. Very, very briefly but he was."

Dan shook his head. "Celebrities and their precious profiles... fucking la la land."

"What time did you post the video?"

"Must have been around twenty to eight, ish..."

"Do you think Gabe might have seen it?"

"I doubt it Dad, but we'll never know. Not without his phone."

"But can't you find out?"

"Not unless he 'liked' the post, then it would show up on my feed. So, if he did see it, he didn't 'like' it."

"Or he just didn't like it." Dan thought to himself. Now he felt uneasy. Nick wasn't here, Jen had stormed off and there was potentially something significant about the timing of the video. He would have to talk to Grace about it, and he would have to choose his moment carefully.

Chapter 27
January 28th 2011

Jen was speeding in the outside lane of the motorway, but she didn't care. The sooner she got back to London, the better. She thought about calling Grace to apologise but it would be easier when she got home, in the safety of her lounge, accompanied by a drink or several. She'd only had a couple at the hotel, but that was hours ago. If she was stopped and breathalysed, she'd pass.

The emotional pressure of the day had taken its toll. Anyone who knew Gabriel properly had had their life shattered in some way and she was no exception. She didn't know where Nick was, that was a truth she couldn't tell Grace. They had argued the night before on a scale very similar to when they were last married. He had been out with some friends and returned in a state of cocaine overload. Jen had recognised the signs immediately. She mistakenly believed he was drug-free, but he wasn't. She left alone in the early hours to drive to Anglesey. She couldn't stop asking herself over and over, "Why did I do it? Why did I marry him again?"

There was no logical answer to that. They had met again by chance in New York at a charity function and they went out to dinner a couple of times after that. After three years apart she noticed he had changed, as she thought, for the better. It was like meeting the mature version of the man she once loved. A romantic, a songwriter, a performer, everything he was before but elevated to another level. Jen had dated several men from New York, but she found them a little too self-obsessed, a little too metrosexual. Not like English men at all. Nick could laugh at himself; he was caring and kind most of the time and he knew how to handle her. They both had creative temperaments, they were both impulsive, so a weekend in Las Vegas hadn't seemed like such a crazy idea. Waking up in a suite at the Venetian, with a mega-hangover and the hazy recollection of a wedding ceremony was perhaps *the* most crazy she had ever felt in her life.

And what about *him*? Why had it been so difficult to be around him at the party? Then again just weeks later at the funeral. Why didn't she feel any shame or guilt? Was it because she still had an overpowering attraction to him? And how did he manage to stay so cool and aloof? She wanted to talk to him about what they had shared. She wanted to know if he still felt the same, but he didn't give her a chance. It was as if nothing had ever happened. Damn it! She hated being ignored. Leaving the funeral party had been a very sensible move on her part. The emotionally charged atmosphere on the day had started to affect her. Being so close to him again without so much as a secret knowing glance or smile was killing her inside. Picking a fight with Grace had been her ticket back to London, which was preferable to getting pissed and making a mistake. If she could get married when she was drunk and hardly have any recollection of it, then anything was possible.

She was returning to the London home that she owned, not Nick. She would tell him to move out and then she planned to contact her solicitor to start annulment proceedings. No divorce, not again. Their short marriage had not been consummated, that was the truth, and he was not going to fleece her for a second time. If everything went to plan, she would sell up and move as far away from the UK as she could and she would never be in his company again. It was the only way to avoid blowing apart a family that she loved. She was just thankful and relieved that Nick knew nothing about her secret.

Chapter 28
April 2011

Dan waved as Grace set off on her journey to York. If their lives hadn't been decimated four months ago, they would have been on a cruise around the British Isles by now. His plan to surprise her with the tickets on New Year's Eve had been tragically taken over and eventually shelved.

Grace was struggling just driving over the water that took their son, and the thought of a cruise had become unacceptable. She had decided to go up to York to spend a week with Michael, and Dan planned to spend the same week fishing, mowing, and overseeing their first paying guests in the holiday lodge. The last few months had been intense and spiritually unpleasant for them both and he was looking forward to spending some time alone while Grace (hopefully) enjoyed a week shopping and dining in York with their son. She was still vulnerable and sad, he knew that, but life had to carry on and he was relieved that she had found some strength, enough to drive a hundred and fifty miles or so to give herself and Michael some much-needed family therapy.

He had some decisions to make this week. Jen had declined Grace's offer to go up to York, that was a relief, God knows what the future held for them all if Jen for some reason decided to tell Grace about their affair. Dan was undecided whether to try to establish what Nick Foster knew, if anything. His throw-away comment at the party could have been just that, Dan had good taste, "especially the women"? It was obvious that Jen had told Nick about his family heritage from his sarcastic drunken comment about the holiday lodge. He could just ask Jen straight out, but he hadn't made any direct contact with her since he ended the relationship, and the last thing he wanted was for Jen to get the wrong idea. Further secrecy between him and her was not a wise move.

He had thought about Jack a lot in the last few months too. His brother had been an arsehole for sure, but he still felt the connection to him that wouldn't break. No amount of seaside rural living, or pottering around on tractor mowers, playing at Lord of the Manor, had diminished his feelings of guilt around rejecting Jack and sending him packing at eighteen. After all, Jack had given him his mother's name. He didn't have to, but he had.

He'd also been having lots of thoughts about Marianne and whether to try once more to establish contact with her. He wanted to meet the woman who had nurtured him in the womb and given birth to him. That was a natural desire for anyone in his position surely?

Following Gabriel's suicide there was one issue that was overriding the grief he was feeling and the burden of guilt he was shouldering. The few seconds of a video taken at the party that Gabe may or may not have seen, minutes before he took his own life. Michael still had the video on his phone and had sent it to Dan just after the last guests had left the funeral. It was much clearer on the big screen than a phone screen, but Nick Foster was definitely in view. There were so many questions he wanted answers to. Why had Nick insisted that the video was deleted from Instagram? Most of Michael's followers wouldn't have recognised Nick or actually cared anyway. Did Gabe see that video and react to it? From conversations with Jamie, it was clear that Gabe was upset about Jamie's unfinished business with Ceris, and it had been confirmed from the post-mortem that Gabe was high when he met his death, but his relationship with Jamie was still intact. It hadn't ended. He was shattered and angry, and he was driving home to lick his wounds. Had he reached the farmhouse he would have been reunited with Jamie and everything would be so different now. Gabe had been sensitive and introverted, but he wasn't unforgiving and stubborn. Then his thoughts had turned to Nick Foster's police interview as part of Operation Starling. He hadn't been charged with any crime, just as Jen had reminded them before she took off to London on the day of the funeral. The funeral that Nick apparently attended but nobody recalled seeing him. The idea that Gabe's death and Nick Foster were connected in some way made Dan rigid with anger. The fact that he had never liked Nick wasn't helping. The boys had occasionally spent weeks in the school holidays with Nick and Jen, right up to their separation and that was now starting to nag him. What the hell was Nick Foster 'researching'? And more importantly what had the Metropolitan Police got to question him about? What was implicating him?

He had wanted so many times to ask Michael about the time spent with his godparents, he just didn't know how he was going to phrase things. How do you ask a nineteen-year-old son if he had ever had any 'creepy uncle' vibes from Nick, or even the unthinkable?

There was something he could do to acquire some answers, so he had decided to use a previously tried and tested method. The private detective firm he had contacted weeks before were sending somebody round that afternoon. He had given them enough information to set the ball rolling and he was looking forward to seeing their first report. He hadn't risked telling Grace that he was having Nick Foster investigated, possibly followed. She probably wouldn't understand as she saw only the good in everyone.

In addition, he couldn't risk Jen finding out that he was paying a company that could uncover potentially unsavoury facts about the man she had recently re-married.

Chapter 29
April 2011

Emma Morgan arrived at 3 p.m. as arranged. She was a senior investigator in the firm, with twenty years' experience, preceded by ten years in the Metropolitan Police. Dan had only spoken to her on the phone previously, so he had a picture of her in his mind on the lines of tweed jacket, frumpy blouse, flat shoes. He couldn't have got it more wrong. She was dressed in casual jeans, a brightly patterned tunic top and knee-length brown leather boots. Her hair was long and dark, tied back in a ponytail. Her face was quite heavily made-up but not unpleasant. Perhaps a little hardened, but not unattractive. She was carrying a battered-looking black briefcase.

He invited her into the kitchen and offered her a coffee. She declined politely, she had half an hour to brief him, and she had a lot to go through. He hadn't been expecting that.

"OK, I'll make a start Mr. Hearn."

"Dan, please."

"Fine, Dan, I'll take you through the first report, then you can decide if you want us to continue with anything."

"Yes, by all means, I've dealt with private investigators before, I know how it works."

"Perfect, right, Mr Nick Foster. What can I tell you about him? Well, he's not living with Jennifer Williams. They did re-marry in December but according to our man in London, he's not living at the address you gave us."

"So where *is* he living?"

"He's staying with one of his band mates in Notting Hill."

"So do you think they're still together?"

"It's hard to say for sure, but he's not eating or sleeping at the marital address. Maybe the honeymoon period ended early? Anyway, he's not an easy man to track. He doesn't seem to have a routine as such. What I can tell you is there hasn't been any activity that would raise any suspicions, particularly with his lifestyle, you know, late nights, drinking, meeting up with friends, sleeping all day. I would say he's a washed-up, more than middle-aged musician who's feeling very sorry for himself right now."

"OK what about…"

"Operation Starling? Right, well, I still have contacts in the Met that are willing to give me information that's strictly off the record so I took what I could. Basically, Nick Foster's credit card details were found on a very, very long list of credit card numbers that were paying an illegal site to download indecent images of children. Everyone on that list was contacted and questioned by the police, and believe me he wasn't the only celebrity that was hauled in. He was very co-operative, apparently. He surrendered his phone and his laptop for forensic testing. What that uncovered was a transaction from a couple of years prior to Operation Starling. He never denied paying for and downloading the images. His explanation was that he was drunk at the time, he had been sexually abused himself as a child and he was doing research."

Dan couldn't help interrupting her flow.

"Fucking research, really?"

"He claimed to be thinking about setting up a charity for victims of childhood sexual abuse and he wanted to acquire some material that would shock people into taking it seriously. Believe it, some people had been caught with thousands of images, but he had downloaded ten at the most."

"Yes, but it's still child porn and it's still illegal!"

"You're right Dan, absolutely, the thing is, the forensic IT people also found evidence that he was researching how to set up a charity at the same time. He had deleted the images, or so he thought, but they can always be retrieved if you know what you're doing. He downloaded at 2 a.m. and he deleted them ten minutes later. He claimed they made him vomit."

"So that's it?"

"Case closed, as far as the Met were concerned. They had much bigger fish to fry than him. He hadn't attempted to distribute or share with anyone. So, they gave him a verbal warning, naughty boy, don't do it again, and that was the end of it."

"So did you find out anything else?"

"Not so much as a parking ticket, not yet anyway. My contact is having one more dig."

Dan couldn't believe it. What else could he do? The information he had now was half-believable, it certainly worked for Nick Foster at the time but as far as Dan was concerned, there was no smoke without fire. He thanked Emma for the report and escorted her to her car.

"Please don't hesitate Dan, if you can think of anything else you want looking at."

Dan had already made up his mind. He would invite himself to York and talk to Michael.

Chapter 30
April 2011

Grace was a little disappointed to see Dan parking up his car on the hotel car park. She had enjoyed the last few days with Michael in York. It was so beautiful, and wonderfully old. They had done some of the tourist sites together and Grace had lit a candle in the magnificent Minster for her very own 'Angel Gabriel'. Dan had called that morning to say he wanted to join them for one night. She didn't really understand why as he hadn't explained in a way that made any sense. Maybe he wasn't coping very well? Whatever the reason, she was glad it was only for one night. He was supposed to be around for the guests at the holiday lodge, just in case they couldn't switch the kettle on, or other such emergencies. She decided to greet him in the hotel lobby.

"Sweetheart, why one night? You didn't really make any sense on the phone?"

"So, arrest me for being guilty of missing my wife!"

"No really, Dan, what about our guests? Aren't we supposed to be around for them, just in case?"

"All taken care of. Our kind neighbour Gareth. He said no problem. He'll be on call for a night. So, that means I can take my wife and son out for a meal, and I'll drive back in the morning."

Grace still wasn't convinced. He wasn't the type of person to divert from his plans, certainly not for a three-hundred-mile round trip. He was usually very organised, so this was for something other than taking her and Michael out to dinner.

A few hours later they were sitting in a small, rustic restaurant, with an open fire crackling, wine glasses chinking and candles flickering on the tables. The atmosphere was pleasant, and the menu was promising a high standard of food. Michael had called to say he was running late, nothing unusual about that, so the first shared bottle of wine was empty. They would wait for Michael to arrive before they ordered food. Dan took a chance and asked Grace if she'd heard from Jen or Nick recently. Grace shrugged her shoulders and sighed. "Jen called me a few days ago, just as I arrived at the hotel. Things have been a bit iffy since, you know, since ..."

"Since she got the hump and left Gabe's funeral?"

"Yes, it's like, things are still a bit strained. She turned down this trip, said she was too busy, but I don't believe her for some reason."

"How's her marriage doing, second time around?"

"I don't think it's doing *anything* Dan. She sounds so down, it's just not like her. I mean, losing Gabe has hit us all hard, but if *we* can sit here and enjoy being in York, why can't she?"

Dan wanted to tell her that Nick and Jen were already finished, but he couldn't give the game away, not yet.

"Maybe she's having some regrets. I mean, she knew who she was marrying, so why do it again?"

"I know, all that 'soul mates' crap didn't wash with me either. I don't think I've really known her since she went to New York. She took off there so quickly. Like she was running away from something."

Before Dan could say anything, Michael walked through the door. What a relief. Dan knew exactly why Jen had taken off to America, it was the month after he ended their affair.

The evening was pleasant, the food was wonderful, and Dan's plan started to take shape. He invited Michael back for a nightcap at the hotel bar. Grace had already drunk a bottle of white and a couple of large gin and tonics.

Compared to him and Michael, she was a bit of a lightweight, so he was counting on her not wanting any more alcohol. He would walk her to the room and join Michael in the bar. Then he would subtly ask his son all the right questions.

The plan nearly worked. Grace opted for a coffee back at the hotel bar. It was only 10 p.m. so Dan didn't push it. He lined up a Jack Daniels and Coke for himself, a Desperado beer for Michael and coffee for Grace. Within twenty minutes she was yawning and after thirty minutes she was saying goodnight to them both.

"I'll be up in an hour." Dan tried to reassure Grace, but she just laughed.

"Is that earth hours?"

"Mum, I won't stay up too late tonight, I'll send the old man to bed soon."

Grace was happy with that, but she knew it wouldn't be just an hour.

They hadn't spent any time alone since the day Gabe was found at Ynys Llanddwyn. Dan was aware that he had told Michael so much that night at the holiday lodge. Things that Michael had absolutely no prior knowledge of. Tonight would be Michael's turn to talk.

He talked about his course and how tough it was. He expressed some doubts as to whether he wanted to carry on at all. A law degree was useful, but it was a long way from being a barrister. Dan completely understood that his son's heart wasn't quite in it. He was also aware that he didn't have long to talk and maybe gleaning some inside information wasn't going to be easy. Then, completely unexpectedly, Michael offered something.

"I got a call from Nick yesterday."

"Oh, really, what did he want?"

"He said we should have a catch-up, you know, I think he's just trying to be a godfather."

"Did you arrange anything?"

"Nothing solid really. Just talked about maybe him doing a charity gig at the students' union."

"Charity? I didn't think he had a charitable bone in his body!"

"Come on Dad, I know you don't like him, but he's ok really. He's trying to help homeless teenagers, there's a lot of them in London."

Dan didn't like where this was going.

"Homeless teenagers? Why?"

"Because it's a great cause Dad and I think, reading between the lines, he had a shitty upbringing. He was homeless himself once, he knows what it's like."

"So how come you know so much about him?"

"I suppose I've spent more time with him than you, you know when me and Gabe used to stay with him and Jen for weekends, when you and Mum wanted rid of us!"

Dan immediately felt defensive. "That was *never* the reason Mike. We were exhausted parents of twin boys, and they were childless and willing to relieve us, now and again."

"It felt like we spent a lot of time there, Dad, not just the odd weekend but I suppose when you're young, time goes slower."

"Absolutely, tell me about it, son. Well at least you enjoyed your time with them, if only for the indoor heated swimming pool. I think that helped."

"That and the fishing, the bike rides, the forest walks…"

Dan thought he should surrender at this point. He lifted his glass. "OK, I give in, Nick Foster, patron saint of homeless teenagers. He's an all-round great guy!"

"He's an all right guy Dad, but he's not a saint. I don't think Gabe liked him much."

"And why do you think that was?"

"Hard to say really. He was reluctant to join in anything, he just came along with me usually. I used to ask him what was wrong? Didn't he like having fun? But you know how he was – sort of the joyless version of me."

"I know Mike, you were always two sides of the same coin. Physically twins, but not mentally. It's just makes me uneasy to think he wasn't one hundred percent happy back then."

"Well, that was when we were really small. It got more interesting for us both when we got to fourteen-fifteen-sixteen."

"Interesting? In what way interesting?"

"Come on Dad. That house was full of booze, all of the time. We knew where it was, and we weren't exactly supervised. Nick and Jen had friends round sometimes for dinner and we'd stay out of the way with a stash. I remember the last time we stayed there, one of their dinner parties ended up in the pool. We got caught spying on them, all naked and drunk, splashing around as if it was normal."

"Holy shit Mike! What did you see? Or more importantly who did you see?"

"I saw everything and everyone there, butt naked. It was so funny Dad."

"I'm disappointed you never told me and your mum. They were supposed to be looking after you, not having naked pool orgies!"

"They thought we were asleep in bed, till somebody saw us. And, come on Dad, what kind of heterosexual sixteen-year-old male wouldn't want to see Jen naked? She's got the body of a goddess. I was pretty transfixed to be honest."

"Please Mike, I don't want to hear any more..." Dan knew *exactly* what his son was referring to. "For Christ's sake she's your godmother."

"I know Dad, but it's not like we're actually related. I remember feeling a bit weird for the rest of the week, you know, being around her? Feeling ashamed for thinking 'certain things'. Just normal things for a horny teenager's brain, but it felt wrong at the same time. She was cool, though I think she knew and she didn't mention anything. She just carried on as if nothing had happened.

"And what about Gabe? What was he doing while you were staring at your naked godmother?"

Michael laughed out loud. "Gabe shot back up to his room as soon as he realised what was going on. He wasn't interested was he? He left me to get a bollocking off a fat bald man in a towel. He went back to his stash and got pissed in his room. He was a bit more withdrawn than usual after that week. I think he was struggling with himself, and who he was, and he was having a hard time with it."

"So where was Saint Nick while all this was going on? I still can't *believe* that not one of you has said a word about it, God, Mike it's off the scale!"

"He wasn't there. Well, not at the pool party anyway. It was that weird time when they'd split but Nick kept turning up unannounced. Like he was trying to catch her out or something."

"What do you mean? Catch her out?"

"Dad, I'm nineteen, I've no idea what went on in the crazy world of my godparents. I think he wanted some sort of proof that she was seeing someone else. Divorce stuff. Pointing the blame stuff, I guess."

Dan didn't keep his son for much longer. He didn't like what Mike had just told him. He couldn't believe how irresponsible the boys' so-called godparents had been. While Michael was still amused at the memories of what went on in that house, Dan was wondering who to ring first. Nick or Jen?

Either way it was going to be very difficult, but it was a risk he had to take.

Chapter 31
April 2011

His phone rang while he was en-route back to Anglesey. It was Emma Morgan. He answered the call hastily and was grateful she had called him now, and not an hour previously. At that time, he had been in the shower while his phone was on the bedside table at the hotel, in close proximity to Grace. She would definitely have quizzed him if she'd seen 'Emma Morgan' popping up on his phone screen.

"Hello Emma, how are you?"

"Oh, hi Mr Hearn, I'm good thanks. I just thought I'd update you."

"Oh, so there's more?"

"Yes, very interesting stuff."

"About Ni......." Emma quickly interrupted him.

"No names over the phone please, let's just say 'our friend'."

"OK, sorry, what about him?"

"He was cautioned back in the late sixties, while he was a student. It cropped up when he was interviewed during Operation Starling."

"I didn't realise he was that old?"

"Well, he was born in 1950, so that makes him sixty-one now."

"So, what was he up to?"

"He was arrested on suspicion of soliciting, it was a well-known meeting place for, what can I say? Anonymous gay sex. A public toilet block in Clapham."

"Why only a caution?"

"He said that he was there to offer help to the rent boys that hung around the place. Thing is they couldn't find a rent boy that could back up his claims. They all tend to disappear when the police are around."

"I fucking knew it!" Dan said under his breath.

"It was only a caution though Mr Hearn. He's never been convicted of any crime."

"That's because he's always got an excuse, hasn't he? Good Samaritan, research? It's horse shit."

"It also might be perfectly true. Maybe he's just been in the wrong place at the wrong time?"

"Or he's a liar trying to hide who he really is?" Dan was now furious inside.

"Can I just remind you Mr Hearn that the police information I received is strictly off the record. You've obviously got some personal issues with our friend, but you can't take what you now know to the police. My informant at the Met has taken a big risk for me, and if they can see unjustified 'fishing' on their computer systems, my friend gets the sack."

Dan pulled into a lay-by as his driving concentration was waning fast.

"Miss Morgan, I'm very grateful for the work you've done, honestly, but my nineteen-year-old son ended his own life just months ago. Now, I can't prove anything, but he was in very emotional state when he left Aberystwyth. Boyfriend trouble. He was also high on ecstasy. Despite that, he was on his way home, I'm convinced of that. Now, just before he did what he did, his brother posted a video on Instagram. We'll never know if Gabriel saw the video, but our friend is clearly in the shot, at my home, attending my party, completely uninvited, the same person that has looked after my boys, countless times over the years. God, if I'd known then what I know now, he wouldn't have got anywhere near them."

"I get what you're saying, honestly, but you still don't have any proof."

"No, I don't have any proof that my son has possibly been abused by his godfather, but I don't think I need it."

And with that, Dan hung up. He understood perfectly what Emma Morgan was trying to say. There really wasn't any concrete proof that Nick Foster had done anything to Gabe, but it was all starting to stack up in his mind. The caution for soliciting, Operation Starling, him appearing at Mike's bedroom door, claiming to be looking for the toilet, his no-show at Gabe's funeral. And now he was contacting Mike to arrange some sort of charity gig in York. Saint Nick, trying to help the vulnerable, again. What a guy.

He had a few more days to work out what he was going to do before Grace returned from York. He definitely wasn't going to share what he knew with her; she was still too fragile. He would call Emma Morgan and apologise as soon as he got home. He didn't want her to think that he was going to act on any of the information she'd given him. He planned to bide his time until Nick Foster wasn't looking over his shoulder. That could take a while.

When he got back home there was a note behind the door. It read, "Dan, I've unblocked the toilet in the lodge. You can buy me a pint tonight if you want!"

It was his neighbour who had kindly volunteered to be on call while he was away. He shook his head and laughed. Unblocking toilets wasn't something he was ready for. Maybe he should pay his neighbour to carry out repairs and maintenance? They could discuss it over a pint later. First of all, he called Emma Morgan.

"Hello Emma, I'm so sorry for hanging up earlier. I was out of order."

"That's OK Mr Hearn, I understand how upset you are."

"I get what you're saying, honestly, I'm not going to do anything, not without proof. I'm a wreck but I'm not an idiot. Could you send me the bill please, to my email address and I'll get it paid today?"

"Fine, I'll sort that out for you."

"Thanks again for your work and tell your insider not to worry."

Then he rang his neighbour Gareth. It went to voicemail, so he left a message.

"Prynhawn da," he made the effort for his Welsh-speaking friend, "that's enough Welsh from me Gareth! Er, thanks for literally dealing with the shit! I'll stand you a few at the Druid's, say seven o'clock?"

Chapter 32
April 2011

Gareth was already sitting at the bar when Dan walked into the Druid's Arms. The only pub in this small village that had survived. It was a mystery to Dan *how* it had survived. After all, Anglesey was a very popular holiday destination and most pubs had totally adapted to cater for the tourists. Not the Druid's. The name itself was enough to put off even the thirstiest holiday makers. On top of that, it looked unloved and grey, offered no food, no wi-fi, and needed a total refurb.

The usual faces were dotted around, mostly older men, the last of the Druid's dying breed of clientele. Once these people were gone, the pub would die too. It reminded Dan of the Ploughboy Inn, back in the day. He could almost picture Patrin and Frank Shaw sitting at the bar, talking scribble to each other after several pints.

He pulled up a bar stool and ordered himself and Gareth a pint.

"How was York?" Gareth was happy to speak English to his friend and neighbour.

"It was nice."

"Nice?"

"Yes, I got to spend some time with Mike. I'm proud of how he's coping, I just don't want him to quit."

"Always handy to have a lawyer in the family I suppose?"

"If he actually wants to be a lawyer Gareth, but I'm not sure."

"And what about Grace? Is she coping all right?"

"It's hard to tell really. She's a hundred and fifty miles away from where her son died, she's distracted at the moment. I'm just worried she'll want to quit this place eventually."

"That would be sad. I won't lie to you Dan, you would be missed."

"We talked about a memorial service for Gabe, later in the year. We've got his ashes, but Grace won't part with them. She's not ready, see? And where would we scatter them anyway? Not the Menai Strait, that's for sure."

"I've seen people throwing roses off the bridges, and wreaths and things. Perhaps you could do something like that?"

"I'll see what Grace says. I think it's a good idea, but she might not."

"Anyway, you can't leave us ordinary folk with our boring parties. We're counting on you to entertain us all, what with your famous friends!"

Dan grunted.

"Not my choice of friends Gareth. Jennifer Williams has been Grace's friend since primary school, and Nick Foster just happens to be her husband, for the second time."

"He seemed like a right prick!"

"You spoke to him then?"

"Yes, briefly, he was pretty drunk though. He was keen to let everybody know who he was. A bit up himself."

"Oh, he's definitely that. I don't think anyone at the party would have recognised him anyway, it's not like he's relevant anymore. I just wish we could get rid of him and his pampered wife."

Gareth nudged his elbow into Dan's side. "I can't say she isn't a stunner though Dan, I bet she's had a lot of pampering!"

Dan didn't laugh along with his friend. Gareth was a typical, thick skinned, down-to-earth Welsh farmer, but even he noticed Dan's change in mood.

"What's up then? Has he overstepped the mark or something? You know how these showbiz types can be? A bit liberal with it?"

"Gareth mate, you don't know the half of it. Liberal doesn't cover it really."

"God Dan, you've got to tell me more now. This is Llanddona, *nothing* happens here."

"I wish I could Gareth, but it's complicated. Really, mate, let's have another pint and plot the perfect murder..."

"I understand you don't like them Dan, but that's a bit drastic!"

"Of course, I'm joking. Saying that, if I knew that there was zero percent of being caught, I'd pay someone, seriously."

Gareth laughed out loud again.

"Dan my friend, I know some rugby lads that would do it for a laugh, I'm not kidding you, fucking savages!"

"Thanks for the offer, I'll have to decline on this occasion, but if I ever get desperate enough to send your rugby mates on a mission, with the absolute certainty that they would get caught and we all end up in prison – I'll let you know."

Then Dan's phone started ringing in his pocket. It was Grace checking if he'd got home, and as usual he'd forgotten to message her. She was also letting him know she was coming home early due to Mike and her exhausting all that York had to offer. He missed her, but he could have done with one more day to do some research without Grace looking over his shoulder. If he was going to establish the truth, one way or another, she couldn't be party to anything, not yet.

Gareth ordered them another pint. This would have to be his last for the evening as his thoughts were wandering to a less inhibited space in his head. It was a space that didn't stop him from thinking about a world without Nick Foster, and a time machine that he would use to go back three years and reject Jen outright. He knew that he'd have to speak to her, there was no getting around it. When and how he was going to do it was evading him for now.

"That was Grace, she's back tomorrow, I'll have to go home and do some cleaning and tidying."

Gareth nearly spat his drink out.

"You're joking right?"

"No Gareth, I'm not joking."

"That's no job for a *real* man."

"Thing is, last time I looked, I was a real man." He wasn't going to let his friend bait him on matters of equality. Then he remembered the repairs and maintenance idea with the holiday lodge.

"Anyway, before I scuttle home to put my marigolds on, what do you think about being my repairs and maintenance man, for the lodge?"

"Depends on what you're offering I suppose."

"Five percent of takings?"

"Ten."

"Piss off."

"OK, seven."

"Deal." Dan put his hand out and Gareth shook it firmly. "I expect an on-call service for our guests though."

"Like I said, I know plenty of handymen, it won't be a problem."

"Great, that'll free up more of my time to tidy a few things up." Dan drained his pint and left home on foot, down the narrow, unlit lanes of Llanddona. He was going to tidy up the mess of unanswered questions that surrounded Gabe's suicide. Emma Morgan had supplied some useful intelligence, but it wasn't going to be enough.

Chapter 33
April 2011

Jen shut her laptop, sighed and poured herself another large glass of red. If there was one thing she didn't like, it was the loneliness that came with solo drinking. Even Nick would be preferable company than just herself, but he wasn't an option anymore. She had let him charm his way back into her life, believing his recovery was genuine, believing his promises of sobriety and fidelity. That had all fallen apart in a matter of months after their ridiculous Las Vegas wedding. Between the tragic death of Gabriel and the day of his funeral, it was obvious that Nick had turned to one of the many dealers he knew, and completely bombed. He hadn't even tried to hide it. When he returned home in the early hours, on the day they should have been travelling to Anglesey together, to pay their respects to their godson, she had told him it was over. Nick had been absent for a couple of days, probably on a bender, and Jen was determined that she wasn't going to relive the hell that had been played out in the death throes of their first marriage. She felt guilty for covering up for him on the day, at the same time she knew that Dan and Grace had not entirely 'bought' the cover story.

She switched on the enormous TV and looked for something, anything, to absorb her and stave off the vulnerability that accompanies loneliness. If she didn't find anything soon, she would probably pick up her phone and call somebody, pour out her feelings, and lift the lid of her very own Pandora's Box. Thankfully she found an obscure channel that was repeating a design and dressmaking competition in America, on which she had been a judge.

"That's perfect, I'll watch myself," she thought.

After watching one episode of herself looking younger, fresher, and full of life and enthusiasm for her craft, she switched the TV off. Maybe she should get an early night? Take her sketch book to bed *and* her wine? It seemed like a good idea. Before she switched the downstairs lights off her phone lit up on silent. It was Dan. She felt an internal jolt of electricity as his name flashed on the screen. She hadn't seen that for such a long time, not since he had ended their affair and she was instinctively very uneasy and reluctant to answer. What did he want? Was her secret out? If so, that would blow apart her life-long friendship with Grace and, God forbid if Nick knew anything, the mood he was in, he wouldn't hesitate to leak it to the press. As she wrestled with her conscience, the phone stopped ringing. After a few seconds it started again. He wanted to speak to her directly and presumably in private.

Dan was sitting alone in the kitchen. "Fuck it Jennifer, answer the call." Then she did.

"Dan?"

"Yes, it's me."

"Is everything OK? "

"Depends on what you mean really, Jen. I could ask you the same?"

"If you're referring to Nick, we're all done." So far so good, that was exactly along the lines of Emma Morgan's information.

"I'm not that surprised Jen, but sorry."

"So, I get the feeling this isn't a courtesy call, Dan? Is Grace home?"

"No, she's in York visiting Michael." He heard Jen take a breath.

"So, she doesn't know you're calling me?"

"No, and I don't want her to know." He could hear Jen's nervous breath. Was she thinking he wanted to re-connect? He would have to put her straight.

"First Jen, I'm not interested in, you know, well, you. It was a big mistake on my part and I'm not calling to try to re-kindle anything." She was silent. Offering nothing.

"What I need to know is, what you know, or think you know about Nick." He heard a sigh of relief.

"What I know? What do you mean? Dan, Nick is an arsehole. We're not together. End of!"

"You were with him a long time Jen. You must know something about his past?"

"If you're referring to that business with the police and his laptop, I told you already he's not like that!"

"What about his upbringing? Has he ever told you about it?"

"What about your upbringing? Have *you* ever told anyone about it? Including your wife?"

Dan knew exactly what she was referring to. He hated how smart she was. He decided to soften his approach.

"Jen, please, I'm still grieving the loss of my son. I'm trying to find out why he took his life."

"So why are you so obsessed with Nick? Then she realised what was happening. "You think he harmed Gabe? You honestly think he may have hurt him in some way?"

"I don't know, I'm asking you again if you ever had any reason to doubt him?"

Jen could feel herself getting angry. She was having a cold, matter of fact conversation with the man she'd once fell head over heels in love with and he wasn't showing any signs of warmth.

"OK Dan, listen carefully, here's what I know. Nick was brought up in the care system. He suffered physical and sexual abuse from all kinds of people who were paid to look after him. By the time he was fourteen he was on the streets. He had a guitar, so he was a busker who spent his nights in homeless shelters. He got lucky one day when he was unofficially adopted by a family that took pity on him. He finished school and went to college to study music. You know the rest."

"Thing is Jen, I don't know."

"What makes you think he could harm a child? Come on Dan, what do *you* think you know? Your turn."

He couldn't tell her what he had obtained off the record.

"There's this video that Michael posted on the night of the party. He posted it on Instagram. I think Gabe may have seen it just before he jumped off the bridge. I'm trying to piece things together."

"What about a damned video? You've lost me now Dan."

"Look, Gabe didn't know that Nick was at the party. None of us knew about your secret wedding, Nick was never on the invitation list, but he is in the video. Clear as day."

"Please Dan, I loved Gabe too. If I'd ever thought for a second that my husband could, could... no, never."

Dan had to throw something else in. He couldn't leave it there. "I know about the parties Jen, the alcohol, the non-existent supervision when *my* sons were in *your* care."

Jen froze. She wasn't expecting that.

"While you and your friends were having fun in the pool, my boys were in your care and drinking."

She was silent again.

"Jen, say something please. Is Michael lying to me?"

"Dan, darling, you knew about our lifestyle, you had no problem leaving them with us. None whatsoever. Now, I'm ending this conversation, and if you don't drop this ridiculous crusade, you'll regret it. You see, I do have proof of something that *actually* happened, remember? Call it my insurance."

"Are you threatening me, you bitch?" Jen didn't hear him say it. She had already ended the call.

Chapter 34
April 2011

Dan threw his phone across the kitchen. An expensive iPhone that hit the corner of a work top and landed on the floor with a smash. He had put himself in a position that he never wanted to be in. His ex-mistress wielding their secret like a weapon, letting him know that she has the proof and that she would use it if she was forced to. Jen was defending Nick, of course she was. The last thing anyone in the public realm wants is to be associated with a monster.

He grabbed his phone up off the floor to inspect the damage, which was a badly cracked screen. That was the least of his worries right now. A phone can be repaired and restored, like nothing happened, but words can't be unsaid, and Jen's words were now hanging over him as if she had cast a spell. She had confirmed that her extremely short-lived marriage was over, and it worried him that she may just say something to Grace out of sheer spite. After all, Grace's marriage, despite the ups and downs, was still intact. His affair with Jen had been purely sexual on his part, however, when Jen started to indicate that she had feelings for him that went way beyond the sex, to the point of suggesting he left Grace, he ended what he saw as the 'arrangement'. Jen's first marriage to Nick didn't survive, Jen's second attempt with Nick was already over. He thought about the woman who had the looks, the body, the career, the house in London, a talent that the fashion -world couldn't get enough of, and yet she was probably sitting alone, separated, childless and bitter.

It always fascinated him how the two childhood friends had taken very different paths in life, had achieved success in very different ways and yet there was still something about Jen that led him to believe there was an underlying jealousy towards Grace. Both women had known each other for longer than they had known him. What sort of value did Jen place on her relationship with Grace? He didn't feel courageous enough to find out.

He poured himself a large whisky and threw in some ice. He would have to bury his fears around Jen, and put a mental tick against her name, which was on the top of the list of people he needed to speak to. He sat in his office and fired up his PC. He googled Nick Foster just to see if there was anything at all that could offer up some kind of clue. He pored over music reviews, concert reviews, and a few, dull newspaper articles about the divorce. There was nothing current, nothing really negative. Even the small article relating to Operation Starling was a statement from Nick's former manager saying: "Nick Foster has co-operated fully with the Metropolitan Police. He has not been charged with any crime and there will be no further action taken."

He thought about Jamie Fellowes who had described Gabriel as the 'love of his life'. They hadn't known each other very long, but they might have had deep talks, personal history, life experiences. The sort of conversations that people *do* have when they're magnetically attached to a new partner. Jamie hadn't been straight with Gabe about his situation, maybe Gabe had poured his soul out and just couldn't cope with the contrasting approaches to a relationship? He had always been so trusting and naive. He still had Jamie's number stored on his now battered phone. It was only ten o'clock, so he rang Jamie's number. He answered quite quickly.

"Hello Jamie, it's Dan Hearn."

Jamie sounded surprised. "Oh, hi, erm, sorry, I just need to turn the telly down."

"Are you still in Bangor Jamie?"

"Yes, I decided not to go back to Aberystwyth. Don't fancy being lynched, see."

"So, what are you doing? I mean, sorry Jamie, I'm not prying into your life, I just wondered if we could have a chat, about Gabriel."

"It's OK, really, I'm unemployed at the moment. I just can't seem to get my head in gear, not since..."

Dan interrupted. "I understand how hard it is Jamie. We're all suffering. We might never get over this."

"So, what do you want to chat about? It's a bit late, not that I care, I stay up till all hours. My mam's despairing with me."

Dan knew he had to be careful. He couldn't let Jamie know anything, he would just have to cast the net with a general question and hope something came back.

"I was just wondering if Gabe ever confided anything in you? You know, something maybe he hadn't told anyone else."

Jamie's tone changed to a little more serious. "Well, if he did, that would still be something he didn't want anyone to know, wouldn't it?"

"I get it Jamie, even if you knew something, you still wouldn't tell?"

"Out of respect for Gabriel's memory, I wouldn't tell a soul. Not even you Mr Hearn."

"Not even if it gave us some answers?"

"Look, Mr Hearn, no disrespect, believe me, but I've been living with the guilt ever since it happened. I can't sleep, I can't concentrate, I just keep going over and over it in my mind. He was very upset, and I should have been straight with him from the start. Then he could have made an informed choice, but I took that away from him."

"But I don't believe that's why he killed himself Jamie, so please, if you can recall, did he tell you anything that he was keeping secret? Anything?"

"No, I swear, he didn't. I thought his life, compared to mine was fantastic. Wealthy parents, big house, travel, designer gear. Brilliant."

Dan sighed. This was going to be fruitless. But Jamie continued.

"There was one night we got really drunk when I thought he was going to say something about his past, but he held back, I didn't push it."

"Why not?"

"Because we hadn't known each other long and I reckoned he'd tell me when he was ready."

"Did you get any clue from him?"

"Not really, but I think it was something he was ashamed of, I could tell. We were talking about our early sexual experiences, but he put a brick wall up. Said something happened that he didn't want, it was in his past and he didn't want to talk about it."

"Did he say who?"

"No. I just got the impression that it was somebody older than him."

"Why do you say older? What gave you that impression?"

"Because I was telling him about a teacher in high school that tried it on with me on a camping trip, and he nodded and started to say something like, he'd had unwanted attention from both sexes, but the worst predators were older. When I asked for an example, he shut down. Said he wasn't ready to tell me or anybody."

At last, a breakthrough. There *was* something that Gabriel was hiding. Some unwanted sexual attention, or even worse.

"Thanks Jamie, that could be very helpful. Please stop beating yourself up. It wasn't your fault."

"I'll try Mr Hearn. I don't know what you think you're going to prove but thanks for trying."

"OK well, I'll keep going, only please, not a word to Grace or anybody. It will finish her off."

"You have my word."

"Oh, and if you don't find a job soon, give me a call, I'm thinking about taking on a new project."

"I will, definitely, what sort of project?"

"I'm thinking of buying a pub."

"Oh, great, which pub?"

"My local. It's not actually for sale right now but when it is…"

"Great, let me know, please. Any way I can help out."

Dan had four people on his call list. One and two were done, and he was going to go straight to four. He had to, now. Three wasn't an option.

Chapter 35
May 15th 2011

Jack Hearn was sitting in his office trying to make sense of a VAT return, prepared by his accountant. It was the part of running a business that he wasn't comfortable with, that's why he paid other people, trustworthy people, to do the sums and let him know where he was up to. It wasn't always straightforward though. The pitfalls of trying to make money whilst paying staff, taxes and business rates were numerous, but despite these annoying barriers, the company was doing well.

He had just bought another small caravan site in Hampshire that was perfect for converting. The plan was to continue with the tried and tested method of turning small, out of the way holiday lets into small, desirable, permanent sites for people who were done with travelling, or anybody that liked the park home life.

It had taken him almost thirty years to build up the business that he was very proud of. The price of houses, decent modern houses, had always been out of reach to ordinary people in this part of the country and he provided the same people the opportunity to buy or rent a luxury lodge on one of his many sites. He was liked and respected by most of his owners and tenants and was loathed by some local authority officials. Despite attempts to block progress with some projects, he now had thirty sites and many, many satisfied customers. His favourite dwelling, despite his wealth, was a lodge, set in its own grounds with a high fence and a security gate. He stood by his product and, despite owning several permanent structures, he was happy to live mostly in this home, that was actually three lodges, carefully joined together and quite magnificent. He had refined taste in just about everything. His clothes, his cars (there were several), furniture, artwork, jewellery. He owned a few racehorses, but that was just a hobby really. He enjoyed entertaining his friends with dinner parties and days out at the races. It was how he lived his life and he loved it. He was a self-made man; nobody could argue with that. From buying his first plot of land, to the present day, he had made it.

He pulled out a drawer from his desk, looking for a new pen. He felt obliged to write a few questions on the VAT return, just to keep the accountant on his well-paid toes. He had to pull the drawer hard as it seemed to be stuck. As he did, a small black and white photograph shot to the front. He picked up the frail, frayed picture gently. He could just make out his mother, kneeling on some grass, with him sitting on her lap. There was a date and place written in pencil on the back that was hardly visible now, 'Hayfield 1965'. He could only have been twelve months old or thereabouts. He didn't really remember much about his early life; except that they were poor and his mother cried a lot. He studied the picture for a few seconds and put it back in the drawer.

He knew and was grateful on a daily basis that this empire, his empire, had started with the money his brother gave him back in the early eighties. He cringed inside recalling how he'd treated Danior back then, his only brother who loved him, and was willing to give him a chance. Years and years later, he was still regretting how he behaved and to some extent felt a sense of shame. He hadn't seen Danior since he left, he had been a disgrace and he wasn't ever going to intrude again. He would wait to be invited, but the wait continued. Jack had kept track of his brother, which was a fairly easy thing to do, just using the internet. He knew that Hearn Logistics had been sold and that Danior and his wife, the wife Jack had never met, had moved to North Wales only last year.

He kissed the picture before returning it to the drawer and said a silent prayer for his deceased parents and his estranged brother. His desk phone rang, a light flashing, indicating it was his secretary. He answered it promptly.

"Hi Caroline."

"Hello, Jack, I've just got back from lunch, and I've got a message on voicemail, well, I've got several actually."

"That's fine, just weed out the crap and give me the important stuff, you're good at that!"

"The thing is, I think you should listen to one of them."

"Very mysterious Caroline. You don't normally do this?"

"I just think you should hear one of them."

Jack popped his head around the door that led to his PA's office. He liked Caroline very much. She was in her early sixties, dumpy, frumpy and grey-haired – not your typical high-salaried personal assistant. He employed her because she was extremely smart, experienced, and took no prisoners. Most importantly, he trusted her. She pressed the replay button on her desk phone.

"Message received today at 13.15…"

A hesitant sounding man's voice could be heard.

"I'm calling to speak to Jack Hearn. Could you please give him a message to call me back when he's free. Please tell him it's Danior, Danior Hearn…"

"Holy Mother of God," was Jack's whispered response.

"Is that who I think it is?"

"I suppose if he's genuine, yes, that's my brother's name anyway."

"The brother you haven't seen for?"

"Nearly thirty years."

Jack sat down on Caroline's desk and put his hands to his head. He felt slightly dizzy.

"Do you believe in God, Caroline?"

"I suppose so Jack, I'm not an atheist."

"So, you think that prayers can be answered?"

"If you believe they can, yes."

"The thing is, *if* that was Danior, I just had a rapid response from heaven. So, here's what we do. You call the number he left and put him through security. Three questions that he has to get right. All three, not one, or two, all three."

Caroline rolled her eyes. Jack was not very trusting, which was understandable in a way. There were so many fakers and con-artists out there.

"The questions are, where was he born? Does he have any tattoos and if so, where are they? And what was the name of his birth mother? If he knows all that, he's my brother."

Jack walked back to his office. He needed a drink. He waited for Caroline to report back, swivelling in his chair and sipping his brandy. He never usually drank during the day, but this was making him nervous with anticipation.

After a few minutes Caroline walked in and placed a piece of paper on his desk with the three answers written on it. He read them in turn.

"New Forest, Romani symbol, top of right thigh, Marianne Fletcher."

It was him for certain. But why now? What did he want?

Chapter 36
May 15th 2011 (earlier in the day)

Dan was sitting in his office staring at the computer screen. He was looking at a photo of his brother, Jack Hearn, millionaire businessman and philanthropist. Despite his efforts to forget the case theory he had in his mind, it wasn't going away. He had thrown himself into several different activities in the last few weeks to try to escape the negative feelings of anger and frustration he still felt towards Nick Foster. He deleted the video from New Year's Eve from his phone just to get the image out of his head, but it was still on the laptop that Michael had used for the slideshow.

No amount of tractor-mowing, fishing, walking or drinking was going to stop him. He had a number four option, and he was going to call him.

Finding Nick had been simple enough, although, when he found Jack, Dan was really surprised at his brother's apparent phenomenal success, according to Google. He had a park home empire in Hampshire and he was patron of more than one traveller charity. He didn't know if the image he was looking at was recent, but it was definitely his brother Jack. Handsome, thick dark hair, and 'the nose'.

It took him a while to take in what he was reading. It looked like the arrogant, entitled young man he'd sent packing all those years ago with a few thousand pounds had rolled up his sleeves, grafted, and built up an amazing business, he was wealthy and successful without losing touch with his traveller heritage. Dan was almost jealous, but most of all he felt proud of his kid brother. It was time to get in touch, whether Jack was willing to help him or not, it was time.

He waited till Grace had left the house for a hairdressing appointment and set about his research straight away. He searched Companies House under Jack's name and found that several businesses were registered to him, not just Thorney Hill Park Homes Ltd. There was a security business called Evergreen Protection. The description was brief, it was a private security business. Dan smiled to himself, wondering if his brother was actually on the straight and narrow, or was he part of something that was edging on the dark side, a Romani trait for sure.

There were so many phone numbers on the Thorney Hill website, it was confusing. Eventually somebody gave him the number of Mr Hearn's PA, Caroline Brownlow. He would have to go through the gate keeper to get to his brother. He was really nervous with anticipation. He hadn't seen or talked to his brother for almost thirty years, and he didn't know how Jack was going to react or what this call could open the door to. There was only one way to find out.

His heart rate increased as he dialled the number, he didn't have a speech rehearsed for Jack but that didn't have to matter now, there was no going back. Disappointingly his call went to an answer machine.

"Thorney Hill Limited. Unfortunately, there is no-one here to take your call, please leave a message for Caroline and she will get back to you as soon as possible."

Damn it! He hated leaving voicemail messages. He sounded so hesitant and awkward. He left his message and sat back in his office chair. If Jack didn't want to know, that would be the end of it. Within a few minutes, his desk phone rang. He could see the number was the one he'd just dialled so he snatched up the receiver.

"Dan Hearn."

"Hello Mr Hearn, I'm Caroline, Mr Hearn's PA." That sounded strange already. "How can I help you?"

"I'd like to speak to Jack please, I'm his brother."

"Yes, I heard the voicemail Mr Hearn. I've spoken to Jack, and he's asked me to ask you a few questions, I know it sounds a bit strange, possibly, but he wants to make sure it's you."

That did sound very weird to Dan. What could he ask? Thirty years had passed, they knew nothing about each other. He had to play the game if he wanted to speak to his brother. The questions were easy enough to answer, but clever Jack. No amount of research could lead anyone who wasn't Dan to answer all three of them.

Caroline politely ended the call. "Thank you, I'll pass those on to Jack and I'll get back to you as soon as he's decided what to do."

Dan couldn't do anything else but wait. If Jack didn't want to open the door he wouldn't. Even if he did co-operate, he was uneasy about Jen knowing *anything,* following her very genuine threat to out their affair. Nick was a problem, and he was hopeful that Jack could provide a workable solution.

Dan was jolted out of his thoughts when his desk phone rang again. It was the same number, but was it the gate keeper or the Lord of the Manor? It was the gate keeper. Never mind.

"Hello Mr Hearn, Jack has a few appointments this afternoon, so he's suggested you call him this evening, after 6 p.m. if that's all right with you?"

He agreed and jotted down Jack's personal mobile number. He could always arrange to meet Gareth at the Druid's later. Grace wouldn't question it. He would then take the Ranger and drive to somewhere sufficiently remote and quiet to make his call.

Chapter 37
May 2011

He found a remote enough place which was the small car park at Point Lynas. Most tourists were there during the day to look at the lighthouse, so at this time in the evening it was quieter. Just before he made the call, he had a flashback to the day he pulled Jack out of the flooded stream and wondered if Annie or Patrin had ever told him about it. He certainly hadn't mentioned anything for the period of time he'd spent working for Dan, and Dan had purposely not mentioned it. He didn't see the point at the time in saying, "By the way, I saved your life once, be grateful you little shit." Maybe he could bring it out of the bag if he needed to this time? The call rang out for a few seconds before it was answered.

"Danior?"

"Hello Jack, Dan's fine, honestly."

"Dan? No problem, good to hear you, honestly, I'm so relieved you found me."

"Relieved? Sounds a bit ominous."

"It's been too long Dan. We parted on bad terms, and I didn't deserve anything from you, nothing."

"Looks to me like you've done all right Jack, with or without me."

"I could say the same about you. You're retired now?"

"Semi-retired, business sold for a fortune, and I've got a few irons in a few fires, but I can't call it work, not really."

"So, why now? Is there something you want to talk about?"

"There's too much Jack, definitely not a phone call's worth. I think we should meet up."

Jack sighed, he knew his diary was usually very full and his free weekends were almost non-existent.

"Where and when Dan? I'll have to book some time. Can you believe it? I'm the boss, there's nobody above me, and I have to ask my PA for permission!"

"I think I'd rather come to you, alone. At first anyway. I have a very patient and understanding wife, she'll be fine with it."

"Whatever and however you want Dan. It's your call, I owe you that much. I'm just texting my PA now. How long do you need? A night? A weekend?"

"A night would be fine and a weekend's fine too. Depends really."

"OK, in three weeks I've got a free weekend. I'd love to have you as my guest. I'll send you my address. Is that fine with you?"

"Yes."

"Alternatively, I'll send you my driver."

"Very grand Jack! I'll say no thank you to that, I'm a terrible passenger."

"He's a professional driver! But whatever you want to do, that's fine."

"Jack, I ran a haulage business for forty years, remember? I'm used to driving up and down the country."

"So, why don't you have a rest at my expense?"

"Very kind, but I prefer to be in the driving seat."

"No worries. I suppose I'll meet Mrs Hearn some other time? Is it Grace?"

"Yes, we got together, then she came to work for me, the rest is history."

"And kids?"

"Two boys, twins, Michael and Gabriel."

"How old?"

Dan's voice started to wobble.

"Nineteen, Jack, Gabriel, well, he, he, took his own life."

"God no! So sorry Dan, when?"

"New Year's Eve, just gone. We're still trying to come to terms with it, but it's so hard."

"I don't have any children Dan, just a couple of horses. I can't even imagine what you're going through."

"Hell, with a thin veneer of normality. Michael's studying law at York but he's flagging. Grace is putting on a brave face, but she's broken inside."

"Please, I hope you don't mind me asking, I can hear how upset you are, but do you have any idea why?"

"Nothing concrete, but I'll tell you what I think when I come over to yours. I'd like your take on it."

"Absolutely Dan. If there's anything I can do, and I mean *anything at all,* it will be done. I promise."

"Will see you in a few weeks then."

As Dan drove to the Druid's, he felt a slight tinge of excitement about meeting his brother. Jack hadn't given much away, apart from he was obviously very wealthy, no kids, two horses, and a driver. He hadn't mentioned a wife, a partner, or anybody else. Very mysterious.

He walked into the pub to see Gareth sitting at the bar – same bar stool, same pint, same bloody coat! He pulled up a stool and sat down.

"Pint please love, and one for Gareth, thanks."

"You in a good mood? I get a pint without asking?" Gareth was very quick to make a joke out of everyone and everything.

"As a matter of fact, Gareth, I feel a little bit upbeat for the first time in months."

"Any particular reason?"

"I just had a conversation with my brother."

"I didn't know you had a brother?"

"Half-brother. Jack. Different mothers. We've been estranged but I got in touch with him."

"Oh, well Dan, family is family, no escaping that."

"I'm going to see him in a few weeks."

Gareth tilted his head and looked thoughtful.

"Jack Hearn?"

"Hey, love, another pint for Gareth for being a genius!"

Gareth wasn't smiling.

"Is he in the business of caravan parks?"

"He is yes. How do you know?"

"I'm sorry Dan, he's *your* brother?"

"Half-brother, formerly estranged."

"I know his name all right Dan. He bought a site near Holyhead, he wanted to turn it into one of them permanent pi… er, traveller sites. Caused a load of shit with the council. Upset a lot of people. He threw a ton of money at it, lawyers, bribes, his name is mud on this island. Be careful, you say you haven't seen him for years, that means you probably don't know him. A lot of people got the feeling he isn't a very nice man."

"Gareth, mate, I'm a big boy, and I appreciate your concern, but I don't care if he isn't a very nice man."

He hadn't quite fallen for Jack's charming and concerned stance over the phone. If he was going to enlist his brother's help, they would have to talk face to face.

Chapter 38
June 2011

Dan's sat nav had directed him for miles and miles through country lanes that were off the beaten track. He had stopped a couple of times for food and a drink which added to his travelling time and made him feel he was on a never-ending journey. The scenery was lush and green, lots of trees, then heathland, then more trees. He imagined what his life would have been like if he'd been brought up in this stunning area. Not that there was anything wrong with Derbyshire. He'd made his life and his fortune there; but growing up in this place would have been a totally different experience.

Eventually the velvet female voice informed him that he had reached his destination, after a four-and-a-half-hour journey, he'd arrived at the huge wooden security gates of his brother's presumably modern-day mansion.

He noticed the security cameras, high on the stone pillars that were either side of the gate, turning inward towards his car. He didn't really know what to do next. He was visiting his brother, not Tony Soprano. Was he going to be frisked by security guards before he could enter Jack's very private inner sanctum? The gates slowly started to roll apart. Somebody, somewhere had pressed the button to allow him in.

The driveway was several hundred yards long, twisting and winding, tree-lined and formal. When the house came into view, he was more than surprised at what he saw. The building was single-storey and looked to be triangular in shape. This wasn't bricks and mortar, rather, this was the biggest and most opulent temporary structure Dan had ever seen. The roof was tiled and pitched, there were sizeable bi-folding doors on the front that led out on to the huge decked area. The land around the home was beautifully landscaped with shrubs and flowers and there was a fountain directly in front that was shooting water up into the air from several pipes.

He parked next to a convertible Bentley that had the top down and wondered where the front door was. If this was a holiday let, it would be *the* most luxurious and expensive ever. It all seemed slightly curious that Jack, the self-made millionaire, lived in a much-glorified holiday lodge and not a castle somewhere. Eccentric came to mind, as well as bona fide traveller, with a lot of money.

Jack seemed to appear from nowhere. He was dressed casually in jeans and a plain shirt. The greeting seemed genuine enough as they shook with their right hands and placed their left arms around each other. They were the same height, although Jack was looking very fit and toned while Dan was sporting a typical 'dad bod'. The eleven-year age difference wasn't really that apparent. They both still had a full head of hair, relatively unlined faces, and straight, white teeth. Jack held on to Dan's right hand.

"It's been too long, way too long. Come this way, I'll show you round."

The tour of Jack's main residence left Dan feeling very impressed. It had four bedrooms, a sauna, a gym, a hot tub and swimming pool at the back. The furniture was all very stylish and new, there was beautiful artwork, figurines, fresh flowers, and a really lovely 'new' smell. Almost as if it had never been lived in. Jack explained that he did own 'proper' houses here and there, but this was by far his favourite. He showed Dan to one of the guest rooms.

"Please make yourself at home. Can I get you a drink? Tea, coffee, whisky? Anything, my bar is fully stocked."

"I'll have a beer please. Peroni if you've got any?"

"Yep, I'll go and get you one, we can sit outside if you like?"

It all seemed surreal that Dan was here, in his kid brother's world that was beautiful, although there was something missing. He still didn't know if Jack had anyone in his life, but if he did, there weren't any clues. All the photos around the place were of Jack with various celebrities, Jack with horses or just Jack. He planned to gently quiz his brother.

He walked onto the palatial decked area where Jack was sitting, sipping what looked like iced tea.

"You're not joining me?"

"Not yet, I don't drink during the day, as a rule. I've got somebody coming over later to cook. I'll have a drink then."

"Somebody?"

"I'm a decent cook, but this is a special occasion, so I've hired a chef."

"There's really no need, I didn't come to be entertained Jack."

"I only do it for special friends, and family. We've got a few aunties left and a ton of cousins. They all live in and around Hampshire, mostly in the parks I own."

"Do they know I exist?"

"Dan, there are no secrets within a travelling community. Believe me, I know the story and if Dad thought that moving you and mum to Derbyshire was enough to give family the swerve, they were wrong. Of course, they knew about you."

"So, how come I never met them?"

"I can't really answer that, except, there was a lot of suspicion and wariness around the old communities back then. You know. Mixing up the gene pool. Babies suddenly appearing was not good for them, their reputations."

Dan sighed and put his glass down. "Thing is Jack, I know Dad tried his best, and so did Annie, up to a certain point in my life."

"Till I was born?"

"Till you were born. I never resented the fact that I had a baby brother, believe it. I looked after you. I was eleven years old, and I didn't know that Annie wasn't my birth mother. Why would I have known that? We were just a 'slightly less than' normal family. Travellers that had put some roots down."

"I know Dan, and when Dad took me and Annie back to the New Forest, I didn't understand why. I was too young I guess?"

"I really thought Dad would come back for me, but he didn't. Have you any idea how that felt for a fifteen-year-old boy?"

Jack finished his drink. "Look, let's talk tonight over dinner. We've got a few hours. Do you still ride?" Dan was tired from his journey, but he could sleep later.

"Not for a while, but I'm still up for it."

"Great! I can lend you some gear and we can do an hour. If that's all right with you? I could give you a history lesson on horseback."

Dan wasn't sure how he would be able to walk the next day but riding through the New Forest with his brother seemed like a lovely idea.

"I'd love to Jack."

"Great, I'll go and saddle up. And don't worry if you're rusty, Amber will take care of you. She's as steady as a rock."

Chapter 39
June 2011

The trek out in the fresh air and sunshine reminded Dan just how much he had loved riding and he questioned himself as to why he had ever stopped. It was obvious to him that Jack was an accomplished rider, he made it look so easy while Dan was less confident, mainly due to lack of practice. He made a promise to himself that he would get back in the saddle properly on his return to Anglesey. He had the land, and there was the spectacular Llanddona beach just down the road. He just needed to build a stable. Another project on his list.

The brothers talked about mainly low-level family issues as their horses strolled side by side. Jack pointed in the direction of various historical family sites, he could name all of Patrin and Annie's siblings, where they had all lived, how many were still around. It was obvious to Dan that he deeply cared for his family, and he looked after them, especially Annie's two surviving sisters, who were both in their nineties and lived in a luxury lodge together, carers paid for by Jack, no question of either of them moving into residential care.

Dan couldn't help tentatively probing his brother about his private life. He talked a lot about the family, but it was noticeable that he gave very little away regarding his own situation. He waited until they were heading back before he posed the question.

"So, er, do you share your life with anyone?"

Jack laughed; he had been waiting for the question.

"Depends what you mean by share really? I'm not lonely if that's what you think. Let's just say I value my solitude."

"Interesting..."

"What I mean is, I *do* have a handful of very close friends that I trust. I made a lot of mistakes trying to make money and I met a lot of people that I wouldn't associate with again. Made a mistake in Holyhead, that's for sure! Your neck of the woods? I was young and naive. Thought money could buy anything. Anyway, I believe that a person can only truly trust themselves."

"You still haven't answered Jack, you know, like a politician doesn't answer!"

"OK, I have one special person that I suppose could be described as my partner. I don't live with this person, we only share good times, it works."

"So, this 'person'?"

"Is out of the country at the moment, China. A business trip."

Dan knew when to give up. Jack wasn't going to say who his special person was. At least not yet.

When they arrived back at the stable block, Dan dismounted in a very undignified way.

"My muscles have lost their memory!"

Jack laughed.

"That was not very good! You need to get fit. I'll sort the horses out if you want and you can go and have a lie-down old man!"

He didn't argue as he felt the stiffness in his back and thighs already.

"Dinner will be about seven. Have a wander about if you want to, use the pool, the hot tub, whatever you want. I've got some calls to make when I've done with the horses."

Dan was lying on a super-king-sized bed, just waking from a very comfortable afternoon nap. He could hear a woman's voice and the rattle of kitchen utensils. It must have been the hired chef making a start on dinner. He decided to ring Grace to let her know how the day was going.

"Hi it's me."

"Hi, I know. How's everything going?"

"Really good, honestly. We've been riding, he has a private chef making dinner."

"Private chef?"

"Grace, he could probably buy and sell us several times over. He's a bit guarded and things feel a little weird but..."

"So, what I still don't get is why now?"

"Please, Grace, I lost a son and I've found my brother. That's all. Please, bear with me. I'll be home tomorrow."

"Sorry I just can't help wondering if he's kosher, you know, if he genuinely wants you there."

"He's been nothing but kind and hospitable since I got here Grace. I don't feel like he's putting on a show just for me, he's just, well, obviously very wealthy and very private about some things. How's everything at home?"

"Fine I suppose. I just spoke to Michael. He's thinking about a trip to Canada in the summer. Apparently, he can have an internship at a top law firm in Toronto. And Jen's running away again, Milan this time. Honestly Dan, she's trying to run away from life, again! I'm not that surprised though, are you?"

"No, I can't believe she re-married Nick, I'm as puzzled as you are, as are a lot of other people."

"And I've been thinking about a memorial for Gabriel. Like you suggested, maybe around September we could have a little service and throw red roses off the bridge? Not his ashes though, he's not going in there again. Not ever."

"Whatever you want love, I'm sure it'll be fine."

"It may be tricky getting everyone together though. Whatever you think of Nick, he's still godfather to Michael.

Jen says she'll be there whatever, wherever she's living, she'll make sure she's at the memorial service. I just hope Nick decides the same, despite what's going on."

"Going on?"

"Jen's trying to have the second marriage dissolved, says it was never consummated. Nick's insisting it was, lawyers having another field day…"

"I'm sure they'll both be there. In fact, I think it's essential that they're both at their godson's memorial."

Chapter 40
June 2011

The private chef had a catering assistant who also served the food to Jack and his guest. They were sitting at a round table, not too big, that had been laid with a white linen cloth, highly polished candle sticks, gold plated cutlery and very expensive-looking cut crystal wine glasses. Dan was impressed that his brother's style was classic rather than completely ostentatious. The chef's assistant looked about eighteen, dressed in a black shirt, black skirt and a white apron. Dan wasn't sure how he felt about being waited on by hired hands in a domestic setting, but those feelings faded as he helped himself to the quality wine and soaked up the hospitality. The conversations had remained quite low-level throughout the day. Jack had expressed his sorrow at Gabriel's death while they were out riding but he was careful not to push his brother for any details. He knew the wine would kickstart that particular topic later.

They talked about life in Hayfield, Annie's illness, Frank Shaw's legacy that had in reality given them both a fighting chance in life. Jack claimed he had no recollection of the incident at the stream when Dan had saved him from potentially drowning. What he did recall was his mother's sad descent into bi-polar disorder and her struggle to cope with it. She had frequent manic episodes that affected Jack as a child. Her dedication to protecting him became intertwined with her illness, resulting in him spending a lot of time with his aunties. The aural and visual hallucinations had wreaked havoc, with the same person fixed in her mind tormenting her, frequently leading to hospital admissions. Dan knew the name; he'd heard it many times.

"Lizzy Cooper?"

"How do you know that name?"

"Because she mentioned, or should I say screamed, that name more than once. Do you have an idea who she was referring to?"

Jack put his cutlery down and poured himself and Dan another glass of wine. He shook his head.

"Yes. She died a long time ago."

"So, who was she to Annie?"

"A Romani mystic, fortune teller, call her what you like. Do you really want me to tell you what I know?"

"Yes, I'm fine with it."

"If you're sure, I can give you the gist of it. And what *I* know has been told to me by the surviving Nevi Wesh travelling community. Some of it may be true, some folklore, you take from it what you want to. Apparently, Annie and Patrin were childless and desperate. Dad was quite a religious man at heart. He considered himself Catholic, although I never saw him go to church. He didn't approve of any sort of spiritual meddling, if you understand? Annie wasn't quite such a pure soul and sought out Lizzy Cooper's help without Patrin's knowledge. She knew he wouldn't approve. Anyway, she asked for a child and a child she got, three months later."

"Me?"

"You."

Dan closed his eyes and held his head back.

"And she thought that I was the result of some sort of hocus pocus intervention?"

"She must have done. She was promised a child and a baby arrived. I suppose she thought that was it?"

"Till you were born? That's when she started to get ill. Not long after."

"In Annie's mind, she should have trusted Lizzy Cooper and rejected a child she knew wasn't hers. She truly thought that Lizzy had cursed her for not being patient. For not believing that she would have a child, with Patrin, before the harvest. She didn't say which harvest. Thing is it was probably a severe case of post-natal depression that got to her. Not some damned curse!"

"That explains a lot. More than I've ever understood anyway. She was convinced that I was going to push you in the stream that day. She was wrong."

"Well, none of that matters now because we're both here. And I don't think it's just for a catch-up is it, Dan? You need help with something?"

The third or fourth glass of exquisite red had just gone down nicely, and Dan was ready. It seemed his brother had timed that question very well.

It was still light as they sat on the decked area to the front of the lodge. It was a beautiful warm evening and Jack made sure the wine didn't run out. After a shaky start, fighting back the tears, Dan was able to recount to his brother the events in his life since New Year's Day. Jack listened intently to the tragic story. Gabriel's struggle to accept himself, Gabriel and Jamie, New Year's Eve, the party, the video, Jennifer Williams, their affair, Nick Foster, everything came pouring out. He surprised himself as to just how much sadness had been festering inside, that had now found an outlet. He had been so strong for Grace and now his grief was spilling out. It was therapeutic. It was necessary.

He was still wiping his eyes and blowing his nose when Jack very quietly and softly summarised what he had said.

"Your son took his own life for a reason, and you don't think it was due to any relationship issues with his partner?"

"No."

"You think it may have been something to do with this guy, Nick Foster? Who I think I met once, years ago at a charity concert."

"Really? Which charity?"

"I think it was a charity for the homeless, can't be certain. He couldn't have made that much of an impression, but it *was* his band that I met backstage for a few minutes. Anyway, you had a brief affair with his wife, and they are both godparents to your children. You've hinted to Jennifer Williams that you think her husband may have harmed Gabriel while he was in their care. She's reacted badly and threatened to tell your wife everything if you don't back off? You want to know the truth? Of course, you do."

"More than anything Jack. It's eating away at me. The things I know are off the record so I can't do anything about it."

"Oh, and let's not forget, he has a problem with travellers. According to you he called you a pikey at a party and you laid him out. Nice one."

"To be fair, he said that before he knew anything about my background. Put it this way, since he found out, probably from Jen, he's sneered at me. Something about my preference for 'temporary accommodation'. He's such a twat."

"So, this is where I come in. Well, not me personally, more a representative of the Hearn family. You know I have a security company?"

"Evergreen Protection?"

"Yes, it's not a massive concern really. It just occurred to me one day that people with money, lots of money, need some extra protection. Bodyguards, door staff, chaperones for their rich kids, drivers. All trained in martial arts, all very professional. I've got them too, but I bet you haven't noticed anyone?"

"Only the private chef and her assistant. Don't tell me, they're your bodyguards?"

"No Dan. Discretion is the mantra. I've got protection out there that none of my guests can see. That's how I prefer it. So, somebody needs to have a conversation with Mr Nick Foster about his life choices? I can arrange that. Very discreet, no trace back to you, or me, or my business. Does that sound acceptable?"

"And if he confesses?"

"You'll be informed, and we can take it from there. Whatever you want. I believe you saved my life once Dan, so nothing is off limits, nothing."

The dark side was emerging as the night fell. Jack was making a sinister offer that Dan, in his less than lucid state, liked the sound of.

Chapter 41
June 2011

As he was coming round in the softness and comfort of the huge bed, Dan could smell breakfast cooking. He'd lost count of how many bottles of vintage red wine had been consumed the night before. As he lifted his head, he had a guess. He slowly lay down again and tried to recall exactly what he and Jack had discussed. There were a few blacked-out moments, that's how he knew he'd achieved 'shit faced'. He had a momentary flashback of Jack walking him to the guest room and helping him to get partially undressed, then oblivion.

There was a knock on the bedroom door, then Jack appeared with a large glass of water and some paracetamol.

"Get this down, breakfast in ten? Full Monty?"

Dan would have to sober up if he was making the drive home today. He politely accepted the offer of a large breakfast, hopefully lots of coffee, followed by a cold shower. He stood up to put on the bathrobe that Jack had placed on the bed. He groaned as his legs and lower back complained about the exercise they had endured the day before.

As he emerged from the room, his brother greeted him with enthusiasm. Like he hadn't had a drink in the last twenty-four hours.

"How come I feel like shit and you're cooking bacon like you never touched a drop?"

"Years of practice, I guess. Anyway, just take a seat and I'll bring it over. Are you planning on driving home today?"

"I promised Grace I'd be back today, so, yes, but I'm not looking forward to it."

"You must still be over the limit. I can't let you attempt that journey, so I'll get my driver to take you home."

"What about my car?"

"No worries, I'll have someone drive your car, someone who's sober, how does that sound?"

"It sounds a bit flash."

"Nothing wrong with a bit flash, just enjoy the ride, it's on me."

Dan gave in to the offer, being chauffeur-driven home was starting to appeal as his head continued to throb. Hopefully the breakfast would soak up some of the alcohol.

Later, as Dan was packing his overnight bag, Jack walked in and shut the door behind him. He sat down at the end of the bed.

"Before you go Dan, there's a few rules we need to agree on, after last night's conversation."

"Rules?"

"If we both want guaranteed anonymity while enquiries are being made, *and* after the fact, we don't discuss anything over the phone or put anything in writing electronically. No email or text messages. We talk face to face or, write to me and use the Royal Mail. I can destroy a written letter, but I can't destroy an electronic footprint. Nobody can. Like you said last night, Nick Foster thought he'd deleted some rather nasty and disgusting images, but he hadn't."

"So, what happens next?"

"My team will take over, probably within the next couple of weeks."

"Team?"

"Trust me Dan, they're very professional."

"How will I know where things are up to?"

"You won't."

"I don't know if I like the sound of that Jack, I mean, will they harm him?"

"Not without your consent, that's a promise. Their job is to try to establish just what his interest is regarding teenage boys, and more specifically just who? If that man had any influence over my nephew, even though I never met Gabriel, I swear to you, Foster will be dealt with."

"I don't want him harmed physically Jack, I want him outed and punished."

"Like I said, we need a confession first, and there's plenty of ways of extracting the truth. It's not all about brute force. He's a cokehead you said?"

"That's what his wife said recently."

"He's not got his act together then. Makes him weak and hopefully more pliable. If he's got nothing to hide Dan, we'll establish that too."

"I'm counting on you Jack. I don't want any mess; I want justice for Gabriel."

With all the rules established and agreed, Dan sat back in the chauffeur-driven Bentley while Jack waved him off. Another driver followed in his Range Rover. He couldn't help wondering what sort of sinister world he was getting into. Jack had more going on than he was willing to talk about, but if he was the key to unlocking some answers, so be it.

He wasn't comfortable with the silence for very long as his driver remained politely on mute.

"How long have you worked for my brother, Ryan?"

"About seven years Mr Hearn."

"Please, it's Dan. No formalities. Is he a good boss?"

"He's a great boss."

"Does he pay well?"

"He pays very well. There are some unsociable hours, so I'm compensated I guess."

"You must really like driving." Dan was starting to irritate himself with his own small talk.

"I like driving, I love driving Mr Hearn's cars. He replaces the Bentley every year. It's my dream job really."

They had at least another three hours travelling, and Dan's head was still pounding. He couldn't keep up this low-level chat.

"Jack said his partner's on business in China at the moment."

"I believe so."

"I've never met her, but I can tell he's happy in the relationship. It seems to suit him and his lifestyle. He's not a grumpy old married fart like me!"

"You haven't met *her?*"

"No, sorry I presumed his partner was a 'her'."

Ryan said nothing else, and by the look on his face in the rear-view mirror, he looked like he'd said enough.

Dan closed his eyes and smiled. "It's OK Ryan, I'm not surprised, he didn't have to say it really. I sort of guessed."

That was a blatant lie. He was very surprised. Jack hadn't given anything away. Maybe he was guarded around family about his sexuality? Surely, he would now know, that to Dan it was an absolute irrelevance?

Chapter 42
July 2011

Grace was reaching into her wardrobe for a handbag when she inadvertently put her hands on the container. She purposely hadn't looked at it for months. All that remained of her angel was in that rather lovely brass and ceramic urn, adorned with images of sunflowers. It was comforting in a way that he was near, not in a cold grave, miles away. They had thought about scattering the ashes on Kinder Scout, a favourite hike they did as a family when the boys were young. Even that seemed too far away now. She wasn't ready to let go, but when she was, it had to be the right place. She had started to wonder if Anglesey was the right place too. Dan seemed settled enough, pottering about, going to the Druid's for a pint with Gareth, building a stable for the horse he was going to buy. He was talking about buying the Druid's, it was only a matter of time before it came up for sale and then he'd throw himself into another project. She didn't *really* like the idea of being the owners of a very inward-looking local pub. There would have to be a lot of changes to make it profitable, which some of the locals definitely would not like. She'd watched enough episodes of *The Hotel Inspector* to know Alex Polizzi's response to "Our customers don't like it." It was the usual, "Darling, you don't have any customers!" Exactly, Alex!

Another element to buying the pub was the further cementing of their lives to Anglesey. This beautiful place had been tainted by the very bridge they had to cross from time to time. Her bereavement counsellor had been really amazing, and she felt much better than she had, but crossing that bridge always put a knot in her stomach. Her counsellor had tried to work with her on the bridge issue, after all, it was only an object, it wasn't directly responsible or had any harmful intentions towards Gabriel. A bridge isn't capable of that. Grace knew all this logic and reason, but it still gave her the shivers every time she drove across it. Despite that fact, the memorial service was set for September at St Tysilio's Church. She was determined to continue her counselling so she could make peace with Britannia Bridge on the day of the memorial, by throwing red roses over the side, and into the water that took her son's life.

It was a very hot day; the skies were clear and there was hardly a breeze. Perfect for the many sailing fanatics that lived here and the droves of people on holiday. The buzz of the jet skis in the distance was constant, all day long, like the sound of an angry wasp. She found Dan up to his eyeballs in concrete as he laid the foundations for his stable block. She'd had a conversation with Jen that morning that he needed to know about.

"Couldn't you pay someone to do that? Looks like back-breaking work love."

"Unlike my brother, I like to get my hands dirty, you know that!"

"Unlike your brother, you're not a gazillionaire, but you could afford a labourer surely."

"It's sorted Grace. Jamie's coming over tomorrow. He could do with the cash and I'm getting too old."

"Is he still unemployed?"

"Not anymore. I've told him he's got a month's work here if he wants it, cash in hand."

"And after that?"

"I'm going to sack Gareth and give his job to Jamie."

"Gareth won't like that!"

"Gareth will have to suck it up Grace. He doesn't need the money, does he? He's as tight as a gnat's arsehole, typical Welsh farmer. In any case, he'll have to be nice to me when I own his favourite pub."

"When? It's not for sale Dan."

"The sign went up this morning, I've already put an offer in."

"Why didn't you tell me? Don't I have a say in it?"

"Yes, my love, *you* are the interior designer. Just think, we can get this done, do the refurb and gather everybody there after Gabriel's memorial. I'm going to re-name it the Angel Inn."

"I think you're getting a bit ahead of yourself Dan. How do you know your offer will be accepted?"

"Because, I made them a damned good offer, trust me. By September that place will be full of people who really cared for Gabriel. Jack said he'd come up, it's in his diary."

"Oh, Jack Hearn is gracing us with his presence, is he? Better make sure the locals aren't invited, he'll be marched to the stocks!"

"Please Grace, don't judge. He's been good to me recently and I know you're going to like him."

"So, is he staying with us? Him and all his servants? Do we have enough rooms?"

"He's staying at Chateau Tryfan, him, his driver and hopefully his partner, we'll see."

"Anyway, pub buying and memorials aside, Jen rang me this morning."

"And?" Dan hated to hear her name.

"She's finalising her move, the house sold almost overnight but she's worried about Nick. Her solicitors aren't getting a response and he seems to have gone AWOL."

"Well, according to Michael, Nick and his band will be at York University in September for a charity gig. So wherever he's gone to lick his wounds, that gig is still on. I checked with Michael a few days ago."

"Why? Why check with Michael? Were you thinking of going?" Grace was very quick to question, and Dan knew he'd almost put his foot in it. He had to think on his feet.

"It's a couple of days before the memorial so I thought Michael could remind him on the night. You know what Nick's like, a bit chaotic? Surely you want him to come?"

"Of course I do. We sit Jen in one corner and Nick in the other, but yes, they should both be there."

Dan felt a wave of relief. He wasn't lying to Grace, he had spoken to Michael a few days ago and he was certain the charity concert was still happening in September during freshers' week. They had also talked about Michael's impending trip to Toronto which would take up the whole of August. He was going to come home for a couple of weeks before he departed. He was in a relationship with a girl in York and he was staying with her in the meantime. Grace would be happy to have him around, if just for a few weeks. Dan had also written a note to his brother, in the privacy of his office, to let him know the date, time and place of the charity concert in York, which he posted the same day. He was sticking to the rules.

Grace still hadn't finished what she needed to say.

"Oh, and Jen's coming up in a few weeks. Just for a few days before she moves to Milan."

He smiled his best fake smile.

"Great, Michael *and* Jen. We should have a barbecue or something, if the weather's OK."

"If you're not too busy building stables and refurbishing pubs?"

Chapter 43
July 2011

Jack welcomed his colleague to the conference room. They sat down next to each other at the huge, oval-shaped table. Caroline had ordered fresh coffee and sandwiches for them both. She usually knew what his meetings were about, but not this time. She hadn't been invited in to take minutes and she didn't ask any questions. He was meeting with the head of Evergreen Security, that's all she knew.

It didn't take Jack long to brief Arran, his long-standing service manager and friend. Arran had listened to every word and not taken any notes. That was the usual arrangement when very delicate matters were being discussed. No records, no audit trail. When Jack had finished talking, Arran put down his prawn sandwich and rubbed his hands together. Jack didn't send this type of work to him too often, but he was delighted at the prospect and the challenge of a covert operation. Even more exciting, this was going after a 'nonce', the sort he'd dealt with in prison, many years ago. Even to the most hardened criminals, there was nothing lower than a paedophile.

He memorised the date and time of the charity concert in September, which, according to Dan's letter, was still going ahead. That gave him more than enough time to send people up to York to establish what the security arrangements would be for the performers. This guy's band were still sort of famous, but a university students' union hall would generally be lacking any serious protection for their acts. He already had a couple of people in mind who would blend in, find out what was needed and leave without a trace.

Jack was extra concerned that any face-to-face contact with Mr Foster had to be discreet, and the conversation had to be memorised, not recorded.

"So, Arran, are you confident?"

"Well, he's hardly Mick Jagger! Before we get to him, we'll know exactly what the university has in place and what he has in place for himself, security wise. I personally don't think he'll have any, but we all know each other in this game, we can find out without raising any eyebrows."

"I'm counting on you Arran. This has got to be invisible. No records, phones off."

"You can trust me Jack, it's not like we're going to take him out? It'll be more like a conversation with an incentive to tell the truth, about his preferences?"

"Exactly Arran. I don't want him dead. I've made that very clear. And no mention of Gabriel Hearn!"

"Have I ever let you down boss?"

"No Arran, so don't start."

"So, what if he doesn't give anything up?"

"Arran, if you're saying there will be an 'incentive' to speaking his truth, I'm confident his choice will be truth or head blown off?"

"Yes."

"But there won't be any live ammunition?"

"Absolutely not."

"So, if he holds out, he's probably telling the truth."

"Yes, either that or he'd rather be dead than outed as a nonce."

"But he won't be dead anyway, according to you."

"No, if he insists, we'll leave it there, just like you've asked."

"Great. Then *we* can leave it there. If you need to tell me anything in connection to this, you come to see me, OK? No calls, no email, no text messages."

"Understood boss."

Jack sent Arran on his way. He was happy to be helping his brother, but it wasn't without risks. He had fully briefed his trusted friend, and now he could step back and wait for the outcome, which wouldn't be till September. He checked with Caroline when Gabriel's memorial service was taking place. It was Sunday the eleventh. The charity concert was Friday the ninth. By that time, either Mr Foster would be turning up for the service, shaken not stirred, or he'd be in hiding for sure. And if he was in hiding, he would be found.

226

Chapter 44
Late July 2011

Jen put her feet up on the sun lounger and tried to relax. Everything was sorted. Her flight was booked and most of her huge wardrobe had already been flown to Milan and delivered to her new apartment. Despite the usual high level of organisation, she couldn't just close her eyes and soak up the loveliness of this place. It would probably be the last time she'd see Grace, even though she had promised to be at Gabriel's memorial service in September, she couldn't really guarantee that her work commitments wouldn't take priority. Being around Grace and her family was not easy, but in forty-eight hours she'd be jetting off to a new life and putting everything, the whole damned complicated, difficult situation, behind her. Grace had mentioned something about a barbecue later. She hated barbecue food, all that potentially lethal, undercooked crap. It just wasn't appealing but she'd do the polite thing and nibble on the salad. She'd made a promise to herself that she wasn't going to drink any alcohol during her stay. It had been alcohol that had allowed her to lower her guard in the past, giving in totally to her desires, and she was very lucky that he hadn't told a soul. If he had, she wouldn't be lying on a sun lounger at his home, about to have some sort of farewell party.

Grace appeared and blocked the sun as she stood over Jen.

"You ready for a drink?"

"I don't think I will Gee. Thanks."

Grace was taken aback. "Excuse me? Hello. Where's my friend gone and who are you?"

"I'm just not in the mood. Honestly."

"Well, you'll have to get in the mood quickly. Dan and Michael will be home in an hour or so. We could just have a couple while we've got some peace and quiet?"

Jen's resolve to not touch a drop collapsed. "Oh God, I'm so bloody weak, go on then, gin and tonic, lots of tonic!"

"Alternatively, if you think it's a bit *too* early, why don't we walk down to the pub and you can see how the refurb's going on. Dan's completely obsessed with it, and he's roped Mike in to help. Can you believe it? Mike's only here for a few weeks before he flies off. I've hardly seen either of them this week. You could give me some interior design tips?"

"I don't understand why anyone would close a pub in the holiday season, couldn't he wait?"

"You know Dan, he gets an idea and he runs with it. There's no stopping him."

Jen agreed to Grace's suggestion. Perhaps she should have that drink first, just to take the edge off her nerves. Why did he always make her feel so nervous?

As they walked down the lane, Grace could sense that Jen wasn't quite herself.

"Are you still worried about Nick, is that why you're unusually quiet?"

"I'm not being quiet, am I?"

"Jennifer Williams! I've known you since you were seven years old, and you're *never* this quiet."

"I'm not worried about Nick. Apparently, he's been in rehab, again. That's why my solicitor couldn't find him. It's all a show though. He'll never get clean. He's a dick."

"So where is he now?"

"He's still bunked-up with his bandmate in Notting Hill. He got half the proceeds of the sale, he could afford his own place but... can you believe it Gee, he tried to get more. Claims he's been diagnosed with a heart condition. All brought on by the stress of me divorcing him again! It's just bollocks Gee."

"Surely he wouldn't lie about something that serious?"

"He's not lying, he produced a letter from a cardiologist, all true, but definitely nothing to do with me. Just a lifetime of booze and drugs. The cheek of it!"

"So I suppose he's taking it easy now?"

"Not if I know Nick. He'll be taking the medication and washing it down with vodka. I shouldn't even be telling you due to confidentiality, medical privacy and all that bollocks. I know you won't tell anyone Gee. Not even Dan. It's just so damned frustrating!"

They had reached the pub, that resembled a building site. The door was open, and they could see three or four tradesmen wearing hard hats, covered in dust of all kinds. One of them saw the two women and smiled.

"Mrs Hearn, er Miss, er,"

"Williams, Jennifer Williams."

"Please don't come in here, health and safety and all that. Are you looking for Dan and Mike? They're out the back chopping a tree down, you can walk round."

As they walked around to the back of the pub, Jen caught sight of him. She hated how she still felt, it was ridiculous. And there he was, wiping the sweat from his brow, chainsaw in hand, covered in sawdust. How could she find that erotic? She just had to make sure she wasn't alone with him at any point before she left for Milan. She would stick to Grace like glue, it was the only way.

Chapter 45
Late July 2011

In contrast to their last gathering, the evening was warm, there was hardly a breeze and the guests were enjoying the outdoor hospitality. True to form, Dan had bought an enormous gas-fired grill, big enough to cook a buffalo, and he was firmly in charge of the cooking. Michael was happy to assist, filling plates with an assortment of steaks, chicken and mackerel. No sausages or burgers at this barbecue, this was Argentine quality.

Dan noticed that Michael had grown his hair back to where it was six months ago. He had shaved his head in January as in his mind, every time he looked in the mirror, he saw his brother. He'd even contemplated dyeing it a darker colour but thank goodness he hadn't. If Gabriel had still been alive, anyone at the barbecue who knew the twins would probably not be able to identify (from a few yards away) just which brother was assisting Dan.

Grace sat next to Jen underneath a gazebo that was strewn with fairy lights. She couldn't help noticing Jen's unusual lack of oomph, just like earlier in the day when she denied flatly that there was something troubling her. She seemed to be gazing into space, in the direction of the monster grill. She took Jen's hand.

"Look, I know how hard it is to look over there and *not* see Gabriel. I keep thinking, any minute he'll walk over and say, "Hey Mum, it's me, this has all been one sick joke. Sorry."

Jen flinched. Was it so obvious she was staring in that general direction? God, she'd have to snap out of this stupid, soppy mood. It was making her feel so lonely, despite the number of people around her, some faces she'd seen before, some new. Jamie was milling around looking like a model for Sauvage. She appreciated his amazing body and brooding dark looks, and if she hadn't known for certain he was gay, she would have pursued him that evening. One last hoorah before Milan. That would show him that she still had it in spades. She had another look around at the guests. They were mainly Grace and Dan's neighbours, dull, boring, countryside types talking about sheep and farm equipment. Jen wished she had stayed in London. At least she could have been lonely on the inside and partying on the outside. Here in Anglesey, she felt so vulnerable. She just couldn't understand why anyone would want to *live* here. One thing she had decided was that she would make an excuse and leave in the morning. Another twenty-four hours trapped in her thoughts and feelings that she couldn't express, mixed with a good supply of alcohol was a disaster waiting to happen.

Grace was not going to let go on her quest to establish why Jen was not her usual self.

"Are you sure you're OK Jen? Are you having doubts about Milan?"

"Are you kidding?

"You don't know anyone there. I thought maybe you're a little apprehensive?"

"I can't wait to get there, Grace. New start and all that. Hot Italian men, all like Jamie, but not all gay."

Well, I hope you find what you're looking for, I really do."

Jen tried not to tear up. It wasn't the right time or place to reveal just how bad the last three years had been, or why. If her parents had moved just a few miles up the road, she would never have met Grace or had any involvement with her family.

"I'll get us another drink, same again?"

"No thanks, in fact, I think I'm getting a migraine Gee. I'll have to go and lie down, sorry."

"Of course, Jen, you go. I don't think this will be carrying on too much longer. Dan pretends he's fine, but I can tell he's tired. The pub refurb's taking up so much of his time and energy. You saw him today, thinking he's a lumberjack!"

"A sexy, middle-aged lumberjack Grace, be thankful."

Jen made her way to the allocated guest bedroom. She sneaked via the kitchen and grabbed a bottle of red. There was no migraine, just an overwhelming desire to be alone with her misery.

As she got to the top of the stairs, he was walking towards her. She hadn't even noticed he'd left the grill. He stopped and smiled sheepishly. She hadn't planned this, but she had to say something now the opportunity had arisen.

"Hi."

"Hi."

"Look, can we have a chat? I think there's something I'd like to share with you, we need to talk."

He shrugged his shoulders and sighed.

"I suppose so."

"Then come with me, this won't take long, I promise, I'll be gone in the morning."

"Come with you where?"

She took his hand and led him to her room. He knew in an instant he should have declined, but he was curious enough to follow her. She shut the door gently and turned to face him. His apron was splattered in barbecue debris, fat, sauce, onions, and he didn't smell too good. Not the most romantic situation but she had to say what she had to say.

"So, we need to talk about what happened before I leave for Milan. It's been eating me away for a long time and I'm tired of the secrecy. You know, when somebody doesn't look at you in the same way they used to, it really hurts."

"Jen, you're drunk, and I really don't care about whatever's bothering you. Now I'm going back downstairs, and I suggest you go to bed."

And with that he turned and left the bedroom. Jen's eyes filled with tears. His rejection was painful and humiliating. The truth was he didn't care. He had said it with conviction and there really wasn't anywhere else to go, apart from maybe following him downstairs and making a scene. She poured herself another drink and talked herself out of blowing the lid off their secret. The sooner she was on a flight to Milan the better.

Chapter 46
September 9th 2011

Nick Foster sat in the poky, not very clean, excuse for a dressing room. He really enjoyed the university gigs. There was so much joy in seeing young people responding to the music that had been written a long time before any of them were born. His band mates had all left the campus while he waited for Michael. He was bringing a select handful of friends backstage for a few drinks. It was a far cry from some of the venues he'd played in his career, but at least he would remember these. Doctor's orders had been very specific, no drugs and as little alcohol as he could possibly manage. He hadn't totally accepted a life of sobriety; he was a realist who knew he would always be an addict, therefore he would always need *something*.

He pulled a bottle of vodka out of his travelling holdall and had a stiff one to counteract the rush he still felt after coming off stage. He had already decided that after his present contractual obligations had been met, which left another four university gigs, he was going to retire. His plans were to use the money from the divorce and buy a house far away from London, preferably with some outbuildings. He wanted his own small recording studio so he could carry on his passion for song writing with no interference from record companies or promoters. His bandmates could carry on without him. He knew some bands from the glory days that only had one original member still touring and playing, but he was done with it now. There were a few more gigs to freedom and the country life, keeping chickens, making his own wine, and maybe he would find someone to spend his senior years with. A seasoned groupie maybe? Not a self-obsessed bitch like Jennifer that he'd made the same mistake with twice. She hadn't blocked him from her social media so he could still keep himself updated with her life and work in Milan. He checked her Instagram page just out of habit. There she was, at some fashion show with a man half her age in tow. It no longer bothered him to see her with other men. All he felt was pity for the empty shell of the woman he knew she was.

There was a knock on the door.

"Mr. Foster? There are some kids here saying they've been invited back-stage?"

It was the pathetic security guard the university had provided. He had learned not to expect much by way of protection in these places. Not like Wembley or the Shea Stadium, where they were usually seven feet tall and scary, no, this guy was middle-aged and overweight.

"How many? Should be about four?"

"Yes, four,"

"OK let them in."

Michael appeared with three of his closest university friends who seemed to be a little starstuck. While Michael gave him a hug, the other boys stood and said nothing. *Now* would they believe that the legend, Nick Foster, really was his godfather?

Nick enjoyed chatting with young people. They usually wanted to know how he got started, where he got inspiration for his songs, how many rock stars' numbers were on his contact list? He told them what they wanted to hear. He'd partied with some of the biggest names in rock music over the years, most of it had been crazy and enjoyable but there were darker forces at work in the world of entertainment that he wouldn't share. He knew he'd got off lightly years ago when the press could have eaten him alive, but luckily they would rather have landed a whale than a net full of minnows, and they got their whale, thank God.

He shared out his vodka with his guests and after half an hour, he thanked them then signed some merchandise. Michael hugged him again before he left.

"Thanks Nick, it's been a blast tonight. We've raised a few thousand, so – brilliant!"

"It's my pleasure Mike, always my pleasure."

"I'll see you in a few days anyway. Gabe's memorial?"

"How could I not be there?"

"The pub's finished now. We've really pulled all the stops out to get it ready for Sunday. Mum and Dad want us all gathered there after, private of course. Doors shut, no locals."

"What about Jen, is she still coming?"

"Well, she hasn't confirmed either way according to Mum. I don't know Nick, sorry. Last time I saw her she was a bit, well, a bit weird."

"Can you specify weird?"

"Quiet, not as pissed as usual and…"

"And what exactly?"

"I don't know, I can't say. Look, it doesn't matter right now. If she turns up, she turns up, if she doesn't, she doesn't. Mum was really upset how she left our place last time. She just vanished, must have got up and left before anyone was awake. She didn't leave a note, no explanation, nothing."

"Fucking drama queen. She probably wasn't getting enough attention Mike."

"Dad seemed pretty much relieved, I always got the feeling he was sort of intimidated by her. He doesn't relax when she's around. I can't believe Mum never noticed."

Nick declined the invitation to party with Michael and his friends. He was very tired and in need of the room he'd booked at a hotel in the centre of York, a generous night-cap, then bed. His age and health issues were no longer creeping up on him stealthily, they were here. He put his head out of the door and shouted to the security guard to call him a cab. He heard a reply, but it seemed to be coming from round a corner.

He sat and thought about what Michael had just said. He'd always known she was cheating towards the end of their first marriage, he just couldn't prove it. He wanted to catch her out, turning up unannounced, hoping to find out just what she was up to. It never occurred to him till now that it could have been Dan. The more he thought about it, the more plausible it seemed. He was a big handsome guy, why not Dan? He was only a man after all? Whatever had or hadn't happened, it didn't matter now. Nick had his retirement plans all set out and he going to execute them.

He looked at his phone again, it was well past midnight, but he could hear the noise from the student union hall as their party continued. Where was this taxi? Had Mr. Dopey Bollocks even ordered him one?

Before he stood up, there was another knock on the door.

"Mr. Foster?"

"What, and where's my fucking taxi?"

The door opened and two people walked in wearing black baseball caps, lowered over their eyes.

The taller of the two men spoke.

"Mr. Foster, your carriage awaits, now follow my instructions and don't do anything stupid."

Nick saw the gun and froze.

Chapter 47
September 10th 2011

Nick followed the instructions to the letter. It wasn't the first time he'd seen a firearm in a dressing room, especially during the tours in America, but these people weren't armed for personal protection, they were threatening his life, but he didn't know why.

After handing over his phone, he walked out of the building knowing that one of his captors was a few yards ahead of him, and the one with the gun was a few yards behind him. His legs started to feel weak with fear. He had been instructed not to speak or look around him, just to follow the person in front and get in the vehicle that was waiting round the corner, out of sight. It was a black Mercedes van with a sliding side door.

He sat silently on the back seat, accompanied by the man with the gun, who had now swapped his cap for a black balaclava, IRA style. The other one got in the driving seat, and they set off. He had no idea where he was going. The windows were blacked out and he had no knowledge of the area. All sorts of questions were racing through his mind. Was he being kidnapped? Were they going to ask for a ransom? Were they going to hurt him? He had half a million or so in the bank, but he wasn't worth kidnapping. After twenty minutes they were off the main roads and into the unlit surrounding country lanes. He could barely make out the tall hedges lining the road as they whizzed by. Whoever was driving must have known these winding lanes well, either that or they were crazy.

Eventually the van stopped, and the driver put on the same style head covering and motioned Nick to get out and walk, to what he could make out as a derelict farm building.

His travelling companion made sure that Nick could feel the gun in his back as they approached the entrance.

His kidnappers had torches which they shined on a few hay bales. The smell of the hay gave him an instant flashback to New Year's Eve and the party. He remembered Michael pointing his phone and waving as he scanned the marquee at some of the already tipsy guests, asking him to wave back. He had asked Michael to delete the video from social media that time. He valued the small amount of free time and privacy he had. He also didn't want his second marriage to Jen getting 'out there'. He knew he'd made a mistake and he didn't want any media intrusion. He was wishing that someone was filming *this* scene for social media. He was terrified.

As a torch was shone in his eyes, the gunman spoke.

"Mr. Foster, I'm sorry that we've had to interrupt your evening. It was a great gig, we both watched it."

"What do you want? Please. I don't know who you are but I'm not worth anything to anybody."

"That's where you're wrong. Please don't undervalue yourself. We're not here to talk about money."

"Is it Jen? Has she put you up to this? For whatever reason? She hates me perhaps?"

"I can't comment on who our client is, however, we're here to talk about *your* life."

"My life? It's just turned to shit!"

"Two words. Operation Starling."

Nick sighed. Why did he always have the feeling that this subject would pop up and bite him one day? He knew that there were people out there, some in the industry, some not, who believed there was no smoke without fire. He could always tell when he was being judged, by a certain look that people gave him. He was never going to completely shake off the label and it hurt him deeply.

"I was never charged; you must know that?"

"That really doesn't prove anything does it?"

"What do you want me to say? I made a mistake. Please believe me, I wanted to help these poor kids."

"So, downloading illegal kiddie porn was your way of helping the children?"

"It made me feel sick, I couldn't believe the depravity, it's not human."

"You know what *I* think, Mr. Foster? I think you were lucky to get away with it. Which was great for you, but unfortunate for others."

"What others? I wouldn't harm a child. I know what it's like to be an abused kid. I lived through it, and I survived. I was lucky."

"So what about the little 'incident' when you were a student? A slap on the wrists for soliciting rent boys, you fucking pervert!"

"How do you know about that? Are you some kind of bent copper? Has *she* put you up to this? Bitch!"

"Like I said, our client cannot be named for legal purposes. So, rent boys, Clapham. Explain."

"I was young and stupid, trying to do some good for those boys. Christ, I wish I hadn't bothered. You look at my track record for fundraising. I got paid nothing for tonight, nothing! All proceeds to charity. Ask my accountant, he doesn't like me doing it. He thinks I'm crazy!"

"Great charity work Nick! Gets you close to all those young boys."

Nick felt his stomach rise, and he couldn't keep it in. He vomited all over the floor. Why didn't these people believe him? And who were they anyway?

"Look, mate, I know what it looks like, but that's not me. It's not my thing. If it's names you want, big names who're on *my* suspect list, I'll tell you, no problem. There are fans out there that worship these guys. They wouldn't if they knew the truth. Some of them are protected for sure, but they need to be found out. They're not gods, they're into some bad stuff, really bad."

The gunman seemed to be listening. "This isn't a trade-off; this is a fact-finding exercise about you." He lifted the gun and pointed it at Nick's forehead. "Just come clean about yourself and we'll leave it there, for now."

"You may as well shoot me then, because I have no sexual interest in children, never have."

The gunman lowered the pistol and knelt beside Nick Foster. "You know what? I think you may be telling the truth so we can leave it there. Now, we'll take you back to the outskirts of town and you'll have to make your own way to your hotel. And we know where you're stopping by the way. We'll keep the phone. And believe me Mr. Foster, if there's anything incriminating on it, we'll find it, and we'll revisit you. Do you understand? Oh, and before we part, you can give up those 'big' names. We could have some fun with that."

Chapter 48
September 10th 2011

Nick was still following strict instructions as he walked into his hotel. He had tried to wipe the remnants of vomit off his jacket, and he was feeling badly shaken. The instructions were, don't look around you, just walk in and act normal. *Do not* report this to the police. They knew where Michael lived, and they would be paying him a visit if the police were alerted.

He was exhausted from the events of the last hour, and he focused on getting to his room and pouring himself a large drink. The receptionist recognised him as he signed his check-in details.

"Mr Foster, lovely to see you. We have a bag for you, somebody brought it here about half an hour ago. Said you left it at the concert venue?"

"Did you see who it was?"

"A young man, say twenty? Tall, blond?" It sounded like Michael. "He hung around for a bit, he thought you should have arrived. He said he'd phoned you a few times, but the number was unavailable."

"It's fine, my godson. I just got a little sidetracked on the way here. I lost my phone actually, that may explain it."

Before he made his way to the lift, he ordered room service. A bottle of vodka and a spicy chicken pizza. Neither were on his doctor's diet sheet, but what the fuck? As soon as he got to his room, he switched the ceiling light on and closed the blackout curtains. His hands trembled as he opened the mini bar. He couldn't wait for room service, he needed a drink right now. His heart was still racing, and he needed to calm down. His phone was gone, for good, and he was told to stay in his room till at least 8 a.m. the following day.

He sat on the bed and switched the TV on to distract himself from his thoughts. Trying to process what had just happened to him wasn't easy. They were dangerous people, and he was paranoid that they were still watching him. They obviously wanted some dirt on him but why? And who was their client? They must have been bent or ex-coppers to know what they knew about him. They could keep his phone; they wouldn't find anything apart from the threads of several unpleasant conversations he'd had with Jen. There was nothing incriminating at all. He had nothing to hide.

There was a knock on the door that made him jump slightly.

"Room service!"

Nick was nervous as he peeped through the spy hole in the door. It was a young woman with a tray. He felt a wave of relief. There was enough vodka to see him through the night, he hadn't figured out what he would do in the morning, but he started to feel safer once he'd locked the door.

The spicy pizza was amazing. He hadn't realised just how hungry he was, since the contents of his stomach had been ejected just a few hours ago. He went through the events again and again in his mind. Two men, a Mercedes van, a gun to his head. Why? Were they some kind of vigilantes? Modern day witch-finders? If they were, they had the wrong man. He knew the pain and mental scars that remained from his early life. It was the reason he wrote music and songs; it was his perfect escape from the nightmare that had been his childhood. What if Jen *was* behind it for some reason? She had tried to have their second marriage annulled but it didn't happen. They had consummated their marriage several times on their wedding night in Las Vegas. She just couldn't remember.

At 3 a.m. the phone next to his bed rang. He had just started to drift into sleep, the TV was still on, and he was lying on the top covers. He felt very groggy and disorientated. Should he answer? What if it was them? He decided not to. He muttered to himself.

"For fuck's sake, leave me alone. You got your answer. Now go find out about them big names..."

As he stood up to take his clothes off, the phone stopped. He rang reception immediately.

"Please, *do not* put any more calls through to my room. Just take a message. Understood?"

"Yes Mr Foster, sorry to disturb you."

"It's three in the morning for God's sake."

He slammed the receiver down feeling more than irritated. He started to experience the effects of the spicy pizza, mixed with vodka. It was a bout of indigestion that seemed to be increasing with intensity. He looked in the mini bar for cold bottled water and drank it down with enthusiasm. This was hurting, he was sweating and he started to feel weak. For a moment he wondered if it *was* indigestion? He sat on the edge of the bed and contemplated phoning reception for help. Was he having a heart attack, alone, drunk, and scared? Before he could pick up the receiver, he fell back on the bed and as his sight faded, he curled into the foetal position, breathing shallowly for just a few minutes before his heart stopped.

The following morning the receptionist called his room to relay a message from Michael Hearn. He had rung at three in the morning, he was concerned that Mr Foster wasn't answering his mobile. After two or three attempts, and given it was half an hour past check-out time, a porter was sent up to the room to check on Mr Foster. He knocked on the door then listened. The TV was on but there was no answer. He let himself in with the hotel's universal key. He could see a figure curled up on the bed, in the reflection of the dressing table mirror. Was he asleep? He took a step closer and waited a few seconds. This man wasn't breathing. He was dead, very dead.

Chapter 49
September 10th 2011

The young porter had been working at the hotel for three months, and this was his first death. He remembered his training and the procedure he had to follow in such an event. He double checked that the guest wasn't breathing, and he was careful not to disturb anything in the room. A sudden death meant the police would have to be called as there could be no guarantees that this was a death from natural causes. He tried to stay focused as he walked down the corridor and into the lift. Protocol stated that staff should remain calm and not alert any of the other guests to the situation. The matter of a guest dying in one of their rooms had to be treated as discreetly as possible. It just wasn't good for business. He found the manager in his office, just behind the reception desk. He looked up to see the young, pale, shaken-looking porter.

"Everything OK Dave?"

"Er, no, er, the man in room 621, er, he's dead."

"Are you sure?"

"As sure as I can be. I mean, he's not breathing."

"Did you touch anything?"

"No, I even left the TV on, no."

"OK, thanks Dave. Do any of the other guests know?"

"Nope."

"Perfect. Find out from reception who we have on the sixth floor, apart from our 'stiff'. And I'll call the police."

Dave found that request really flippant and disrespectful, but he couldn't say anything, he valued his job too much.

"The man, it's the singer, you know, Nick Foster."

"Nick who?"

"You know, the old guy, still touring with his band."

The manager put his head in his hands.

"Shit, that's all I need on a Saturday morning. This place will be full of people trying to check in in a few hours. Shit. A celebrity stiff in one of our rooms is *not good*. Anyway, here's what I need you to do. The police will ask anyway so if we're prepared it won't take up too much of our time. Find out who was on reception duty last night and get their number. Tell reception not to allocate any rooms on the sixth floor for the time being. We're not too busy at the moment so it should be do-able. Oh, and close the sixth floor to anyone who isn't staff or police."

Three hours later, one of the responding police officers was sitting in the manager's office.

"I'm sorry but we're still waiting for the police pathologist. He's a bit jet-lagged apparently, just flew in from South America yesterday. He should be here in the next half-hour."

"Nice. While *I'm* trying to keep a hotel running on a Saturday in York, with a corpse in one of my rooms. Not just any old corpse though, apparently he's quite famous?"

"Yes, I suppose he is. A bit last century, but yeah."

"I hope his identity isn't made public. That's not good for my hotel. People can be very funny about things you know."

"We're not going to release any details at all. Not officially, but we can't stop some things just getting out there. People talk, it's human nature. If you can see an upside, think about the cranks, the fans, strange people who'll want to book the room that Nick Foster died in?"

"I get what you're saying, but they are in the minority. Most people don't want to know if someone's died in a particular room and what they don't know won't bother them. He's not the first guest to gasp his last in my hotel, and I'm sure he won't be the last. God forbid though if he's been murdered!"

"I can tell you this much, it's not looking that way. There are no injuries, just a body on a bed, a near empty bottle of vodka, no sign of any drugs, apart from some heart medication in a toilet bag. Oh, and a half-eaten pizza of some sort."

"That's on our room service menu. You can check when he ordered that on the system."

"Already done. We'll piece things together. Like I said, this isn't looking at all suspicious. The guy probably had a heart attack. We just need the pathologist to sign things off, then we can let the ambulance people remove the body."

"We have a service lift and a back door for anything like that."

"Don't worry, they're professionals, they'll be as discreet as they can."

"Good, then I can re-claim the room, and open up the sixth floor?"

"Hopefully sometime this evening."

"Great."

"There are just two things that are puzzling us at the moment, which may or may not be significant. We can't find his phone. Is there any chance he's stored it somewhere else in the hotel? I know it sounds weird but there's no mobile in his room, it's been checked thoroughly."

"All our rooms have safes; we don't provide anything more than that for our guests."

"It's just that everybody has a mobile these days, and he'll be no exception, I'm sure. Do you have his number on your records?"

"Absolutely, I'll check our system now. Yes, there it is, room 621, Mr. Nick Foster." He wrote it down and handed it over to the officer.

"Great, thanks, I'll ring it, see what happens."

He pressed the number on his keypad and listened.

"Sorry, the number you are calling is unavailable."

"Nothing. It's either out of charge or switched off. I suppose we could check phone company records, see when his phone died, but if he's natural causes it won't really be an issue. He might have lost it, simple as that."

"These things happen. Can you imagine the contacts on *his* list?"

"I certainly can. He'd just done a gig at the university. Maybe one of his band mates picked it up by mistake? Maybe a student helped themselves? Elton John could be getting crank calls as we speak!"

"You said there were two things?"

"Again, it may be something and nothing, but his clothes reek of sick, but there's no evidence in the room that he's thrown up anywhere."

"I'd check every drawer, you wouldn't believe where some guests deposit their stomach contents! Do you have his next of kin?"

"That's the thing. We don't know who that is, but we're working on it."

Chapter 50
September 10th 2011

Grace was feeling tired and tense simultaneously. The weariness brought on by Dan's relentless resolve to finish the pub refurb was running alongside her feelings around *why* he was so determined. As she ate her breakfast alone, she tried to imagine what the next day would bring. She knew *who* it would bring, that's if all the invited guests turned up, but how was she was going to cope on the day was to her an unknown. The last few months had been so frantic as she had unwittingly been drawn into a project management role she hadn't ask for. Dan meant well, he wanted her to be fully occupied with trades and deadlines, budget control, staff recruitment, all the stressors that accompanied a project like this, but tomorrow could not be halted. It was almost as if she were anticipating Gabriel's funeral all over again.

Dan had left the house hours ago with Jamie to oversee the final bits and pieces of decorating at the newly named Angel Inn. Jamie had stayed with them for the last week, which had been lovely. He was practically Dan's right-hand man now and was set to become the pub manager. The accommodation upstairs had been completely modernised into a two-bedroom apartment, which Jamie would be moving into. His steady employment with Dan had enabled him to pay child support for Bronwen and she would be staying with him for one weekend per month. Grace looked forward to being a part of Bronwen's life, not in a big way, more in the way of supporting Jamie when Bronwen was spending the weekend with her dad. He had worked hard to pull his life together while still dealing with grief and Grace had grown very fond of him.

She looked in her notebook at the guest list. Not all the names were ticked off as confirmed. Jen was still indicating 'definitely maybe', even at this late stage. Grace was still a little pissed at Jen's sudden departure from her last visit. There hadn't been a plausible explanation as to why she had sloped off without a word, after what seemed like a bit of a weird evening. She had tried to blame it on being stressed about her move to Milan, but Grace wasn't buying it. Jen was impulsive and adventurous, not usually anxious about turning her life inside-out. She thought about calling Jen one more time to confirm either way, but she put her phone down. Jen knew all the details, day, times, places. It was up to her now, so if it was going to be a no-show, she would be seriously reconsidering their life-long friendship.

Grace had talked Jack out of staying in the hotel. Although she still hadn't met him in person, she had spoken to him and insisted that he and his guest should stay with her and Dan. They had the room after all, and Dan had been so well looked after when he visited Jack earlier in the year. She wouldn't have to cook anything other than breakfast on the morning of the memorial. All the guests would be fed at the pub later in the day, and they were taking Jack and his guest out to dinner this evening. Dan's even wealthier brother sounded perfectly lovely, so why was she feeling apprehensive about meeting him? Was it him or his mysterious guest that was making her feel uneasy? He still hadn't confirmed if it was his partner or a friend, or even a business associate. For now, it was just Jack plus one. So cloak and dagger.

Then there was Nick to consider. He *had* confirmed. Not even the prospect of being face to face with Jen again was going to stop him. He had asked if he could stay with them, rather than having to travel down to London from York on

Saturday, then London to Anglesey on Sunday. Grace had politely declined. Jack was arriving today, and she didn't want Nick to be in the house at the same time. Not the first time Dan had his brother round to stay, things were tense enough. Then she had an idea. Nick could stay at the pub. There were two bedrooms, both decorated and furnished, so why not? Jamie wouldn't mind, surely? It was only nine a.m. so there was a chance that she could contact Nick before he set off for London. She tried his phone a couple of times, but he wasn't picking up. She phoned Michael without considering how early it was. He answered, sounding extremely groggy.

"Hi Mum, do you realise what time it is?"

"Sorry Mike. I forgot you were at the gig last night. How did it go? You obviously had a late one?"

"It was great, really Mum. I'm a bit whacked to be honest. Yes, it was a late one."

"With Nick?"

"I saw him after the gig, took a few friends backstage, then we went back to the bar."

"Did he go with you?"

"No, he went to his hotel. Then I got collared by a steward, said Nick had left a bag in the dressing room. I called him a few times but no answer, so I took the bag there myself."

"Did you see him at the hotel?"

"No. The receptionist said he hadn't arrived, which was a bit odd by most peoples' standards but we're talking about Nick aren't we?"

"I want to offer him a room at the pub tonight, and tomorrow night if he needs it. Save him a journey to London. Thing is I can't get through to him."

"Well, I wouldn't worry too much Mum, he's probably still in bed, like me."

"OK, well, when you surface properly, perhaps you could try to contact him again, for me? I'm on pins here waiting for your uncle Jack plus one. Whoever that is! If Nick ends up back in London, so be it. I can't afford to stress about him today, not really."

"Whatever Mum, I'll be with you around five. I can't wait to meet Uncle Jack. We still going out for dinner?"

"Yes."

"Awesome, see you later! And don't worry about Nick, he's a big boy, he can take care of himself."

Chapter 51
September 10th 2011

Dan answered his phone without letting go of the paint brush. It was Grace and she was probably anxious about something. It was barely past 9 a.m. and they still had a lot of finishing touches before the pub could be declared ready for opening. He had committed his time till around 2 p.m. when he planned to go home and change in time for his brother's arrival. This was a big deal in more ways than one. He wanted Jack in his life, and that was definitely what was happening, however, things were already complicated. He wouldn't be able to relax properly till Nick Foster turned up. The code of silence that Jack had insisted on had been kept, which was good for any potential audit trail for sure, but Dan couldn't help feeling anxious about the things he didn't know.

He answered her call.

"Hi, look, I'm up to my eyeballs in paint here! Are you OK?"

"I think so Dan. I just wondered if the apartment was ready?"

"Why? You're thinking of leaving me?!"

"Ha, ha, now there's an idea."

"So, the apartment has everything except a functioning kitchen at the moment."

"Could somebody use it, without a kitchen?"

"Well, when I say kitchen, I mean oven and hob. Last minute hitch. Suppliers sent the wrong one."

"I just thought Nick could use it tonight? Save him a trip to London and back?"

Dan felt a flicker of fear at the mention of his name.

"Nick? Have you spoken to him, I mean recently?"

"No but I've tried, several times. So has Mike but he's not answering, either that or his phone's switched off. Not just that, it's been off for a while."

"How do you know?"

"Because Mike saw him last night at the gig and he's tried to contact Nick, like me, several times since, but he's not getting through.

He felt a small amount of relief that Nick and Mike had been together not even twenty-four hours ago. That was reassuring. Jack had made a promise that Nick wouldn't come to any physical harm, whatever the outcome of the 'fact finding' exercise. He would only know when and where this had been carried out when he could talk to his brother face to face, and that was going to be very soon.

"Yes, I suppose Nick could stay here. Jamie's not moving in for another few weeks so, yes, I don't see why not. Why are you so worried about him anyway? You know how he is?"

"I know how he is, but the thing is Dan, him and Jen, and the divorce, the whole thing, it's been pretty messy again. I just want to keep them as far apart as possible. That's if Jen turns up at all."

Dan was praying that she wouldn't. He didn't want her around anymore.

"I don't know why you're so bothered about other peoples' stress Grace. Haven't we had enough of our own this year? I'm pretty tired of the whole Nick and Jen circus. Tomorrow is about being thankful for having Gabriel in our lives for nineteen years. I don't care if neither of them turns up. I really fucking don't!"

"All right Dan! I hear you! And I agree totally. We don't need their crap! It's just…."

"What Grace? It's just what?"

"Well, I shouldn't be telling you this, Jen asked me not to say anything, but, Nick's not a well man."

"What do you mean? Since when? And why would we be so surprised anyway? He's never been health-conscious has he?"

"No, that's why he has a heart condition. Jen told me. She thought he was making it up for some sort of financial gain, but she's seen the consultant's letter. He's under doctor's orders for sure."

Dan closed his eyes. Holy fuck. Nick had better turn up some time soon.

Chapter 52
September 10th 2011

Jack arrived at his brother's house alone. He had thought about bringing his partner, but this was not the right occasion. There would be plenty of time in the future to introduce him to the family, happier times hopefully. He had driven himself up to Anglesey which had made a nice change. Arriving in a chauffeur-driven Bentley seemed a little too ostentatious and beside that fact, it gave Luke a long overdue weekend off.

He pulled the iron cord at the door, and he could hear the bells ringing in the hallway. Dan appeared almost instantly. He opened the door and looked over Jack's shoulder.

"Please, Luke can come inside, I insist."

"Luke's having a weekend off Dan, I drove myself here. Believe it or not?"

The gave each other a hug.

"Welcome to our home Jack, please, treat it like your own."

"It's a lovely place Dan, I'm almost jealous."

"We love it, despite, well, you know, despite everything that's happened."

Grace appeared, looking and feeling slightly apprehensive. She had seen photos of Jack on Dan's phone. He looked like a younger, slimmer version of her husband and seeing him standing in front of her she realised that he was so much like Dan, darker skin and eyes, even thicker hair and extremely handsome. He had an energy field around him that Grace could sense immediately. It felt quite menacing and powerful. As he gently shook her hand she felt a tingle inside, just like the feeling she had when she first saw Dan at her cashier's till, all those years ago.

"Lovely to meet you Grace, my brother married well."

"Thanks, I think I got a pretty good deal too. You're here alone?"

"Oh, yes, I thought it was best, given the occasion."

"That's fine, whatever you're comfortable with, please make yourself at home. Can I get you a drink?"

Jack looked at his watch. "Is it too early for a gin and tonic?"

"Absolutely not, you must have been on the road a while, time to relax now."

Jack sat on the massive L-shaped couch that faced an inglenook fireplace he could have stood up in. Grace brought him his drink in a huge gin glass with ice and lemon, and he was more than ready for it. She excused herself quite quickly, she had to get ready for their evening out.

Dan had played things very coolly in front of his very innocent and trusting wife, however, he was more than ready too, and not just for a drink. As soon as Grace disappeared upstairs, he fixed himself a large whisky and sat down next to his brother.

"She's a lovely woman Dan, I can tell. You'd be a fool to lose her."

"You don't think I know that? God, I wish I could turn back the clocks."

"Well, I'm not going to tell, you can trust me."

"I hope so Jack, because I don't know if I can trust Jen. She was acting really weird the last time she was here. I'm starting to feel a bit trapped by her. You know? Like the veil of secrecy is getting thinner and all it's going to take is her getting drunk and emotional, then it could all come out. It's terrifying."

"So why do you keep inviting her back into your life? She sounds a bit unhinged?"

"You're not kidding! She approached me the night before she left, tried to say she was sorry, at the same time she was trying to put her arms around my neck. It was embarrassing. Whatever she wanted to say, I didn't let her finish. I've lived with the guilt for a long time, and I'm not prepared to let *her* pile any more on me. I swear she's jealous of Grace, her life, her family, everything Jen hasn't got. She could really do some serious damage if she wanted to."

"You could make yourself a promise though. That if she turns up tomorrow, you politely get on with things, send her back to Milan and never see her again."

"I wish."

"So, what's the alternative? You have a jealous ex-lover, your wife's best friend, hanging threats over you? For ever?"

"I don't see a way out, Jack."

"Oh, there's always a way out, Dan. Speaking of which, our friend, Mr Foster. He's been interviewed."

"I'm glad you mentioned it. I've got to admit, it's been playing on my mind. So, did he confess anything?"

"No, he didn't. Interesting though, he gave up some big names, you know, people in the business that he knows are involved in some pretty disgusting stuff."

"So, he wasn't giving up anything himself?"

"No, and believe it Dan, he was subjected to some pretty strong persuasion. And before you ask, no, he wasn't harmed. He shit himself, apparently, well, not literally, he threw up."

Dan was relieved. God knows what he'd be thinking if Nick *had* confessed to anything. He'd have bought a gun himself.

"So, when he gets to the service, we all act normal, like nothing's happened. I presume he *is* coming?"

"That's the thing Jack, nobody can contact him, not since last night. Mike was with him till he went back to his hotel, after that, nothing."

Jack's face changed. It was a look that Dan hadn't seen before. Almost like a mask had been removed.

"They took his phone Dan. That's why. Call it insurance."

"Last night?"

"Yes, last night."

"Shit."

"Dan, don't worry. They didn't harm him. I made a promise that wouldn't happen."

"I get what you're saying Jack, I'm grateful for your help, it's amazing, but I found out today, Nick's under some consultant, heart problems. You said he threw up. That's a lot of fear Jack."

Jack cleared his throat and drained his drink. "If he's healthy enough to do a charity gig?"

"I agree, but he's a dick head. Off the scale. Probably doesn't care about his health."

"Not wise at his age, don't you think?"

"So where's his phone?"

"It's switched off. It'll stay switched off till it's in a place where there are no masts, no signals. It's called a bunker. Then we can see just what's been going on in his life. May even have to re-visit him, you never know."

"Hopefully you'll meet him soon. You could give me *your* personal take on him."

"Believe it Dan, I would love to meet him and his crazy ex."

At that moment Michael appeared. Dan stood up to greet his son.

"Mike, you're here! Can I introduce you to Jack Hearn, your uncle?"

Michael was beaming as he shook hands with Jack.

"Wow! Dad's brother! Very cool."

"It's a pleasure, way overdue, but still a pleasure."

"So much I want to ask you, honestly. I'll go get changed and we can catch up tonight?"

"Absolutely."

Mike ran upstairs and met Grace coming down.

"Mike, so glad you're here. Have you met Jack? He's downstairs."

"Yep, and he's a younger, slimmer version of Dad! Bit better looking too!"

"I don't agree! Any news? About Nick?"

"Nothing Mum. I'm clueless. But don't worry, he'll turn up, you know how he likes to keep us all guessing."

Chapter 53
September 10th 2011

Dinner was to be one of Dan's 'no expense spared' events. The Michelin Star restaurant in Porthaethwy was usually fully booked for months in advance so he had pulled a few strings to acquire a table for five at relatively short notice. Jamie was a last-minute guest at Grace's insistence, given the hard work he had endured to enable the pub to open on time. He arrived slightly later than the other four, suited and booted for the occasion. Grace had only seen him in work clothes for the last few months, so when he approached the table looking so smart, a real head-turner, she smiled. Gabriel had found love with this man, and it was obvious to all just why that had happened.

Jamie was nervous for more than one reason. He'd never set foot in a restaurant of this calibre, he loved the Hearn family, but seeing Michael was difficult due to him basically being a clone of Gabriel and he wasn't great at meeting new people. The new person being Jack Hearn, a multi-millionaire, and from what Michael had told him on the phone earlier, a little bit intimidating.

Jack watched him walk over to their table. It didn't register immediately who this beautiful young man was, not till Grace called to him.

"Jamie, so glad you made it, please sit down."

Jack stood up and offered a handshake before Jamie sat in his chair.

"Jamie, I'm Jack Hearn, Dan's brother. Very pleased to meet you, I've heard a lot about you."

Jamie felt himself blushing. Thank God he had a beard, hopefully nobody would notice. Jack Hearn was dressed in a Versace shirt, his watch had diamonds on the face and whatever aftershave he used, it was powerful and magnetic. He noticed a resemblance to Gabriel, something about his nose, his smile. His skin and hair were darker, but he was hot, very hot. Jack then made an announcement.

"Please everybody, order whatever you want, drink whatever you want, this is on me."

Dan was quick to respond. "Sorry Jack, you're our guest, I can't allow that."

"I just want to thank you all for allowing me back into your family, it's an absolute privilege and I am truly grateful."

Dan shook his head. "Jack, please, let me do this, you can pay next time."

"Fine, I promise you though, I won't be holding back!"

"Thank you. Tonight, we are privately celebrating the life of Gabriel Hearn, tomorrow we do it publicly." He raised his glass. "To Gabriel, our angel."

Everyone followed suit with tears in their eyes, including Jack. There was so much love around this table he could feel it. He almost felt jealous of his brother who was surrounded with loving, caring people. He almost wished he'd brought his partner to share this heart-warming experience. Then again, there was Jamie Fellowes sitting opposite, and he was finding it hard not to stare at this amazing-looking young man. He loved his softly-spoken Welsh accent, his seemingly shy demeanour, and dazzling smile. God, if he was twenty years younger! When it came to ordering, Jamie seemed a little out of his depth, he obviously hadn't eaten in *this* place before. Then Jack's fantasy mind started to whir as he imagined taking Jamie to all the best restaurants, dressing him in designer clothes and travelling the world with him. He was in a committed relationship, and although he didn't live with his partner of fifteen years, he couldn't recall looking at anyone else, not like this, and certainly not anyone as young as Jamie. Now and again throughout the meal he caught Jamie looking at him, then quickly looking away. It was obvious that Jamie's 'gaydar' was working well. Jack hadn't told Dan he was gay, he didn't want to, this wasn't the right time. The visit was about honouring his nephew, not getting 'pheromonal' with a lovely piece of eye-candy. There may be time for that in the future though.

After a few hours of great food and polite conversations, Dan insisted on taking everyone to the Admiralty Arms in Beaumaris. It was only nine-thirty and he wanted to introduce his brother to some of the locals. To his surprise, Grace and Michael declined. Grace wanted to be in one piece for the memorial and Mike wanted to add a few more photos to the slide show he'd made for Gabe's funeral. He was going to run it again at the Angel Inn for the guests. Grace had objected at first, but she backed down. It had felt too soon at his funeral, but she was OK with it now.

Jack felt a little uneasy as they walked into the pub. He kept his jacket on as he was suddenly conscious of his very expensive shirt and watch. He was also aware that some of these 'locals' may suss out who he was. The battle for Holyhead may still have been in the memories of some of these people and he knew his name was mud. Dan had dismissed his worries completely, even though he knew Gareth had put two and two together, but Gareth didn't drink in this pub, too many ex-pats for his liking.

Dan was at the bar while Jamie and Jack took their seats. Jack could hardly believe how nervous he felt. He had never been promiscuous, he loved his partner, although lately life was becoming a little predictable. He *never* drank in pubs, and when he did go out back home, he always had security lurking somewhere in the vicinity. He realised that he was feeling vulnerable, and he didn't like it. He was Jack Hearn, nothing and nobody ever made *him* feel vulnerable – till now.

He tried to put on his very best heterosexual front for Jamie.

"So, Jamie, you work for Dan now?"

"Yes, he's been fantastic since, you know, since we lost Gabe. I didn't function for a while, couldn't even get out of bed. Dan's a top bloke, he's helped me with everything."

"He certainly is. I know it's been really hard for him and Grace, trying to figure out why. I never met Gabe, but I can't help feeling curious, as if he were *my* son."

"Do you have any kids Jack?" His heterosexual front wasn't working. Jamie could tell.

"No kids, just two horses. I never wanted children."

"Me neither, well what I mean is, it was never in my plans, but I've got a little daughter, Bronwen. She's amazing. Lives with her mum in Aberystwyth. I was living a lie, but I wouldn't change anything I suppose. It's not right to wish your kids away."

"Of course, and nobody should ever have to live a lie."

Just as Jack said that, Jamie gave him a knowing look. Then Dan arrived with three pints.

"Cheers gentlemen, good beer and good company. None of my usual friends are in here. Never mind, you'll meet some of them tomorrow."

"Thanks Dan, so I get lynched tomorrow instead!"

"Nah, nothing will go wrong tomorrow, unless a recently divorced couple both turn up then it's anyone's guess?"

Jack raised his pint. "Well, here's to a fitting memorial, and the hope that only *one* of them turns up."

Chapter 54
September 11th 2011

Grace sat at her dressing table and sighed. It was a beautiful sunny day with no clouds in sight and the heat of what had been an amazing summer was now a warm remnant in the autumn air. She'd been up since 6.30 after a night of fitful sleep, dreams about Gabriel, some of them not pleasant, and she was already feeling tired. Breakfast had gone down well, given she hadn't cooked for that many people in a long time, full Welsh, which was full English made with locally-sourced Welsh produce. Jack had complimented her cooking, very politely, and followed up with an invitation for her and Dan to spend a weekend with him at his lodge. Grace had accepted the offer, however, she had some nagging doubts about Jack Hearn. He was charming, a little too charming, polite, intelligent, he had a good sense of humour, and despite his obvious huge wealth, he seemed quite grounded. Grace just couldn't pinpoint exactly why she felt he was putting on a show, and that somewhere beneath the surface was a very different animal. Dan seemed to be a little on edge around his brother, which wasn't like him at all. She had questioned him when he got in and had tentatively pointed out that he seemed a little apprehensive around Jack, and he had outright denied it. Maybe Dan was just feeling like she was about Gabriel's memorial? Everything was organised to perfection, the church service, his friends, including Jamie, who had prepared their heartfelt tributes, red roses to be thrown off the Britannia Bridge, catering at the Angel Inn, free bar for their guests, everything. In a similar fashion to Gabriel's funeral, this was supposed to be a celebration, so why was she feeling so low? Probably because it was too soon. Maybe in a year's time she'd still feel like this, so today was as good a time as any.

The service was due to start at 3 p.m. so there was plenty of time to prepare herself. The roses were being delivered to the church, one for every guest, which included the professional people who had been involved in their New Year nightmare. Ian Roberts, now retired, Joanna Draper, Dewi Jones the off-duty paramedic who had found their son at Ynys Llanddwyn. One thing she had learned about the indigenous people of Anglesey was that they were, in the main, warm and respectful people who may not seem so at first, not till they trust you, but once you're in, you're one of their own. These three people had kept in touch with Grace and Dan, the odd phone call, text messages, periodically checking in to ask how things were going. They didn't have to, the case was closed as far as the police and the coroner were concerned, but they had all been touched by this awful tragedy. She would make a point of thanking them today for their attendance and their continuing support.

Dan and Michael were already at the pub, getting everything ready for later. Michael had made some additions to his slide show, which he wanted projecting on a wall and Dan wanted to make sure the wide screen TVs were working – all the Sky channels, all singing and dancing. The locals wouldn't recognise the old place but, hopefully they'd like it, eventually. The locals, apart from some of their neighbours, wouldn't be stepping through the door till Monday lunchtime. Jamie would have to be in a fit state for the opening day and he'd already promised them he wouldn't be touching a drop today. He would probably be on his own in that respect. Who could turn down free alcohol? Certainly not Nick and Jen. That was quite a worry, given their recent second acrimonious divorce. The only chance of peace was if they both stayed away, or just one turned up. Jen still hadn't cancelled, and Nick was proving unreachable.

Just as those disturbing thoughts were fleeting through her mind, her mobile started to ring. It was Jen. "OK, this is it, what's your excuse Jen?" was the next thought.

"Gee! I'm so sorry I haven't been communicating properly. I'm so busy I can't tell you."

"Hi Jen, don't tell me, Milan Fashion Week? Must be coming up soon?"

"Two weeks to go, everything's gone bonkers. Total mayhem."

"It's fine Jen, I understand how it must be. You don't have to explain."

"Explain what? I've just picked up my hire car. Should be with you in a couple of hours, tops."

"Oh, Jen, really? I didn't think you were coming."

"I thought about it Gee, but I couldn't be *that* selfish. Just keep Nick as far away from me as possible."

"I will if he turns up. Nobody can contact him, not since Friday night."

"God he's such a prick. Anyway, see you soon."

Chapter 55
September 11th 2011

The small church of St Tysilio's was full. So full that people were standing up due to the small number of pews. To the left-hand side, the Hearn family and representatives of the Farley family took up the only three pews. Grace, Dan and Michael at the front, Jack and a couple of Grace's cousins behind them, and on the third pew sat Jen, Grace's ageing godmother and Jamie.

Grace had struggled with Dan's choice of church for this memorial service, given it was on a small island in the Menai Strait. There was a clear view of the Britannia Bridge on the approach which made her slightly uncomfortable. Just knowing that her son's body had been swept along the same body of water, and out into the Irish Sea didn't bring her any comfort. Despite her unease, they were opening a pub and their future was Anglesey. She would make her peace eventually. She looked over her shoulder at the people gathering behind. Almost the same crowd as the funeral, still, Nick was absent. As the Reverend Williams cleared his throat to start the service, Michael's phone started to buzz in his pocket. Grace poked him in the side with her elbow, this was not the time to be taking calls. He whispered to her. "It might be Nick, I'll have a look."

He looked at his phone and shook his head. He whispered to Grace again. "It's Ned from uni."

Grace was slightly irritated. "Just switch the damned thing off Mike, please."

He followed his mother's instructions. He couldn't upset her, not today.

The service went very smoothly as family and friends paid tribute to Gabriel with funny anecdotes and heartfelt words of sadness at his passing. Everyone attending was given a red rose on arrival for the next stage of the memorial. After the service they made their way to the bridge and, following a final prayer from Reverend Williams, they all cast their roses over the side into the twinkling and seemingly calm waters below. It was very moving occasion that brought tears to most of the eyes there. Dan had his arms around his wife and his son, while Jen looked on. God, he wished she'd stayed in Milan. When the ceremony had finished, Dan made his announcement.

"Please could everybody make their way to the Angel Inn, Llanddona. There's a free bar, just for the next couple of hours, and we've laid on some food as well. Feel free to critique the establishment, especially the cask ales, you're our guinea pigs!"

Dan was excited at the prospect of his pub being full, even if his guests weren't paying. He'd tried to keep the place true to itself, a rural seaside local that now had tasteful décor, really great beer and a varied menu, using as much local produce as possible. There was also a surprise for Grace that he'd managed to keep quiet. The sign hanging outside the pub was a copy of an original drawing of an angel in flight, taken from one of Gabe's sketch books. It was beautiful and radiant, just like Gabe had been. Grace was going to love it, hopefully.

When she saw the sign, she cried again. This time it was happy tears, for the talent her son had displayed as a fine art student, and way before that.

"It's so beautiful Dan, how the hell did you keep *that* from me?"

"You've got Jamie to thank, he sorted everything. I think we should have it as the official logo, you know for menus and napkins and things?"

"Hey! We haven't made a profit yet! Slow down!"

"You watch, I've got a great feeling about this pub. Look. Gareth's already propping the bar up!"

Sure enough, as they walked in, they saw Gareth had adopted his usual position at the bar. Most of the seats were taken in the front half of the pub where the bar was situated, and more were standing in the back half where the bi-folding doors were open to the beer garden.

Dan looked around the room for Jen, who had been more than happy to accept a lift from Jack to the pub. Of course she had, her eyes practically lit up when she was introduced to him outside the church. It was promising to be an entertaining afternoon. Jen looked as stunning as ever, so what?

Jack was head to toe in Armani, smelling great, a younger, slimmer and better-looking version of Dan, obviously extremely wealthy, just Jen's type. He already knew she would be commanding his attention. He spotted them sitting together in a corner. Jen was animated and laughing while Jack looked past her towards Jamie, busily pouring drinks behind the bar. Conditions were perfect for Jen to make an absolute fool of herself with his gay brother. He was almost looking forward to it.

Dan found himself sitting at the bar with Gareth, while Grace kept her elderly godmother company in the back room. Gareth was very approving of the refurbishment, and even happier with the quality of the beer.

"I won't lie to you Dan, this place is cracking. Good pint too. It's still officially my favourite pub. Cheers!"

"Glad you like it Gareth, here's to many more pints at the Angel Inn! Cheers!"

"See your designer friend's found a comfy spot, right next to your brother. She's ordering wine by the bucket. Gonna cost you a small fortune this, Dan."

"It's fine Gareth, just sit back and watch the entertainment unfold. Thing is though, she's staying in *my* house tonight and I know what she's like when she's hammered. It's OK though, Jack'll handle her."

"I wouldn't mind 'handling' her Dan. Do you think he'll go for the bait?"

"No Gareth, I don't think my brother could ever be baited by a woman."

Gareth's eyes widened. "Really? You've got a very colourful family Dan, no doubt about that. So, if he's, you know, a gay, where's his other half?"

"No idea. Jack's a very private man. He hasn't even told me he's gay."

"So how do you know?"

"Just something his driver let slip."

"His driver?"

"Yes, his driver. Never mind Gareth, with your grumpy Welsh farmer life. He's seriously wealthy."

"And in serious trouble. Look."

They looked over to see Jen putting her arm around Jack as they sat against the bench-seating. He took her arm off his shoulder and excused himself. He approached Dan and motioned for him to go to the beer garden. "Can I have a word? Outside preferably?"

They walked to the end of the beer garden together.

"She's a bit full-on Dan? I can't believe you went there. Not now I've met her. I mean she's an attractive woman, she's stunning I suppose, but come on?"

"Thanks Jack, I know what you're saying. Honestly, I'm still terrified she'll say something to Grace, you know, if she gets pissed and angry?"

"So, you made a mistake? I'm not happy you've got this hanging over you Dan. You and Grace are an amazing couple and I'm not going to let an out of control, jealous bitch spoil anything. Especially not today. So, here's the plan. I'll keep her entertained, I'll make sure she's drinking a lot, then I'll escort her back to yours. Call me a decoy."

Dan looked his brother in the eyes. "I *know* you are Jack, it's OK. And thanks."

"That's the least I can do for my brother. There's more chance of me sleeping with one of Gareth's sheep than her."

"I *know,* Jack, I *know.* You don't have to tell me."

Chapter 56
September 11th 2011

Jack smiled as he made his way back to the pub. He was used to female attention, mostly unwanted, and Jen was no exception. He could have some sport with this. As he walked through the bi-folding doors he saw Michael and Grace, watching the slide show, pictures of the twins, family holidays, happier times. He still couldn't quite believe just *how* identical the boys were. Wild blonde curls, beautiful smiles, enjoying life under the guardianship of their amazing parents. He stopped when he spotted Jen at the bar, ordering her second bottle. He wanted to see the whole show, so he asked Michael.

"Is it OK if I join you?"

"Sure, sit down, you trying to escape from Jen? Jeez, she's on her way already."

"She's not there yet, but she's trying. It's a pity her ex didn't show, has anyone heard from him?"

Michael suddenly remembered his phone had been switched off for a couple of hours.

"Shit! He might have tried to call me, I've tried his number dozens of times. Maybe he's ill or something?"

Jack watched as Michael's phone screen came back to life, followed by several 'pings'. It was a fairly large screen and Jack could see the messages, at least five, all from someone called Ned. Michael scrolled through the messages speedily.

"My mate Ned, he rang just as the service started, Mum ordered me to switch my phone off!"

Grace defended herself promptly. "I should think so Mike, talk about rotten timing!"

"He's asking if I'm near a TV? Then he says, switch on the 24-hour news, you won't believe it!"

"Do you have to? Right now Mike? It's probably a joke." Grace wasn't in the mood for Ned's student mentality.

"We've got the TVs all up and running Mum, please, just for a few minutes?"

"If you absolutely must Mike, go upstairs to the apartment, I'm not turning on TVs down here, it'll spoil the atmosphere."

Jack had to agree. "Your Mum's right Mike, you should go upstairs. In fact, I'd like to see the apartment too, if that's OK?"

"Yes, come up. Just make sure Jen doesn't follow us!"

"Why do you say that?"

"Oh, just, never mind. There's a separate entrance round the back. She won't see where we've gone."

Jack followed his nephew up the stairs to the apartment. Jen was still sitting where he left her, talking to one of Gabriel's fellow art students. If they were quick, she wouldn't have time to notice his absence.

The apartment was bright and tastefully fitted out. Jamie would be living here soon, and he wasn't going to be disappointed. The huge TV was mounted on the wall and Michael took a few minutes to figure out the remote control and where to find the 24-hour news channels. They sat on the couch and waited. It was the tenth anniversary of nine eleven, Sky News was showing the same horrific scenes from a decade ago. As with most of these channels, the current news was on a loop at the bottom of the screen. There was nothing significant at all that stood out. Michael was bemused.

"God, Ned's such an arsehole. What is he on about? He knows what I'm doing today!"

"You could try another channel? BBC maybe?"

Michael flicked over to the BBC 24-hour news channel. Again, all nine eleven, sad stuff, but nothing that Mike would take a personal interest in. Then it came. Across the bottom of the screen.

"North Yorkshire police have confirmed that the singer, songwriter and performer, Nick Foster, has died aged sixty-one. He was found in a York hotel room on Saturday. The police are satisfied that there are no suspicious circumstances and are treating his death as natural causes."

Michael stared in disbelief. Jack didn't flinch at all. He was silently relieved that Nick Foster's sudden death was a natural one. His team had done their job, without the knowledge that he had a heart condition. None of this could be traced to him, his associates, or his brother.

Michael was obviously in shock. "But I was with him, he went back to his hotel, then he died?"

"Sorry, Mike, these things happen. I never met him but I'm sure he was a terrific godfather."

Michael was crying. "He was the best, honestly, not like *her*, fucking weirdo."

Jack stayed with Michael till he composed himself. "Thing is Mike, we've got to get back to the other guests, especially Jen, she doesn't know, for now, but she's going to know any time soon. And then what?"

"I wish it was *her*, that's all. I mean, talk about predatory. You've seen her today, the way she behaves. You know, the last time she was at ours, before she went to Milan, she, she..."

"She what?"

"She was drunk, as usual, and she asked me to go to her room. I was confused but I didn't know what she wanted. She said we needed to talk about something that had happened. I thought she meant Gabe. She said it had been eating away at her. She was tired of the secrecy. Then something about when someone doesn't look at you in the same way they used to, and how upsetting that was for her."

"That's very odd behaviour Mike."

"Tell me about it. I just told her she was drunk and that I didn't care about her troubles basically. I suggested she went to bed and walked out."

"Did you tell anyone?"

"Nope. I thought about telling Mum but she's been through enough this year without me telling her about her very best friend coaxing me into her bedroom, apparently about to confess something?"

Jack shook his head. Had Jen been attempting to tell Mike about her affair with his father?"

Then they both heard a scream downstairs.

"News travels fast, come on Mike, we need to go."

Chapter 57
September 11th 2011

Jen had just received the call from Nick's manager. She was feeling woozy, Dan's impossibly handsome brother had found her resistible, and *he* had once again taken his stance of sheer aloofness. All her sadness broke free with one loud scream. Nick was dead. It could only be reported in the news after his next of kin had been informed, his younger brother. At least somebody had had the courtesy to call her personally, hopefully before it made national news.

The whole room fell silent as Jen continued to weep. Gareth ran to find Dan who was still outside in the beer garden.

"Your designer friend, she's having a meltdown, you'd better come!"

This was just what Dan had been dreading. As he approached, he could see that Jack and Michael were standing in front of Jen, while Grace was trying to comfort her friend.

Jack nodded his head at Dan. "Upstairs, the TV's on, you need to go and watch. In fact, I'll come with you."

The two men sat together watching the breaking news roll across the screen. Dan felt sheer panic rising up in him.

"They weren't supposed to kill him Jack, you promised!"

"They didn't kill him, not directly anyway. He was already in a bad way. And why is *she* so upset? I thought she couldn't stand him?"

"She can't, it's all for attention. We need to get her away from the pub. She's way too emotional, can you help me Jack? Please?"

"I'll offer to take her back to yours. Try to calm her down. Give her a few more drinks. Hopefully, she'll keel over eventually. And there's something I'd like to talk to her about."

"Like what?"

"Just something Michael said while we were up here. Very odd. Leave it with me. You go back and join your wife and son, they need you."

"Nothing would surprise me now Jack, nothing."

Jack Hearn placed Jen's coat around her shoulders as he escorted her out of the Angel Inn. She was stumbling on her tall, thin heels and sobbing. He hadn't had much to drink so he walked her to his car and helped her into the passenger seat. His suggestion to her had worked instantly. She was more than happy to leave the pub and go back to the farmhouse with him. Of course she was.

When they got back, he walked her to the sitting room with the huge couch and offered her another drink. She slumped in a corner and kicked her shoes off.

"Any red in Dan's wine cellar?"

"I'll have a look; I'd be very surprised if he hadn't got *any.*"

"Thanks Jack, you didn't have to leave the family gathering just for me, I really appreciate it."

She had no idea just how very necessary it had been to separate her from the other guests. He returned with two full wine glasses. One contained red wine, one contained blackcurrant cordial, she wouldn't notice what he was drinking. He had slept with women, one or two in his life. Enough to know that they were not for him.

Jen stretched her long slim legs out onto the couch and leaned her head back on a large cushion. Jack knew what she was doing, he found it amusing but he managed to keep his face straight and serious.

"You must have loved him once?"

"I suppose I did, in a way, but it never felt *completely* right. It's still a shock though. Poor Nick, alone in a hotel room. *Nobody* deserves that."

"And today of all days? I'm not sure how much longer the guests will hang around at the pub now. It's a shame really, Dan and Grace put a lot of planning into today's events."

Jen was already halfway down the large glass of red. "Believe me Jack, Dan couldn't stand Nick. And Grace? I'm not sure, but she was never keen. They'll soon get over it."

"What about Michael?" Jen froze temporarily.

"What about Michael?" she echoed.

"He seems to be really fond of his godfather. It's hit him pretty hard from what I could see."

"Poor Michael, poor, poor Michael."

"You don't sound very sympathetic?"

"And *you* don't know Michael."

"True, I only met him yesterday but from what I can surmise he's a great guy."

Jen held her glass up. "To the great guy, Michael, and his wonderful father, Danior."

Jack decided it was time for a fill up. He had to time this properly and she was probably one drink away from emotional truth-talk.

As he handed her the refilled glass, he made sure he looked her in the eye.

"I know about it, Jen. He told me."

"*He* told you about *it*?"

"These things happen Jen. I'm sworn to secrecy though. This can't get out."

"I may be a bit pissed Jack, but I'm not as stupid as you think. I've made a few mistakes, so what?"

"So, you call an affair with your best friend's husband a 'mistake'?"

"Of course! Especially when he dumps you because he never loved you anyway?"

"Trust me Jen, I'm not judging, we all make mistakes. As long as we *learn* from them."

"But will I ever learn? Hearn men, handsome, magnetic, seductive. I'm a complete sucker."

Jack's phone rang, it was Dan.

"Excuse me, I need to take this call. I'll get you another bottle. May as well?"

"You go for it, Jack."

Chapter 58
September 11th 2011

Jack walked out of the farmhouse towards the holiday lodge. He had to be out of earshot from Jen, who was getting there, but not quite. Dan sounded anxious.

"What's going on Jack? I'm worried. What you said earlier, about Michael. What's it about? Because he won't tell me."

"Don't push him Dan, Miss Williams is starting to become a little more pliable. Trust me, she's about to spill something. I told her I know about your affair. She doesn't seem to care that I know."

"I suppose she's got *you* in her sights, that's why. Some sort of revenge shag?"

Jack laughed out loud. "Well, that's not going to happen, I can assure you. How's Grace coping?"

"She's a bit shocked but not altogether surprised. It's just the timing is lousy. Half the guests have gone, I reckon I can keep them here for about another hour, tops."

"Fine, I'll be done here soon. Then I'll come back to the pub."

"Done? What do you mean, 'done'?"

"She'll fall asleep soon. Trust me."

Jack sauntered coolly back into the sitting room. He had another bottle of red in hand and when Jen saw him, she squealed like a child and held her glass out to him. He refilled her glass and sat down on the couch, next to her feet. He started to massage them, which did absolutely nothing for him, while Jen started to whisper gently.

"Jack Hearn, are you trying to seduce me?"

"I don't think I'll have to try too hard, anyway it's not my style."

"And you're free and available? Please say you are."

"I'm in a long-term relationship but, I suppose I can be a bit of an opportunist, you know, when the chance comes along."

"Perfect, you Hearn men, either too married or too young, usually."

"Too young?"

"Oops, now I'm saying too much, but I swear I've not done *anything* illegal."

"Sounds interesting."

"Oh Jack, I regret it so much. First, I have Dan casting me aside as soon as I expressed any feelings for him. He just turned so cold, so quickly. It ended my marriage – it's just Nick didn't know it. He was totally bloody oblivious. I was in bits, then I noticed Dan wasn't the only Hearn male to take an interest in me."

"Michael?"

"Michael. Gorgeous, tall, blond, muscular Michael."

"You've slept with Michael?"

"Not exactly, I wouldn't call it sleep darling."

Jack felt repulsed inside, but he kept going. "When did this happen Jen?"

"It was three years ago. No, I shouldn't be telling you this. I've never told a soul. It's crushed me inside."

"Jen, it's OK, I need to know who I'm being compared to. Like you said, you've not broken any laws."

"Ha, not UK law anyway. I saw him gazing at me, I was naked, he shouldn't have been there, it was a private pool party, but he was there, spying. I was drunk, upset, rejected and I did something very bad, very, very bad."

"You seduced a sixteen-year-old boy?"

"That's pushing it a bit. But I suppose part of me wanted revenge on Dan. I was a complete fucking mess Jack, and I'll regret it for the rest of my life."

"And have you talked to Michael about it since? How do you know he hasn't told Dan and Grace?"

"How do I know? Because I wouldn't be sitting here right now. Michael just acts as if nothing happened, and I just go along with it. Although I did try, a few months ago, before I left for Milan. It was pointless though, he's still in denial. Just walked away. It was embarrassing."

Jack tried to sound sympathetic, however, this just wasn't adding up. Was she a complete fantasist?

"Sounds like you've had a rough ride, Jen. So where did all this happen?"

"It happened at our place, er, mine and Nick's. We were virtually over. He wasn't even home that night."

"OK Jen, what if I tell Dan and Grace what you just told me?"

"Then the whole rotten truth will come out, Jack. I've got all the proof I need on my phone about the affair with Dan. I'll go back to Milan and Dan will have to suffer the consequences of just what happens when a marriage breaks down."

"I'll tell you what Jen. Why don't you go to your room, and I'll bring us up another bottle? I'm not in the business of fucking marriages up, especially my brother's. You've tried the rest, now you try the best." He cringed as he was saying it. Cheesy wasn't his style at all, along with women in general. He watched her slowly climb the stairs and called to her.

"You get comfortable, and I'll be up in five. Just need to make sure we're not going to be disturbed."

Five minutes later he crept up the stairs and quietly opened the door to her room. She was semi-naked on the bed, dress discarded on the floor, and completely unconscious.

Chapter 59
September 11th 2011

Jack drove as fast as he could back to the Angel Inn. Thankfully it wasn't far, and he didn't meet any cars travelling towards him on the impossible, narrow and winding lanes. He had Jen's phone that she'd carelessly left on the bedroom floor. At least she wouldn't be woken up by the potentially hundreds of people offering their condolences. He felt a slight twinge of guilt about the sudden demise of Nick Foster, but that came and went very quickly. The guy could have collapsed at any time with his health problems. He just thanked God that it didn't happen in a barn, in the middle of nowhere in North Yorkshire. Now Jack had to have an important discussion with his nephew, then an even more important one with his brother.

As he entered the pub, he could see that half the guests had already left. Dan was sitting with Grace, who had an ashen, shocked look on her face, and Michael was nowhere in sight. Jack grabbed a beer and joined them. Grace seemed puzzled that Jen had left so quickly. She was as shocked as anyone at the news, but even more shocked at Jen's reaction.

"I just can't believe he's dead, Jack. I'm not going to pretend I liked him much. The whole godparent thing wasn't very well thought out, do you agree Dan?"

"We just asked Jen, and he more or less presumed the role was his *too*. We didn't even ask him."

Jack shook his head. "Where's Michael?"

"He's upstairs, he's very upset. Losing Gabe has been *so* hard for him and now he's lost Nick."

Jack stood up. "I'll go and check on him, are you two OK?" Grace nodded and smiled.

"We've had tragedy in spades Jack, this doesn't compare really. How did you leave things with Jen?"

"Don't worry about Jen, she's already sparked out."

"Did she try and seduce you, Jack?"

"I'd rather not say. She's a bit of a mess. Let's leave it there."

He made his way around the back of the pub and up the stairs to the apartment. He found Michael lying on the couch watching a YouTube video of him and Gabriel on their travels in Australia. The tears were rolling down his cheeks.

"You miss him?"

"More than I realised. Sometimes it just hits me, it's really, really, cruel."

Jack studied the screen. "I just can't tell you apart, he's your double."

"I know, we had some fun with that, when we were younger. Not even Mum could tell us apart sometimes. The doctors put one embryo into Mum, and it split into two. Monozygotic twins. How cool is that?"

"Did you ever swap around? You know, school, dates?"

"*Did we*? Gabe seemed to get all the girls in high school, you know, he was shy and quiet, not like me. I think he knew from about the age of fourteen he wasn't interested in girls, so that's where *I* stepped in. God, we had some ridiculous times, hilarious though."

Jack suddenly felt quite emotional. He remembered feeling the same as Gabriel, back in a time when he couldn't let his parents, or anyone in his family, know about his sexuality. He had dated girls just for appearance's sake, he even got engaged once. Much to the delight of Patrin and Annie, their son was a black blood and he was set to marry a girl with similar credentials, some distant cousin. They had been very disappointed when he called off the wedding and never explained why.

Michael sat up and wiped his eyes on his sleeve. He switched off the video that was obviously torturing him.

"Mike, I just had a very strange conversation with Jen. She's asleep now, hopefully for the rest of the night, but..."

"Really? Jen? Pissed? Talking shit? Nothing new about that." He was still feeling highly emotional.

"Mike, listen to me. I've met countless 'Jennifers' in my life. Beautiful, smart, talented, crazy women. Like Gabe, I'm not interested, but quite often *they* don't realise it. Too wrapped up in their own egos. Needy little vampires that want constant affirmation of their looks, their bodies. Very rarely does anyone say 'no' to them. Don't get me wrong, I've met plenty of men like that too, it's not just a woman thing, it's a personality thing."

"So, what's Jen saying now?"

"She made it clear to me, just half an hour ago, that you and she have slept together."

Michael shook his head. "She's nuts. Why would she say something so crazy and potentially destructive? Have you told anyone else?"

"No, I think it's best we keep this away from your parents Mike, they've been through enough. She mentioned a pool party. You were spying?"

Michael nodded in acknowledgement. "OK, some truth there I suppose. I was there, sixteen, spying on her and her friends. They were all bollock naked, and I saw her get out of the pool."

"What happened next?"

"Some fat bald guy saw us, started shouting. Gabe ran off upstairs. Left me to take one for the team."

"Gabriel? He was there too?"

"He went back to his room, left me to it."

"And then?"

"I apologised, then went and found Gabe. He had a bottle of vodka in his room, so we drank most of it."

"Did you stay with him?"

"No, I went back to my room, I was sixteen and pissed on vodka, I must have passed out."

"So, Jen didn't attempt to enter your room? Would you have remembered anyway?"

"I wasn't that bad; I think I'd remember something like *that*. She was a bit weird with me after that night, just odd really. And ever since. Why's she lying Jack?"

"I can't say. Maybe she's just a complete fantasist."

"Or, maybe, oh God, I just had a flashback. Oh God, no."

"Take your time, what is it?"

"I, I, woke up in *Gabriel's* bed. It was *him* that came to my room. Some kind of throwback behaviour from when we were kids. He *hated* us being separated at night. Especially if he didn't feel well. He would get in bed next to me, fall asleep, then I'd get up and go to his empty bed."

"Is that what happened, are you sure?"

"Yes."

"So Gabriel spent the night in *your* bed?"

"Yes."

"Now things are starting to add up. Do you understand what I'm saying?"

"Yes."

Michael picked up his phone. He scrolled through his pictures and videos till he found what he was looking for.

"Look, I recorded this on New Year's Eve, posted it on Instagram."

Jack watched the five-second video, the one Dan had talked so much about. There was Mike, waving and panning around the room, and there, quite clearly was Nick Foster *and* Jennifer Williams. Jack felt nauseous.

"She *thought* she was with you that night Mike, but she wasn't."

Chapter 60
September 11th 2011

Jack asked Michael to stay put and say nothing. He ran downstairs and found Dan, sitting at the bar with his friend Gareth. He tried to look and stay calm. Things were certainly adding up now. Dan's case theory had been way off the mark. Jen thought she'd had sex with Michael, but she hadn't. Gareth shook Jack's hand.

"I don't care what they say, I quite like you."

"Well, I've come back to Anglesey and I'm still in one piece. Luckily, we live and learn." He then asked Dan if he could pop upstairs for a 'chat'.

In front of Michael, he recounted his conversation with Jen. Dan closed his eyes as he listened. He didn't want to witness his only son pacing up and down the apartment, becoming very angry. He couldn't confront Jen. She had threatened him recently with outing their affair. He couldn't tell Grace, it would kill her, and he had no words to console Michael. Only Jack knew the extent of this torturous situation and he had to prevent Michael taking any action. Jen had nothing to lose now her deepest, darkest secret was no longer a secret, so, she would be at her most dangerous.

Michael started to get vocal. "That bitch got in bed with *my* twin brother, thinking he was me? Believing that I somehow 'wanted' her, at sixteen years old? She should be arrested. Dad, why aren't you saying anything?"

Dan was rooted to the spot. He was speechless.

"And, I mean, Gabriel, he was gay, I mean, is that even possible Jack? Do you know if that's possible?"

Jack nodded. "I suppose that would depend on a few things, you know. I had sex with a girl when I was sixteen. It's a tough time, especially if you're not completely sure.

Maybe he was trying to prove something to himself? Either he was or wasn't gay? Maybe he decided he definitely wasn't after, you know..."

"After he'd been molested by his own godmother? It's disgusting. But it explains *everything*. He was so quiet after that."

Dan decided to speak. "I think he nearly told Jamie, but he stopped short, and Jamie never pushed it. He went as far as saying he'd had an experience with an older person, a predator, those were his words."

"And you presumed it was Nick? And now he's dead too? While *she's* comatose in *our* home? I need to speak to her!"

Jack held up his hand. "Michael, please, sit down. Let's think this through calmly. Now, if you confront Jen, she's going to deny it. She'll say it *was* you, it *was* consensual, and it was a drunken one-off. Nobody can prove otherwise. Not now. That's what she believes, and she'll stick to it. Meanwhile your lovely mum will have to live through another unbelievable nightmare, and she's had enough. What I suggest is you stay here tonight, with Jamie, and I promise you she'll be on the first flight back to Milan tomorrow. In fact, I'll drive her to the airport myself. Grace doesn't need to know anything, but I promise you this much, you'll never see her again. Not if you don't want to."

"How does that work, she's Mum's best friend?"

"You'll just have to trust me and your dad. Yes Dan?"

"Yes, Mike, believe me, we'll be putting some distance between us and Jen. I can't bear to look at her again. What she did to Gabe, well, he couldn't deal with it. When he saw she was at our party, he was high and distraught, and he did what he did."

"So, it's *my* fault really? I posted that video. Oh God, I posted that video. He saw *her* and couldn't face up to it. Oh God… I killed my brother!"

Michael was sobbing uncontrollably when Grace walked in.

"No, Michael, you didn't kill your brother. What's going on here?"

Jack was quick to intervene. "He's very emotional Grace, you know, it's been a hard day for him, for all of us. I think he means he should have been there for Gabriel. He had no idea about Jamie, or the situation. Is that right Mike?"

"I suppose so."

Dan escorted Grace out of the room. "Don't worry, he's upset about Nick too. Jack's been brilliant today, he really does care about us all. You have no idea how much."

Chapter 61
One year later

Jennifer Williams opened the doors onto her sun terrace. It was the most beautiful autumn day in Lombardy. The scent of the bougainvillea that was hanging in abundance from the balcony was rising up in the warmth of the morning. The ever-present Lombardy poplars were swaying in the distance and the crickets were in full chorus.

This was the calm before the storm, as it had been last year. Fashion week was nearly upon her, and everything that went with it. Long days, interviews, temperamental models, catwalk terrors, photographers, critics. It was full-on and crazy, but she loved it. She had a few more days to relax with Marco in their beautiful villa. All she had to do today was glance at her itinerary and remind herself of what was coming. They virtually had the day to themselves, which was rare.

Marco was still asleep, wrapped in luxurious Egyptian cotton sheets. She looked at him as he lay peacefully on the huge bed. He was young, very young, but she'd never been happier. Her Italian was coming along nicely with his help, and she loved to show him off on every occasion. At twenty-five he was a man; nobody could argue with that fact. She smiled as she recalled the day they met, just a few weeks after her return to Milan the previous year. He seemed to appear from nowhere, randomly in a restaurant, he wasn't really Italian, even though he could pass himself off as a native. Marco was born in England to Italian parents and had moved to Milan to work for a wine merchant the same week they met. He made her feel young and sexy again, even though she was approaching fifty.

She thought about calling Grace, momentarily. They'd hardly spoken since last year. She hadn't appreciated being frog-marched to the airport by Jack Hearn. She could hardly remember the day of Gabriel's memorial. It had been so traumatic and sad to find out Nick was dead, and her over-reaction was to drink herself into a stupor. Telling Jack about her night spent with Michael had been a huge mistake. He made sure she left the country, without saying goodbye to any of the Hearn family. He insisted on driving her to the airport while she protested about her hire car. He said he'd take care of it. She realised on the way that Jack Hearn was not all he seemed to be on the face of it. She remembered feeling vulnerable and intimidated by him. He insisted she sat on the back seat, and he didn't say a word to her once the journey was underway. When they got to the airport, he handed over her luggage and whispered to her, "Goodbye Jennifer, now, stay away from my family. Do you understand? There'll be no more invites to parties, weddings, funerals, christenings, nothing. And that includes Nick's funeral. Get it?"

She had tried to tell him he couldn't stop her but his only reply, with cold, dead eyes had been, "Don't put me to the test Jen, you won't like it."

So here she was, finally enjoying her life with Marco in this fantastic place. She hadn't attempted to attend Nick's funeral. His brothers hated her anyway and she didn't want to upset Jack Hearn. She believed he could be dangerous.

A walk into the village to pick up some bread and olives seemed like a good idea. Getting back into bed with Marco was tempting, but she felt they'd spent every second together since they met, and he looked so peaceful lying there. The walk would do her good anyway.

He watched her from the balcony, walking towards the village down a tree-lined avenue. Today was the day, the first anniversary of Nick Foster's death, and he had no time to waste. Pretending to be asleep for an extra hour hadn't been easy but finally she'd left the villa. He rummaged in his wardrobe for the burner phone he'd been sent and switched it on. The number he had to call wasn't stored on the phone, he had memorised it. Life had been a blast with Jen. She was a bit unhinged; she drank too much, and they argued a lot. He'd enjoyed playing the part of Marco, the wine merchant. Jen was so caught up with herself she hadn't really questioned where or how he actually did his job. His real name was Steve Pugh from Hammersmith, a hired hand, an actor who happened to speak more than basic Italian. He called the number and gave the code. That's all he had to do.

Jen was walking back to the villa, swinging her basket and humming to herself. She really was happy, for the first time in a long time. She didn't pay any attention to the van parked twenty yards from her home. It was a typical farm vehicle for transporting sheep, and she could smell the contents as she approached. A very unpleasant smell, coupled with the noise of unhappy, uncomfortable sheep. She saw the ancient man in the driving seat and smiled. He smiled back, weather-beaten and toothless. God, she loved this rustic place. She didn't even sense the man approaching her from behind. He stealthily put a black cloth bag over her head and punched her so hard, she blacked out. When she woke up, she knew she was lying on the floor of a very smelly van, and she wasn't alone. The sheep were treading on her and their excrement was all around her. As she tried to call out, she realised that the sheep were making more noise than her and the van's engine was louder than the sheep. It seemed to be travelling for hours. When it stopped, the back door opened and the sheep were ushered out. She begged for somebody to help her, but nobody spoke. She lay on the floor; her feet were bound and after another few hours she sensed it was getting dark outside.

Eventually somebody opened the back door again. She was pulled along the floor then the same person untied her feet. She didn't have the energy to shout for help. With the cloth bag still over her head, she was taken to a building, and told to sit on a chair, in Italian. Then she felt the blast of cold water. She was being jet washed, presumably to rid her of all the sheep shit.

Whoever was doing this eventually took the cloth off her head, but she couldn't tell who it was. He was wearing a mask, the sort of mask worn by a medieval doctor, with a long, protruding beak-like nose. She was shivering as she tried to ask him a question.

"Who are you? Please, I've got money, are you kidnapping me?"

No answer. He just placed the cloth back over her head and led her outside. It definitely was dark now. He forced her into the boot of a car, and they set off again. Jen had lost the energy to stay awake. She was exhausted, hungry, dehydrated. She thought about Marco, their amazing relationship, and how much she loved him. She'd been gone for hours now, surely, he would have raised the alarm and the police would be looking for her.

When the boot opened, she could hear running water, fast running water. The man pulled her out and made her stand. He removed the cloth again, and he was wearing the same gruesome mask. Then she saw the gun. He placed it to her temple and walked her towards a bridge. She could hear the torrents of water below. She'd had a swimming pool for years, but she couldn't swim. She only had the confidence to splash around with her feet firmly on the bottom of the pool.

He made her climb up on to the side of the bridge. She felt her bladder give way. Then the man spoke, English with an Italian accent.

"My client wants you to know something."

"Your fucking client?" she snarled as she shivered.

"Yes, my client says, Jennifer, you didn't sleep with Michael, it was Gabriel. You got the wrong twin. You fucking whore."

She had just a few seconds to take in what he said. She saw in her mind for a split second, Michael in her room, bewildered, claiming not to understand what she was talking about, and walking out.

"Did Jack Hearn send you?"

He didn't answer.

"Now, it's time for you to join Gabriel in his death. Goodbye Jennifer."

He didn't have to point the gun at her, he didn't have to push her. She threw herself over the side, knowing this was the end for her.

Chapter 62
September 2012

Grace sat alone in the small church. There were a few people dotted around, talking quietly to avoid the echo of their voices tainting the sombre atmosphere. She felt out of place in this picturesque Italian village, miles from her family, or anyone she knew. As a representative of the Hearn family, she had travelled to Milan to attend Jen's funeral and she was feeling uncomfortable. She rarely travelled far without Dan, so flying solo to spend a few days in Lombardy hadn't been easy. Trying to guilt-trip him into accompanying her had been fruitless. As she sat in church, she still couldn't quite figure out why he was *so* adamant that she attended this extremely sad situation without him. He knew how much she hated flying; he knew how long Jen had been a part of her life and of the lives of their children. At the same time, Grace had always sensed that he was intimidated by her, which seemed to manifest in his unease when she was around. Maybe he just disliked her, so much so that attending her funeral just didn't sit right with him. Curiously, Michael had displayed the same attitude towards his godmother. He excused himself from accompanying her due to running the pub, having a staff problem, and wanting to stay at the helm of what was becoming a popular destination for locals and holiday makers alike.

She took the quiet time to reflect on the many changes that had happened over the last year. Michael's decision to quit his law degree had been a sensible one in Grace's opinion. He was burdened with course work and grief whilst in a fragile state, so when Dan suggested he take over the manager's role at the Angel Inn, he had accepted immediately. He was now living in the apartment above the pub and seemed to be in his element. The vacancy arose when Jamie announced he had accepted a job offer from Jack Hearn. Dan hadn't been too pleased at the time, his brother had poached one of his staff with the offer of a better salary and better prospects, running the new site Jack had acquired on the outskirts of Caernarfon. The silver lining was the opportunity for Michael to continue life without Gabriel, in a positive frame of mind.

There was an element of guilt creeping into Grace's conscience where Jen was concerned. They hadn't spoken much over the year, but when they did, Jen hadn't given any indication of her depression. She had a new job, new partner, new life and on the couple of occasions they had spoken, Jen seemed happier than she'd ever been.

When Grace received the call from Marco, he had told a very different story. Jen's bouts of severe depression, her drinking, her addiction to prescription pain killers. It all sounded far from the picture Grace had in her head in relation to Jen's new life. Marco had sounded distraught at the loss of his 'Bellissima'. She had left their villa on the anniversary of her ex-husband's death and disappeared. He had found the suicide note several hours after she went missing and he had alerted the police. Poor Jen, who hadn't seemed all that stable following Gabriel's suicide, but Grace hadn't thought for a second that she was *that* desperately unhappy, especially at Nick's passing.

A bell sounded and the guests stood up. Grace waited till the procession walked by. Marco was the first person behind the pall bearers, weeping and distraught. Jen's coffin was stacked with beautiful floral tributes, and by the time it had been placed on the trestle, the church was packed.

Grace looked down, closed her eyes, and said a silent prayer. "Goodnight Jennifer, God bless you, you crazy bitch, please give Gabriel a massive hug from me and Dan and Michael."